HUSH LITTLE CHILDREN

by Hayan Charara

Flexible Press
Minneapolis, Minnesota, 2025

Print ISBN: 979-8-9914928-8-1
eBook ISBN: 979-8-9914928-9-8

Flexible Press LLC
Minneapolis, Minnesota
www.flexiblepub.com
Editors William E Burleson
Vicki Adang, Mark My Words Editorial Services, LLC

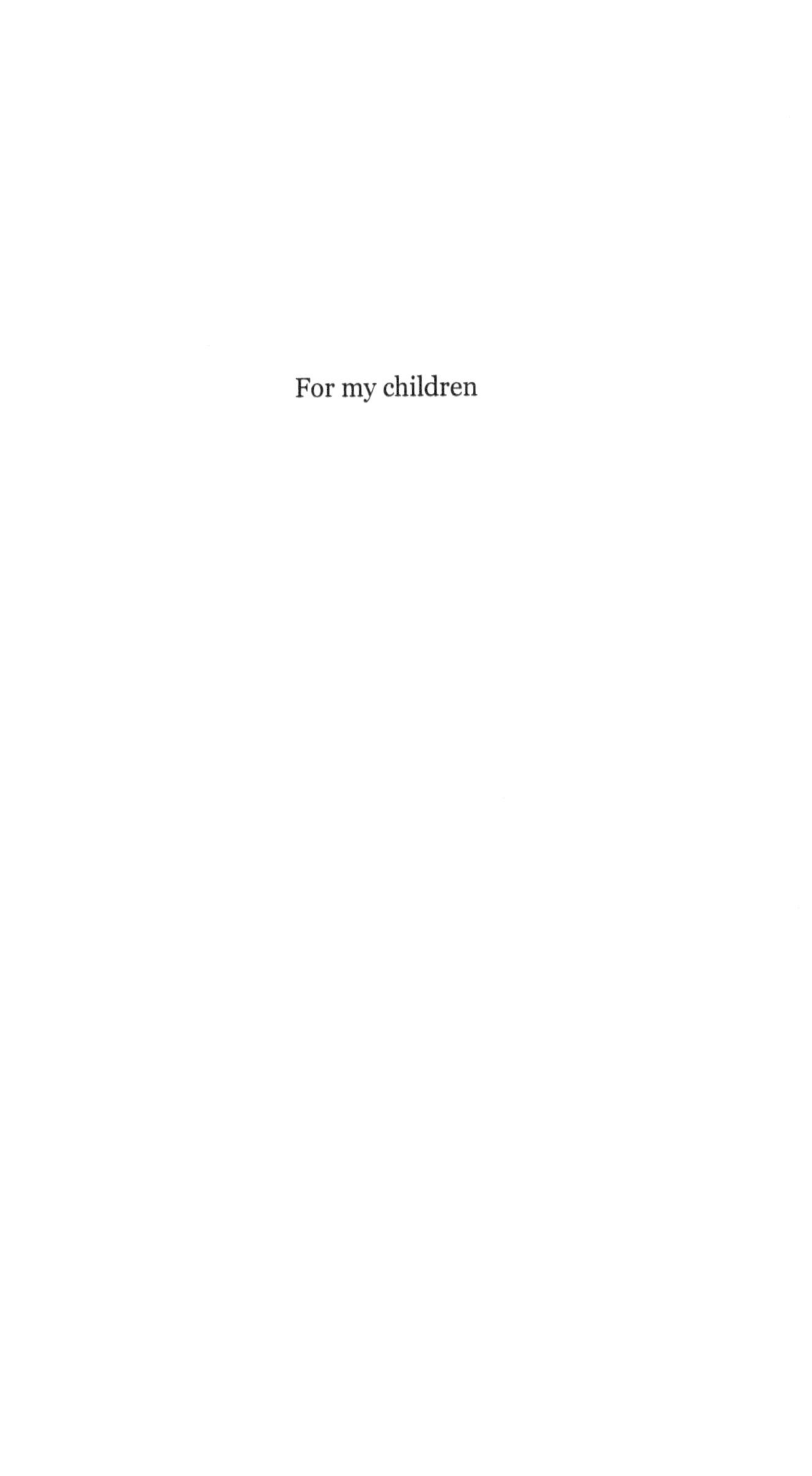

For my children

In ancient times a story could end in only two ways: having passed all the tests, the hero and heroine married, or else they died. The ultimate meaning to which all stories refer has two faces: the continuity of life, the inevitability of death.

 —*Italo Calvino*

ONE

THE FIRST WAS a girl, eleven years old.

By all accounts she was a happy child—socially engaged, physically active, slept well. She was smart, too, a child who remembered everything she heard, and rumor was she had heard that women were less successful than men in the task she would undertake, men often resorting to more definitive and spectacular methods.

The day she became the first, a Saturday, her mother and father must have been sitting across from each other at a small table in a breakfast nook. Because it was early when it happened, they were both still wearing the clothes they had slept in, and they were either barefoot or in slippers. I like to imagine slippers because of the weather at that time of year—the cold against their feet would have been at odds with the warmth they had shared in bed. Slippers on, then, they existed simply as a husband and wife, still waking up, their talk polite and necessary, subdued by the early hour and their slow rise to wakefulness.

If they were anything like M and me, they were waiting eagerly for the coffee maker to beep, a welcome interruption to the morning's tranquility. Though unlike M and me, they would have sipped their coffees together, sitting beside each other or across from each other. At the very least, they would have been in the same room, and that kind of proximity would not have been an issue. It certainly wouldn't have felt like some sort of imprisonment.

"Good morning," the wife would have said to the husband, realizing she hadn't yet said so. Though the greeting was barely audible, the husband would have heard and nodded in return—he was the type who listened to his wife.

Here and there, over the next three or four minutes, they would have lodged a handful of minor complaints, the kind that people utter out of habit or for lack of anything else coming to mind.

"My neck is stiff," one would have said.

The other, "The neighbor's dog was barking last night. Did you hear it?"

To call the remarks complaints would be making more out of them than the husband and wife would have. Everything about their morning routine—the wife turning on the coffee maker, the husband pulling down two porcelain mugs from the cupboard, spooning sugar into one and tearing open a packet of artificial sweetener for the other, and finally pouring milk into both cups—attested to the comfort they had grown into and maybe even wanted in their life together. Whether about body aches or noises in the night, their conversation echoed their hard-earned contentment.

After the husband nodded yes about hearing the dog bark, he said nothing else to his wife, and she said nothing more to him, not until the coffee maker beeped. After the beep, she yawned and told him how much she needed coffee to start the day. In response, he stretched his arms wide. And from the nearby room they both made out the sound of cellos, violas, violins, flutes, clarinets, horns, pianos, cymbals, and then a very loud crash.

Their daughter was watching cartoons.

They would later admit to a news reporter that they both believed this to be true, about their daughter and the TV.

Took it for granted, in fact. The belief that their eleven-year-old was watching a cartoon was so strong, a litany of thoughts ran through each of their minds, and given the years they had spent raising the girl together, living with her and with each other, knowing more about her than the girl at that age could possibly know about herself, it took very little effort on my part, or M's for that matter, to imagine the husband and wife's thoughts overlapping, for the two of them at exactly or nearly the same moment to think or to say out loud about their child, "She's sitting too close to the TV."

M and I disagreed on a lot, but on this point we did not. In each of our separate childhoods, we, too, had heard our own parents grumble about watching television. We also agreed that the only discrepancy between the husband and wife about the girl sitting too close to the TV would have been the exact distance between her eyes and the screen—either one or two feet from the screen or else so close that the girl could make out the picture's red, blue, and green pixels.

Whatever the case, the husband and wife wanted to break the girl of the habit. Long ago they had convinced themselves that plopping down so near the blue glow of a TV screen would lead to poor eyesight, and from there they foresaw a downward spiral. Poor vision would trigger the need for eyeglasses, which would then give rise to a domino effect of troubles, anxieties, traumas, burdens, heartaches, and miseries to last the girl's entire life. These included taunts from classmates at school, "four eyes" and the like. These would then lead to low self-esteem, depression, anger, truancy, bad grades, detention, and so on. From there, in no time, the girl would suffer the ravages of alcohol abuse, drug addiction, and ultimately an unwanted pregnancy, a bad marriage, a divorce, more bad marriages, et cetera, et cetera. A vicious cycle of hope, failure, despair, and then start all over again.

Did they really need to worry about such things? The girl wasn't even technically preteen yet. In the end, it did not matter. They worried she would go blind watching TV, and on any other day or at any other time of day, they would have put down their coffees, and one of them, most likely the wife—she usually the calmer of the two, the more patient parent, the one who better hid her irritation or exasperation—would have walked into the TV room and said, "Honey, please don't sit so close. It's bad for your eyes." Or, if husband and wife chose not to interrupt the serenity of staying put on a Saturday morning, of caffeine finally taking effect, or of feeling their bare feet on the cold tile floor—if they were indeed the kind of people who did not wear slippers—then one of them, probably the husband—who was usually less patient, more easily agitated, and more prone to want to nip problems in the bud—would have pushed his chair back, and then, to let the girl know he was coming, stomped his way toward the room with the TV. Stopping halfway and loud enough for her to hear, signaling that he meant business but thinking to himself that he was hardly coming off as cruel or mean, he would have yelled, "Missy, don't make me come in there."

On that day, neither husband nor wife did any of these. The wife remained calm, and somehow the husband kept his patience, the pair unruffled by the idea of television ruining their daughter's life. They allowed her to go on sitting too close to the TV.

After seeing the couple on the news, I imagined the reasons why that morning they chose to let go rather than intervene. On this morning, I told myself, they happened to feel themselves more than the usual tired they had often quibbled about since becoming parents. If the day before they had been asked to describe their fatigue and answered, "Worn out," then on this day they would have upped it a notch or two. "Drained," the wife might have said, and the husband, "Dog-tired." That their daughter was only eleven meant that the husband and wife probably slept terribly and that most mornings they counted themselves fit to drop. I expressed this opinion to M, explaining that because of how badly children slept, parents suffered the kind of sleep deprivation that would cause pilots to crash airplanes. M outright rejected the opinion. The girl was eleven years old, she told me, not eleven months, and would have been sleeping through the night for a long time.

Maybe, then, I told M, the husband and wife had been up late the night before for some other reason, one that mirrored our life together. Each of them could have been engrossed in a book. They *were* voracious readers, a fact confirmed by a friend or relative of theirs who later appeared on a podcast about the growing crisis. Exactly what kind of readers they were, what kinds of books they liked to read, the friend or relative did not know or else knew but didn't think it mattered enough to reveal.

Let's say the father favored stories that brought to life scenarios about which certain philosophies only hypothesized, especially events, people, and ideas that the great political thinkers considered catastrophic. More than once over the course of their marriage, the wife, I'm sure, must have asked her husband, "Why do you read books like that?" With each instance, having answered a version of the question so many times before, he would have replied with something along the lines of, "Because I'm a human being," to which, obviously, she would have rolled her eyes and retorted with a snide or sarcastic remark, probably, "Some human you are."

Given this, let's say then that the mother preferred to read books not so heavy on philosophy or catastrophe. She called the books she preferred "leisurely reading," whereas her husband preferred to call her literary choices "brain candy." The point is, they had stayed up late reading, and in the morning, they woke up exhausted, and when they realized that their daughter, the first girl, was watching TV with her eyes glued to the set, rather than do or say something, they let the girl be.

Or, maybe, they had in fact put their books down at a reasonable hour, each reaching over to the nightstand on either side of the bed to turn out the lights. Then, yawning, they turned in early, early enough to anticipate a good night's sleep. Yet through the long hours of the evening and into the morning, they found themselves sleeping fitfully, the lapses of rest and rejuvenation interrupted by neck pain, a sore back, a bad dream, a nagging worry. Instead of tranquil slumber, the husband and wife tossed and turned, and this proved to be the reason they let their daughter ruin her eyesight watching cartoons.

Or else they had slept just fine but fell asleep late and didn't get enough hours of rest because for the first time in days, or weeks, or even months they found themselves in the mood and had sex.

I can tell you this: M did not think my bringing up long bouts of abstinence funny or appropriate. Not at all. I can also tell you that I wasn't trying to be funny, not at all.

I said to her, somewhat under my breath, "I'm deadly serious," and M told me to go fuck myself.

Ultimately, whatever the reason for their overtiredness, it led to their not calling to the girl who was sitting too close to the TV, and not going in to check on her, either. The fact was, had they done so, it might not have made much difference. The moment the husband and wife heard the cartoon music and thought simultaneously or nearly so about their child sabotaging any hope for a good life and twenty-twenty vision, the girl was no longer where they thought she was, doing what they took for granted she was doing. All along they had imagined her nearby, within earshot, and they were completely wrong.

The girl had already left the room, and left the TV turned on, and headed upstairs at the same moment the coffee maker beeped.

At that moment, too, the girl decided not to bother with pills, razor blades, or her head in an oven. Instead, she crossed the threshold into her parents' bedroom, where the night before her mother and father might have undressed each other, touched each other, and climaxed together. From under the mattress on her father's side of the bed, the girl pulled out the handgun her father had purchased before she was born and, for all the years since her birth, held onto for fear of the unknown. And then, because the floors were carpeted, the girl walked soundlessly out of her parents' bedroom, down the hall, and into the privacy of her own room where, facing a mirror, she raised her right hand to her open mouth, and over posters of boys and girls much older than she could imagine herself ever becoming, she blew her brains out and became the first.

For days on end, the first girl's mother and father found pieces of skull embedded in the walls, buried in the carpet, scattered about in the nooks and crannies of the girl's bed-room. The most devastating discovery came almost a week into the cleaning. Inside the girl's dollhouse, a bone frag-ment the size of a small tooth had come to rest atop a doll-sized bed in a doll-sized bedroom custom-crafted to be a replica of the girl's bedroom.

They kept picking up the pieces until, a couple weeks af-ter the funeral of their only child, the father stopped the mother. Or maybe it was the mother who put her hand on the father's shoulder and signaled that they needed to talk. Or, aware of each other's misery, it was possible that the two came to a halt together and, for the first time as husband and wife, truly thought of themselves as soulmates, forever bound to each other by the tragedy the daughter had heaped onto their lives. Simply, they stopped, looked into each other's eyes, and one or both asked the only question that ultimately mattered.

"Should we go on?"

They must have come to an agreement quickly.

Had they been asked and gone on record with an answer, their neighbors would have claimed the husband and wife's quick, like-minded arrival unusual for their marriage, as the two argued regularly and loudly, sometimes with windows cracked open and usually about trivialities. The price of eggs was one such incident. The wife willingly paid extra for organic, cage-free, and free-range eggs, and the husband would come close to losing his mind when he saw brown eggs in the refrigerator. Other flashpoints included debates over which was more wasteful, hot showers or baths, doing dishes in the sink or the dishwasher. They argued incessantly over the temperature setting on the thermostat. And when they drove somewhere together, the wife invariably brought up her husband's tailgating, and when she was behind the wheel, he complained about her rolling through stop signs.

The point was this: When these and other pet peeves occurred, they constantly complained to each other about the other. However, they never fought over the girl, not how to raise, feed, or dress her, which remained the case to the very end, and so, when the wife brought out into the open the subject of their self-destruction, then and there the husband knew he had married the right woman.

What I gathered about them from reading news and online opinions was that the realization the husband came to about his wife did not strike him as romantic in the least. In terms of appearances, which sometimes are no less and no more accurate than what lies beneath them, he didn't look like a sentimental man. The wife did not seem to be a sentimental woman. Yet, when they decided to head into the twilight together, they must have felt immediate satisfaction and fulfillment. In any marriage, after so many years with countless ups and downs, with hours, days, weeks, and sometimes months of uncertainty and demoralizing doubt about whether the marriage will last, nothing would be more rewarding than for a husband and wife to carry out the final obligation of their wedding vows together, hand in hand. They must have relished the achievement.

They left a note on the dollhouse. But so not to desecrate the sanctity of the daughter's bedroom, they took their task to the basement. Unlike their daughter, and maybe because of her, they thought through the aftermath of their decision and opted for a cleaner approach: rope, rafter beam, two chairs, and the count of three.

❦

The first girl, and her mother and father, too, of course, lived—had lived—in the East Side. The local newspaper published an op-ed about the tragedy and more than insinuated a relationship between the self-murdered family and the neighborhood in which they lived and died. "The successive misfortunes that have beset the East Side should set off alarm bells," the op-ed argued. "Is this a pattern?" it wondered. "Keep your eyes on the East Side," it warned.

For enough people, that the fear articulated by the op-ed sounded like a truth—which was that the suicides, the young age of the first girl, and the fact that they lived in the East

Side—was hardly a coincidence. A relatively small number of people began to repeat, no doubt privately but more importantly publicly, that the suicides in the East Side, especially that of the eleven-year-old girl, were not due to the usual circumstances behind underage suicide (mental health, trauma, trouble at home, and school or peer-related problems) but rather that an underage suicide crisis was underway in the neighborhood. The most vocal proponents of the supposed phenomenon (the neighborhood a breeding ground for suicidal youth) were a group of parishioners in a small church on the edge of the East Side led by an old preacher, a man with beautiful blue eyes and white hair who always wore a gray suit jacket and almost-matching gray pants. The church where the old man preached matched the simplicity of his dress. It was a small one-story building with a nondescript exterior and plain, unadorned windows and doors. The church did not even look like a church. To anyone unfamiliar with the East Side, and maybe even to the residents who had lived in the neighborhood all their lives, the church could have been easily mistaken for a storefront or a health clinic, a shoe repair shop, or a local politician's election headquarters. The church lacked distinction. It wasn't special in any way. In a word, it was unremarkable.

Outwardly, the old preacher also appeared unremarkable, mundane even. Gray suit coat, gray pants, plain shirt, plain shoes. Except for his eyes, which were a radiant blue. Even more striking than his eyes, his voice. His words were extraordinary and imaginative. In sermons at the small church, the old preacher predicted that the East Side's disgraced children would continue to kill themselves for no reason other than to claim bragging rights. He told the small congregation that while the first girl had singularly and for always and ever attained the title of the first child suicide of the suicides to come, the other children who would follow in her footsteps ("theirs, not ours") would outright murder themselves for glory or its less glorious cousin, celebrity, so to go down as the first of their own making. He told the gathered fearful that in addition to the first girl, there would eventually be a first boy, a first with brown eyes, a first with red hair, and on and on. This trend would not stop, either. Soon there would come the first with blue or green eyes, the first teenager, the first set of twins. He told his congregation that he believed the first girl and her parents, and East Siders like them, signified all that was wrong with the world (it was corrupted) and its inhabitants (they were contaminated). He told them that the children of the East Side—not their own children, not the children who belonged to the church, who were somehow immune to the virus ready to infect the rest of the neighborhood's young, but these other people's children—were a threat.

The congregation believed him. They believed because they were afraid, and they were afraid because for a long time they had heard and then came to believe this, that, and the other about the East Side and the people who lived there, people like M and me.

The this: The East Side was once a good neighborhood, but it had become unsafe, dangerous, and crime-ridden, the sort of place that, if they could—and some of them did—people like the old preacher's congregation would leave. The East Side came to be that way, the preacher and the congregation believed, because people like M and me had moved in, overcrowded the neighborhood, overtaken its essential character. Once, the East Side resembled its sister neighborhood, the West Side. Not so much its houses or churches or the vehicles parked along it curbs, but its people—they looked the same. Little else had changed in the East Side, but in the eyes of men like the preacher, it had become the sort of place a person only ventured into if they had something illicit in mind or otherwise had made a wrong turn or two and inadvertently ended up on one of our streets. Was any of this true? The truth didn't matter. What the old preacher wanted to believe, what he wanted others to believe, that's all that mattered.

The that: The people of the East Side, the ones who looked like M and me, were innately dangerous, uncivilized, and barbaric, hostile to everything that people like the old preacher and his congregation held dear. We were incapable of reason. We were only capable of understanding through violence and brute force. We showed little to no regard for human life, especially the lives of innocents. The men among us were misogynistic and oppressive—to women, families, and communities outside of our own. The women among us were complicit in their own oppression and repression. "Am I oppressing you?" I once asked M, to which she replied, "Not the way the preacher thinks." The preacher thought we were anti-human, anti-modern, politically militant, uneducated, backwards, weak, illogical, and overtly emotional. We were intolerant of difference and change, particularly if the change was viewed as progress, and our values, even the best of them, were stuck in a distant, outdated past. To make matters worse, even though not a single person in the East Side had ever enacted the kind of violence the preacher warned about, a few times some guy who kind of looked like me had done just that. And as a result, people who looked like him had been named public enemy number one. That was all his believers needed to think that people like M and me were also their enemies.

And the other: The East Side and the people living in it, those who looked like M and me, were a menace in the imagination of the other people living in the East Side, those who looked like the old preacher and his congregation. In their minds this impression had been so deeply engrained, so pervasive, they could hardly see us or read about us without going there. So when a girl killed herself and was identified as one of "them" by the preacher, every fear, every threat, and every harm that he and his congregation had only imagined became, in an instant, real. People like us believed in the wrong god, the wrong afterlife, the wrong sacred text. Mind you, M and I hardly believed in anything we couldn't see with our own eyes, but when the preacher and his congregants saw us, they saw *all* of us, and they saw a menace to everything good.

"Why are they even giving this guy the time of day?" I asked M.

"You watch too much TV," she answered. "That old preacher's a crackpot. He's been a nuisance forever, talking nonsense about people like us ever since I was a little girl—and before that, too. The only people foolish enough to listen to his gibberish are those other crackpots in his church—no one else—and they're probably the only ones who believe a word he says."

I wanted very much to take M's word for it, except the old preacher was on TV. Local TV, yes. Cable TV, sure. But TV, nevertheless. Obviously, someone who knew something about the medium's reach and about TV-viewing habits believed that enough people *would* want to listen to the old preacher, and besides, the old preacher wasn't the first guy to talk this way, and his congregation wasn't the first audience to buy into his talk. "But what do I know?" I asked myself. Maybe in the East Side, the world worked differently than outside of it, where crackpots weren't ignored but taken seriously. When it came to the East Side and the old preacher, I settled on taking for granted that M knew much more than me, a fair and reasonable assumption to make. She'd lived in the East Side her whole life, just like her father and mother before her, and her grandparents before them, and before that, her great-grandparents—they had come here first, and as far as I could tell, from the little I knew about them from a few framed photographs, a handful of stories told about them, mostly by M's father, they were the only people in M's line about whom the old preacher and people like him could actually say were unlike them. Yet no one in M's family, or mine, bore any resemblance whatsoever to the menace described by old preacher. Our predecessors had simply spoken a different language and had unfamiliar names, and to better fit in, not only did they learn a new language, they also legally changed their names. But when it came to the East Side, M knew infinitely more than I did, and so, I presumed, she must have known better. The only lingering questions: Why had she never mentioned the old preacher before, and if he had always been a problem, then why hadn't I heard about him, not just from my wife but from anyone else?

I wasn't from the East Side, but I had been living in the neighborhood for more than a decade, ever since moving to the city to take a teaching job at the college. In that time, I had heard all sorts of terrible things about all kinds of people, me included, which is typical for any community, anywhere. About the old preacher, though, or his small church, not a peep. Not even from M's father, a man who talked too much and for whom the concept of restraint was either foreign or else made him ill—the man could not hold back an opinion about anything. M's father could have set the record straight about the old preacher, and I would have asked him, but all that was left of him were the bungalows he willed to M after his death, four of them, all in the East Side. One white, one yellow, one pink, which was M's favorite, and the one we lived in, the blue bungalow.

I resented the old man—M's father, not the preacher. All I knew about the old preacher, at that point, was that he wore an ill-fitting suit jacket, and he thought the world was a terrible place, and we were the cause. Who doesn't own an article of clothing in the wrong size? Who hasn't thought, *The world sucks?* Who hasn't blamed the ills of the world on other people and their children? M's father, on the other hand, I knew much more intimately. While he was still alive, he had done his absolute best to ruin my life. On top of that, he excluded me from his will. A shameless man, he went so far as to tell me why I hadn't been willed a cent: He hoped M would come to her senses and leave me for a man who could get her pregnant. That fact—that I hadn't or couldn't impregnate M—the old man took to the grave, and I must admit, it gave me some pleasure that he died without a grandchild.

M has read every word of this. No secrets exist between us. Not anymore, at least. There weren't that many to begin with—only a handful—but with secrets their capacity for ruin dwells not in their quantity but their quality. Of the few secrets I had kept from M, only one truly mattered, and I would reveal it to her near the end of our story—not because I am good or honest, though I like to think that on my best days I could be such a man. No, I confessed to M because I believed that only the truth would save us, that the truth would steer our story toward the ending she wanted more than any other: life with children.

❧

For years, we tried to have one of our own.

In the first year of our attempt to make a baby, we tried a lot. Daily, nightly, at unanticipated times of the day, in unexpected places. Our efforts, if they can be called that, stemmed just as much out of a desire to have a baby as they did the desire M and I shared for each other. We didn't set a schedule or a deadline. We abided by a simple equation: If the one form of desire (lust) immediately led to the other (progeny), then great, and if it took a few weeks, a month or two for M to conceive, so be it. In having gone about it in this way, we thought we had freed ourselves from worry.

Months and months after we began trying, M still wasn't pregnant. I started to wonder if the reason the pregnancy sticks kept showing up negative (one red line, not two) had nothing to do with bad timing or luck but rather a shortcoming. While I didn't dare bring it up at the time, I did wonder to myself who the guilty party was. I won't say on whose shoulders I hoped responsibility would fall—mine, M's, or the two of us—but I can admit this: Because I knew M well, I suspected that at around the same time, she was entertaining the very same thoughts, and because she knew me better than anyone else, she also kept those thoughts to herself.

In the second year of our unexpectedly prolonged unwanted childlessness, I took to believing that seeing M pregnant might be an unlikely scenario. This time around, I told her so.

"Maybe it isn't going to happen."

She mulled over what I said. No words, just thoughts. The only discernible hint of her hidden deliberation was when she shook her head ever so slightly. This presented itself as a crisis of interpretation. I couldn't tell if the gesture meant she was agreeing, disagreeing, or still considering the proposition. At long last, she took a deep breath, which M usually did right before making a definitive statement, and said, "Anything's possible. And if anything is truly possible, then one possibility is that you, or any other man, is *not* going to get me pregnant. So, yes, maybe me getting pregnant is not going to happen."

That wasn't exactly the answer I had been hoping for, and I asked her, "Why are you talking about other men impregnating you?"

"All I'm saying is that I'm a healthy woman, and you're a healthy man. There's no biological, physiological, or medical reason preventing us from making children. That's an undeniable fact. But I'll grant you that in the world we live in, it's probable that you and I will never have children, that you won't impregnate me, and that I don't ever become impregnated—not by you, not by anyone. So, to your original concern, yes, I can imagine it being the case that I never get pregnant. I can fathom that. My imagining it alone makes it possible. After all, that's the difference between people and animals—the imagination. We have one, they don't. It's what separates us from all other living things."

We had just finished eating dinner and were straightening up the kitchen, putting away dishes, forks, spoons, pots, pans, and she was talking about metaphysics as if it were the weather. But then she hesitated and stopped talking—no doubt, I figured, on account of the pallor of disbelief that overtook my face. Honestly, I didn't know what she would say next. In her right hand she was firmly holding a knife she had just wiped dry. She cast her eyes downward, at the floor, which was over a century old, made of wood boards that would outlast us all. She began nodding, and then she started in on the head shaking again, this time with more force, leaving no doubt about its significance. I was momentarily frightened of my wife.

"All that may be true," she said, "but not for one second, not the tiniest bit do I really believe that I'll never have a child."

She looked up and straight at me, right into my eyes, widening hers. Intentionally, I now think. She took a step closer, and because she had inched forward, so too had the knife in her hand—they were both nearly touching me—and she said, "I'm going to have a baby. I am one hundred percent sure." She smiled and put the knife away. With her fingertips she brushed my cheek, which under most circumstances (but not this one) I would have taken as a sign of affection.

Hesitant, I asked, "How do you know?"

She started to walk away without answering.

"How?"

She kept moving, out of the kitchen and into the living room, which had the same old floorboards as the kitchen. They creaked as she walked over them.

I asked once more. "How can you know that?"

At the bottom of the stairwell leading to the second floor, where our bedroom was, she shook her head one last time, and in case I wasn't clear about what she meant by that, she told me.

"Don't ask."

Then up she went, the house announcing with creaks every step she took farther away from me. A moment later I heard a door close, a door lock, and then the bathtub filling up with water.

For a while I tried hard to keep my mouth shut and my opinions to myself, at least those about M getting pregnant, or not getting pregnant, which in retrospect I regret because my silence must have been understood as not only acquiescence but acceptance. Surely, this affected the conviction she held concerning her imminent pregnancy. It grew and grew and grew.

Those days, the first few years of our marriage, I loved M more than I loved anyone. I loved her even more than I loved myself. This might have been a problem. Dedication of this sort, to one person above all others, turns a husband or wife into a believer, a follower, a devotee—it makes a religion out of marriage. Out of love, or a form of love, or a perversion of it, or a misunderstanding of love, or—it was possible—out of the only true love I had ever experienced, I listened to M say things that most of my life I considered to be completely stupid, the sort of statements that, had anyone else uttered them, I would have questioned, even shunned the person. But when M insisted, contrary to all available evidence, that she was going to have a baby, no ifs, ands, or buts about it, I simply said, "Okay."

If you could have seen us that day, and in the days, weeks, and months that followed—really seen us go about our life, uncensored, unedited—you would have wondered why we stuck it out at all. The ideal married couple may be two people opening themselves up to each other despite the consequences, revealing to one another every insecurity and weakness, every inadequacy. Some people call this "trusting one another." Some call this "intimacy." To M and me, such notions, and the people who believed in them, epitomized the exact opposite of who we thought ourselves to be and what we thought our marriage could withstand. Simply put, we were incapable of saying what had to be said when it was most necessary to say it.

On the face of it—that is, the censored and edited version of our marriage—our life together looked much like the lives of happy sitcom men married to happy sitcom women, or the lived-happily-ever-after pairs in romantic comedies, or the devoted, committed husbands and wives whose marriages grew stronger for having suffered trial and tribulation. The few friends or acquaintances we used to have wouldn't have dreamed us otherwise. For all I knew, they might even have envied M and me, envied what they mistook our marriage to be, what they saw on the exterior. Every so often even I fell under such a spell. I would stand back and tell myself, "We've got it good" or "We can't complain." But if I were being honest, and some days I was, I knew the words and sentiments behind such comments were disingenuous. More often than not, I kept undeserved flattery like that to myself, mostly for fear of what appears painfully and shamefully evident when, in retrospect, any marriage comes to an end.

In the third year, a handful of doctors ran test after test on M and sometimes on me. The first time I went in to have my sperm sampled, I worried about how much time I should spend in the bathroom producing a sample. What would the nurse or doctor think of me if I came out too quickly? Would it be better or worse to linger longer than it took to finish the job? The nurse who called me in caught me eyeing her, too. She'll think I'm picturing her while I masturbate, I thought as she reviewed my forms and copied down my insurance information. She handed me a clear plastic cup with a screw-on cap, a label on the side, no name (only a number) to identify the sperm I would put in, and with skillful indifference that presumably a person gains with years of practice, she told me that next to the chair in the bathroom I would find a stack of magazines, just in case I needed help.

"Take as much time as you have to."

In the bathroom, I locked the door, checked the lock twice, and spent at least half the time I was in there assessing the degree and depth of my embarrassment and the other half imagining the nurse imagining me bringing myself to climax, which was not pleasant. Fortunately, the clinic had the foresight not to require those of us producing samples to check out with the same nurse we checked in with, or with anyone. The clinic didn't even require us to exit through the lobby, sparing countless men from showing their faces to complete strangers only moments after gratifying themselves.

Whatever I felt after these visits, be it embarrassment or its more overbearing cousin, shame, I couldn't complain too much, not in comparison to what M endured during and after her visits. She was analyzed, X-rayed, scanned, sampled, dyed, probed, and needled, then all over again and again, and like this it went on and on for months and months. After seeing everything she had gone through merely to confirm whether her body would be capable of conceiving a child, I had no doubt that life was infinitely easier and simpler as a man. Under no conceivable circumstances would I ever trade places with a woman.

In the end, none of the doctors found anything keeping us from one day creating one of the world's three to four babies born every single second of every single minute. "You should be able to reproduce," we were told. "Other than a change of mind or an unforeseen circumstance, there's nothing keeping you from having children."

We tried for another year before finally going the artificial insemination route. Once more I locked myself in a private room, this time allowing seven minutes to elapse before coming out, too much time for what I needed to do but an amount of time I had arbitrarily determined to be neither too little, too much, too fast, or too slow. I also convinced myself that the nurse, who was again a woman, really had no clue how long it took for a man to masturbate. More than anything, I just wanted time to do nothing at all but be alone. I had been at home and without a job for so long that the freedom I had initially felt began to feel a lot like captivity. M was always home, too—she always had been, even when I was still employed by the college, which meant that when I was home, she was there, too, with me. Always. Being locked away in an enclosed room without windows might look like confinement, but it felt like escape. Seven minutes of escape.

I left the sample cup on a metal tray in the bathroom. A minute or two later, a nurse picked it up. She delivered the fruits of my loins to a doctor in another room without windows, with M lying on an examining table, wearing only a hospital gown. There, the doctor sent my semen on a journey through a sterile catheter into M's body.

"Conception should proceed normally," the doctor told us immediately following the procedure, M still on the table, the white paper rolled out beneath her crinkling with the long, hopeful breaths she took. "Give it another forty-five minutes, then you can go home and do what you normally would on a night like this, but take it easy. No marathons tonight. Watch a movie. Read a book. Two weeks from now, come back and we'll see if you're pregnant."

Two weeks later, we got the news that our first attempt at artificial conception had failed.

So did the second, the third, the fourth, and the fifth attempts. M scheduled a sixth try, but last minute she canceled. I didn't ask why, and I didn't get the sense that she wanted me to argue otherwise.

I didn't argue.

For a year, we gave up on creating life artificially. We still had sex, though not with the intention or hope of conceiving, and not nearly as often as we used to.

I thought this would pass.

I thought wrong.

M regarded the time off as a hiatus, a year of healing. She never repeated out loud the cliché about time and healing, but she must have mulled over its hackneyed proposition until it became a belief. She must have received all the other clichés, too, wholeheartedly, welcoming every bit of hope they promised: only time will tell, all in due time, good things come to those who wait.

That same year, I resigned myself to having tried and failed. Like M, I also succumbed to clichés: As far as M getting pregnant, on us having children, on me becoming a father, I had thrown in the towel, called it a day, admitted defeat. By the time the earth had just about completed another orbit around the sun, M began bringing up wanting to give it one more shot, but by then I was finished. She kept pushing, I kept pushing back. She urged and urged, and I refused to budge. It cost too much money, I argued. The procedures were too invasive, too traumatic to undergo again.

"We're happy the way we are," I told her. "We're doing fine," I also said. "Remember how hard it was?"

She did remember, but she didn't care.

"I don't want to try anymore," I said finally.

"Please," she begged.

"No."

"Please."

"No, no, no."

"One more try. That's all. I swear."

In the seventh year, given that she was a young, healthy woman living in an industrialized nation, M's chances of having a baby through in vitro fertilization were 39.6 percent. Two weeks after a doctor slid a tube through her cervix and implanted an embryo in her uterus, we drove to the doctor's office for the pregnancy test. A receptionist smiled at us when we checked in. A nurse smiled at us when she called M to take the test, and the same nurse, when she called the two of us back about a half-hour later, smiled one last time after leading us down a hallway to the doctor's office and opened the door to let us in.

The doctor was seated behind a beautiful mahogany desk, an antique Persian rug beneath her feet. The office had artwork on the walls, one of which was an original drawing by a famous artist about whose paintings I had heard a bunch of dumbasses say a hundred times before, "My kid could paint that." The drawing was on the wall behind us. The doctor was facing it. We sat in overstuffed chairs facing her.

Like her nurse, the doctor smiled at us. But unlike the smiles of the people she employed, the doctor's lasted far too long. I bet myself, silently, that she was counting the seconds in her head. I felt the need to look away. I glanced sideways at M. She had been living a life of infinite hope. She looked thoroughly exhausted. I was tired, too. I had already given up on doctors, and I didn't want to go through any more procedures or read any more articles on infertility or try any more home remedies. I did not want to do, think, say, or feel anything M was still willing to feel, say, think, and do.

The doctor began talking, and I arched my neck to get another glimpse of the famous artist's drawing on the wall behind us. I had been sure it was a Picasso, but I second-guessed myself because I couldn't make out the signature from where I sat. The doctor said, "Yesterday, I saw a woman with half a uterus. Technically speaking, she can get pregnant, but if she does and carries a fetus full term, in a uterus that's half the size that it should be, there's a good chance the uterus will rupture and both she and her baby could die. She's one of my better-off patients. I have another patient who doesn't have a uterus at all. She was born that way and didn't know it and didn't find out until she was in her thirties. How all her life a thing like that went unnoticed—well, it happens, more than you would think it does. Not that it would've made any difference had she found out earlier or someone in her family knew about the deformity from day one. Not in terms of her getting pregnant, at least, except, of course, not knowing about her condition she lived a life of false hope until she was an adult, a grown woman. Anyhow, you can't add what's not there, not with a uterus, not that I've read in the medical journals, so that's that with her. Another patient of mine, she doesn't have fallopian tubes. Same story, different reason."

I turned around just as the doctor nodded sympathetically at M.

"You, you're a healthy woman," she went on. "You're not getting pregnant, but technically, you *should* be able to. Honestly, I can't tell you why you're not. I'm puzzled, frankly, and I wish I wasn't. I wish I could tell you exactly why this isn't happening and what you can do about it. What I can tell you, though, is that the women who come to me, they would kill to be in your shoes. They would kill to have your reproductive organs."

The doctor kept talking, but I gradually stopped paying attention. What I heard her saying was what I wanted her to say, even if the words coming from her mouth did not match the sentences forming in my mind. "You need to let go," the doctor's voice in my head told M. "Be done with it. Move on. Besides, too many people already populate the world. Too many of them are children, and the overwhelming majority go to sleep hungry and grow up malnourished. You've seen the TV commercials. More flies around the eyes, ears, and mouth than on a dog-dropping steaming on a sidewalk in the middle of a hot and muggy summer day. That sidewalk is cleaner than where some of those kids eat or sleep. Those kids, they're doomed to a hopeless, hapless existence. They will never grow up. They'll die young. Did you know that? They're going to endure all kinds of wretchedness, the sort of hardship and suffering stray animals hardly go through, the kind of misery that only..."

A person could say all sorts of things to another person, deplorable, unspeakable utterances, and he could still apologize for letting them loose, he could beg forgiveness, he could insist he didn't know what had come over him, he could turn red with embarrassment, he could cover his face out of shame. Or a person could imagine and only imagine saying the deplorable, the unspeakable, saying whatever the fuck he pleased, but ultimately keep his mouth closed. I made that choice, the easier of the two available, the one sparing me from having to beg for release from any guilt that might have come about, from having to apologize for how I truly felt. Regardless, I wondered about the thoughts living on the tip of my tongue, which was the place where simple human decency most often faltered and where, I had been telling myself for a long time, human decency sometimes needed to falter.

As for the doctor, because I had stopped listening to her, I had no idea what she was saying, but I knew M was paying attention because the words she heard were making her cry. And that—M's sorrow—pulled me back. The doctor said, "I'm sorry," and I turned toward M and placed my hand on her shoulder and squeezed sympathetically. The doctor slid a box of tissues across the beautiful mahogany desk. I thanked the doctor, pulled out a few tissues, and handed them to M. She took them but didn't use the tissues, just let them drop into her lap, even though her weeping turned into muffled sobbing. I moved my hand from her shoulder to her knee, and again I squeezed so she could feel and know that I was doing the right thing. The doctor stood up and shook her head the way she must have done hundreds of times before, expressing sympathy but also finality. She knew exactly how to let a couple down, how to be the bearer of bad news, and finally, how to make a graceful exit.

She walked around the desk, shook my hand, and said she would leave us alone. "Take your time." Again, I thanked her. Moving a little too quickly (she must have had another client waiting), she headed out of the office and said in a tender and steady voice, "The nurse will come to get you," and then she disappeared behind the door, which she closed on us gently.

I applied more pressure on M's knee. While doing so, I glanced back at the drawing maybe by Picasso. It was possible that the drawing was of a human figure or a tree or an insect. The marks on the canvas could have been birds in fall, diving into the ocean, falling out of the sky, attacking, hovering, or swooping. They could have been scattered words or letters that may have meant something to the artist, or else they were only marks and meant nothing at all. They could have been the nothing that was not there, the nothing that was.

The doctor's words all but extinguished any hopes that M had harbored and kept alive. In the days that followed, her talk of babies, children, and being a mother gradually ebbed. All the same, once a month, every month, she took a pregnancy test, and every month, once a month, the test in her hand revealed a single red line, not the two she kept anticipating. She took the tests in the upstairs bathroom but brought them downstairs to show me. Usually, she would find me sitting at the kitchen table, drinking coffee, and almost always she interrupted an aimless thought, like whether we would ever change the white square tiles that made up the kitchen countertop or if they would be here long after we were gone. She would sigh and say something like, "I took a test," and I would think to myself, "This kitchen has looked the same for a hundred years."

I took to responding to the single red lines with gestures that must have become familiar to M, yet she accepted them as genuine. To demonstrate commiseration, I would sigh. When I wanted to express compassion, I would sit beside her for a minute or two. Some months, I would do both, and in the most empathic tone I could muster, I would say to her, "Maybe next time."

M must have known that I didn't believe in a next time. She must have known that I was simply grinning and bearing her sadness and sorrow. She must have also known that I had become comfortable with what I considered to be a simple, sensible, and easy-to-live-with explanation for why our marriage had been, would continue to be, and would ultimately end childless: There was no explanation. Things either did or did not happen. One thing led to another, or it didn't. No one and nothing willed anything into existence. I found this approach not only practical and burden free, but reliable. Why aren't you pregnant this month? Because you did not get pregnant, that's why. Why is there only one red line on the pregnancy test? Because there aren't two. To M, this way of thinking was completely unacceptable. It did not matter that hope and desire had not yet ushered in a new beginning or a new life, metaphorically or literally. I knew that they could have, but they hadn't, and there was no guarantee that they ever would. I was beginning to think like a philosopher, a pessimistic one: The beginning of life, and quite possibly every instant over the course of a lifetime, was a shot in the dark. Once, such an idea might have frightened me. Now, I welcomed it. I was tired. Tired of trying. The idea of becoming a father wore me out. Just being who we already were—husband and wife, no more—that was so much easier. It was a way of life we had already attained. No extra effort required. If we were to become something else, something more, or even less—parents, divorced, widowed—then I would accept and welcome the change. Pretending that I had any control over what our lives would or could be was exhausting work. And impossible to achieve. I began to believe that our marriage depended on submitting ourselves to this notion. There was one problem, though. M had convinced herself of an altogether different way of seeing things.

I still loved her very much, but around this time I thought she was being foolish.

In the ninth year, on a Tuesday, the temperature mild, the sun bright, a good day to be outside, relaxing on the porch, gardening in the yard, strolling under a canopy of trees, eating lunch at a park, or drinking coffee on a bench downtown, we were in the house. I was on the green couch against the wall, reading a book. We had picked out the sofa together at a thrift store the year we married. M was seated across from me in an antique armchair, the seat and back cushion brown leather, the wood solid oak. The chair had belonged to her father, who inherited it from his father. Supposedly, a master woodworker made the chair for him, the wood from an oak tree cut down to make room for the blue bungalow to be built. I doubted that. I wanted to doubt her grandfather's ability to commission furniture and houses not because it wasn't true but simply because we couldn't afford to do the same. M was in the heirloom armchair, and I was on the secondhand sofa reading about Apollo chasing Daphne through the woods and Daphne begging her father to save her and her father saving Daphne by turning her into a tree. As for M, she was, again, waiting for a pregnancy stick to show her two red lines. There are few things more agonizing than having to hold in an opinion, especially when the opportunity to express it comes about regularly. Month after month, I had succeeded. But on this beautiful day, finally I caved.

"Why do you keep doing this?"

Without a word, without a groan or sigh, without acknowledging me or my question—she didn't turn toward me, she didn't raise an eyebrow—M set the pregnancy test on the coffee table, the indicator face down, and reached over it for the remote. She turned the TV on and the volume up, making it all but impossible for me to keep reading. On TV, a woman was overjoyed at how white her teeth had become. She called the product being advertised "life changing."

"Why?" I asked again, raising my voice to compete with the TV.

She looked once more at the pregnancy test, set it back on the coffee table, this time rearranging it right next to the remote control but still face down, and said, "Everything happens for a reason. Nothing happens without purpose."

She knew precisely which ideas would infuriate me. Somehow, miraculously, I resisted the urge to push back. Drop the subject, I told myself. Go back to your book. I went to the sentence where I had left off, and I began reading again. I went over the same sentence half a dozen times, at least, but all I heard in my head were M's words: "Nothing happens without purpose." Without bothering to mark the page in my book, either with my finger or dog-earing the corner, I closed it and asked, "Do you mean, there are no coincidences? If that's what you mean, then you're talking about destiny, fate, God's plan."

"Whatever you want to call it, everything around us says so."

"Says what?"

"Take a look at the plants and the animals, the heavens, even atoms and electrons."

"You want me to look at atoms and electrons through a microscope?"

"I want you to see that everything is organized and ordered, that there's a rationale to everything under the sun, even the sun. And if there's an explanation for everything before our eyes—why trees grow leaves, why water turns into ice, why ice melts at a given temperature, why the ocean looks blue in some places, green in others—then why not for what's happening to us? Why wouldn't there be a rational explanation for why this and not that, why something is and why something isn't? Mysteries have their own reasons, and we just don't know them—not yet. As for you and me, as to why I'm not pregnant and why I keep trying, I'll tell you why: The fact is we *can* have babies. Every doctor we've seen says there's nothing wrong with me or with you. I can get pregnant. You can get me pregnant. We can have children. Yet all these years later, of trying month after month, I haven't gotten pregnant, we haven't had children, and I…"

"That's exactly my point," I interrupted her too loudly. "That's what I've been talking about all these years, month after month after month of one red line after another red line."

"No, that's not exactly right," she said calmly. "All these years, you've been telling me *the facts*." She made air quotes. "I already know *the facts*. I just reiterated them to you. I'm not talking about facts. I'm talking about something else."

"What are you talking about?"

"A higher purpose."

"A higher purpose?"

"Yes."

I stood up, astonished by the remark. M remained seated. In her father's armchair. Looking comfortable and rested. I hated that chair. It was too big for the room. And the room was too small. Maybe at the turn of the century, when people were smaller, the room was the perfect size for a man and woman, along with a child or two. Today, the chair, the room, the house itself, they symbolized a bygone era and its antiquated notions, one of which was a certainty in a grand scheme to the universe, to existence, to the fleeting, arbitrary, and inconsequential happenings we call life.

"Okay," I said, my voice even louder than before. "What if our higher purpose is not to have babies? Or what if someone or something—God or nature, the universe—what if everything that's around us simply wants to tell us, to tell you, 'Hey, you, you're not having any babies. Babies are not in your future. No babies for you. Stop trying. Get over it.' What if that's our higher purpose?"

Again, calmly, which I could hardly believe, and which made me more furious than I thought imaginable, M said, "I've thought about that, too."

"Oh, okay. Please, love of my life, enlighten me."

"If we weren't supposed to have a child, then obviously there would've been a sign."

"There's a sign?"

"Yes."

"You're right. There is a sign. An obvious one. You're not pregnant. That's the only sign we need. What else do you want? Jesus Christ's face on a burnt piece of toast?"

Still calm, she said, "If we weren't supposed to have children, the doctors would have found something wrong with my body, or you would have had a low sperm count, or something—there would've been that kind of sign. But there were none. Not even one."

Later, I would be ashamed for yelling at this point, but in the moment, I hardly cared.

"What about the biggest sign of all? What about all those pregnancy sticks you toss into the trash every few weeks? How many times have you done that now? Aren't all those disposable no-you're-not-pregnant sticks the clearest goddamn sign of all?"

"Please don't talk to me like that."

I made an unintelligible sound and stomped off to the kitchen. I stopped in front of the refrigerator. I clenched my fists and grunted again, loud enough for M to hear. Then I opened the fridge and yelled, "Maybe there's a higher purpose for why I want to pull my hair out."

M was smarter than me—she didn't reply.

I grabbed a beer and stood over the kitchen sink and looked out the window into the backyard. The grass needed mowing. The flower beds needed weeding. The bushes along the fence needed trimming. The fence was leaning where it should have been straight; a few of the boards were rotted and needed replacing. Above the fence, I saw a squirrel and watched it run across the top of the fence to a telephone line to a tree. I heard a dog bark somewhere out of sight. I had no clue which of my neighbors owned a dog. How was that possible? How could I not have noticed something so plain to see as a neighbor with a dog? From behind me, I heard M turn up the TV volume again, and I said under my breath, "Holy shit, now she's trying to drown out my thoughts." She started flipping through the channels. I heard voices, then white noise, then more voices and more noise. Then the channel-changing stopped, and M called out my name.

I ignored her and continued to hover over the sink, gulping beer, and sizing up the world outside the four walls I called home.

She called again.

I think I might have stood there for the rest of the day, just to prove that I could, but M screamed, "Come. Now. Quick. Hurry."

She was standing in front of the TV. On the screen, a breaking news story.

A teenager from the East Side had stolen his mother's SUV, drove across town to the West Side, the Museum

District, where the houses were a bit grander and the lawns in front of them more lush and the cars and trucks parked outside more expensive and where, high above the streets, which on the West Side were called boulevards, the oak trees, majestic like the houses they shaded, stretched their gnarled limbs from one side to the other, sunlight shimmering between the leaves. There, on a quiet corner far from the East Side, far from where the teenager was born and with his mother lived, at a high speed he careened across the parking lot of the West Side's elementary school and jumped the curb and slammed his mother's SUV into a wall of windows behind which sat a classroom of first-graders.

The teenager smashed headfirst into the windshield. Upon impact, the windshield turned into a spider web of glass, its center shaped like a human head. He died on impact.

The person on TV said that the vehicle's airbag did not deploy. The same person on TV speculated that the now-dead teenager might have intentionally disabled the airbag. This person on TV also said that the children in the elementary school had probably been celebrating the last day of classes before the summer break, and then, simultaneously touching his earpiece and interrupting himself, the person on TV said, "I'm sorry to say that we can now confirm a number of fatalities, all of them children."

M turned to me and said, "We need to talk." She began to say something but cut herself off. Then shook her head no. "I take that back. I need to talk. You need to listen."

She was breathing deeply, and her hands were trembling.

"Everything has come to this," she said. "Every meaningful thing. Every meaningless thing. In my life and yours. All of it has come down to this. To right now." She swallowed her breath, and I mimicked her, involuntarily. She said, "At first, I thought I understood and that you didn't. Now I realize that I didn't understand either, not entirely." She glanced at the TV. "Everything just changed."

The person on the TV, who was still talking, I heard him say "a rash of suicides." M, with her eyes still on the screen, said, "Everything is perfectly clear now." She paused for what in the moment, and in retrospect, seemed to be an unnecessarily long amount of time, but the pause had the desired effect: Like her, I was also taking deep, long breaths, and I saw that my own fingers were trembling.

M held her hand out, presumably to calm me, to reassure me of the thing I didn't yet know but would find out. That's how I read the gesture. Instead of taking my hand, she opened her palm and held it out for me to look.

M said, "There are no coincidences."

I looked down at the pregnancy test. There were two red lines.

Then she said, "We're going to have a baby."

Then the person on TV said, "Our children are under attack."

TWO

LATER THAT NIGHT, after we went to bed, a good five or ten minutes after M fell asleep and started snoring, around ten o'clock, ten thirty, I left the bedroom. As always, the floor sounded my footsteps with creaks, but M didn't stir.

In the bathroom, I dug through the trash can and found the package that the pregnancy test had come in. I checked the date on the label. Maybe M had used a pregnancy test past its expiration date, and that was the reason it had produced a false-positive result.

The suspense was brief. The test was not due to expire for almost a year.

I sat on the edge of the tub, which, like the rest of the house, was old. A cast iron claw-foot tub, the tub painted white, the feet black. It matched the mosaic floor tiles. I was impressed the first time I saw it. Old-fashioned charm. After using it, I realized how impractical the tub was: too small for me to take a bath in it, shitty for taking showers, nowhere to put soap and shampoo, took up half the bathroom, added chores (we had to get on our hands and knees to clean beneath it, and after every use, we had to mop up the splashes on the tile), and added worry (not M, but I was convinced, because it must have weighed a ton, that the tub would one day collapse the floorboards beneath it and crash into the kitchen).

I sat in the bathroom until the silence was interrupted by noises filing in one by one: first, my own breathing, then my heartbeat, and M snoring, and the faint hum of the bathroom light, then crickets chirping in the yard. I tiptoed back to the bed, which squeaked when I lay back down. A while later, around midnight, the dark and quiet of the bedroom interrupted only by the ticking of our old-fashioned alarm clock (M was no longer snoring), another possibility popped into my head for why the test revealed two red lines and not the one I had been expecting and had grown accustomed to seeing: Maybe M had administered the test in the wrong way, maybe she hadn't properly or thoroughly followed directions. As much as I wanted to believe this—and finding out would have meant retrieving the package from the trash again, and reading the fine-print instructions, which I had not before considered doing—I outright rejected the notion. I had no trouble admitting to myself that M making *that* mistake was highly unlikely. She had tested herself so many times already she could have written a guidebook on how to use a pregnancy stick. She could have tested herself with her eyes closed. She knew the procedure like the back of her hand. You get the idea. So I waited for more reasons to come. Around 2 a.m., I gave up waiting on their arrival. I got out of bed, grabbed the laptop, and headed downstairs.

According to the Internet, one possibility for why and how the test came up positive when it shouldn't have: M had tested too soon, either a day or two or even a week early. How was M managing to keep track of her menstrual cycle, I wondered, when I didn't even know which day of the week it was?

Another possibility: M's urine had been too diluted from drinking large amounts of fluid right before taking the test. "She *is* always drinking water," I said to myself.

A third possibility: that in all the years we were together, I somehow did not know that my wife suffered from seasonal allergies and, again without my knowledge, all those years she was popping Benadryl tablets, daily, and if that were true, then the presence of an antihistamine in her bloodstream could have caused the positive test result.

Even though I was sleep-deprived and bursting with wishful thinking, both of which have led even the smartest men to errors of judgment, I knew full well that none of these could be true.

I went back upstairs, defeated. Or, more accurately, at a loss for not having found a satisfactory explanation for the two red lines. Yet I was sure that a why and a wherefore waited out there for me to stumble upon. While M continued to sleep soundly, happily snoring away again, not so much sawing logs but scraping chair legs, I remained gripped by doubt. I got out of bed once more and took the pregnancy stick from M's bedside table, where she had left it the way a child tucks a tooth under a pillow, expecting something magical to happen, and I tiptoed into the bathroom. In retrospect, I could have stomped in there and M would not have heard a thing over her snores. I locked the door behind me—like the tiptoeing, probably unnecessary, but better to be safe—and I scrutinized the pregnancy test, looking for a defect, for something, anything unusual.

I focused on the two red lines. I studied them from different angles. Held them against the light. That was when I noticed that one of the two lines, the one on the left, appeared fainter, its color closer to pink than red.

"That could be a sign."

Instantly more alert, and hopeful, I returned the pregnancy stick to M's bedside table and headed back downstairs, carrying the laptop with me. In the kitchen, at the Formica table, I went online for confirmation. "This is it," I told myself. I typed a few words into the search bar, hit return, and in a split second the Internet gave me a definitive answer. Regardless how dissimilar the two red lines appear, two lines equal pregnancy. Always.

I closed the laptop, and the kitchen went dark.

Why was I so insistent on finding an error? I've had plenty of time to come up with an answer, and the answer may not be definitive the way two red lines are, but it's good enough for me. The test result upended what had become an undeniable fact of life: *not* that I didn't want children but that having them would be impossible, that a life with children belonged to someone other than me, other than M. I grew accustomed to this idea the way most people get used to their own face in the mirror. I was relieved. One less thing to stress over. Then the test let me down. One day it's yes. The next it's maybe. The day after that it's an outright no. And it was no, no, no for nine years straight until, out of nowhere, came the yes. I was perplexed. I didn't know what to do or who I was. And I had already gone through something similar—one day I was a college professor, and the next I was not. Then, just as now, I had M. All along, she had perceived things so differently than me. My bewilderment she met with joy, and with wonderment she tempered my disbelief. I had leaned on her then, and I would lean on her now. That's what I told myself, and a new greater sense of relief washed over me. I would come around to her way of seeing things, a journey made easier, I supposed, because we had worries to deal with much more pressing than my hesitancy to accept reality. We had bigger distractions than a miracle pregnancy. We still had the suicides. We had the teenager who killed himself, who took seven kids with him. We had the dam that his suicide broke wide open. Nothing like that had happened before. Not here. Not with children. Not with very young children. Not in recent memory. And as far as I knew, not on TV or in film or in poems, plays, stories, or novels.

As a professor—a former professor—I knew more than the average person about child murder-suicides not taking place in literature. My job was to read books, to talk and argue about them, which I did, each year, with men and women who became younger and younger each year and who were, eventually, young enough to be my offspring. But I don't remember ever coming across a single book in which children killed themselves either in large numbers or in succession. Somewhat similar stories existed. A novel about children killing other children, yes, that exists, but the children in that story are isolated, on a remote island, a strange land far from the place they call home, and they aren't killing others by killing themselves. A story in which young people take their own lives? Yes, at least a couple of these have also been written. In one, the media misrepresents the speech of a young man about his own suicide as a message championing mass suicide, and then teenagers across the country begin writing death poems and offing themselves. In another story, a group of suburban teenage boys (now men) reminisce about and try to make sense of a group of teenage sisters (forever girls) who, one by one, bring about their own demise. None of these are quite the same kind of story because while teenagers of a certain age might legally be children, they are socially, emotionally, and cognitively no such thing, which is to say that what had happened in the East Side (or what seemingly everyone supposed would be happening) differed both in degree and kind from what I had read in these books. At least I thought so.

Was a child suicide taking place?

To this question, I received an answer the day after M found out that she was pregnant, which was also the day I committed to changing my outlook on life to match M's more closely, which was also the first day the mothers and fathers of the seven children killed at the elementary school in the West Side woke up to the nightmare called the rest of their lives. That day I lowered the temperature on the thermostat, the first ritual of the muggy and hot season ahead. I also plugged in the dehumidifier. The AC and the dehumidifier performed a daylong symphony of white noise with few intermissions, and they would soon enough be accompanied by an orchestra of cicadas. More importantly, that day I was watching a TV program, an interview with an expert of some kind who was wearing a gray suit, a white shirt, a solid blue tie, and slightly oversized black eyeglasses that made him look both intelligent and urbane. Because of all the ambient noises, I turned up the volume, which brought even more attention to the expert's slightly modified Midwest accent—the lack of a drawl. This lent a tone of unpretentiousness to his voice, offsetting or else balancing his cosmopolitan appearance. He explained to the man interviewing him, "Children simply don't kill themselves." What did he mean? He said, "There's a reason why a child—why anybody—chooses to end their life." He took a deep breath, ready to mount an argument, but the interviewer intervened and asked him a follow-up question. He asked if, by claiming that children did not kill themselves, he meant to get at the socioeconomic antecedents leading up to the suicide of children, in particular the East Side teenager who had killed seven grade-schoolers.

"No," the expert said. "That's not what I said. All I mean is that it's an extraordinary occurrence for a child to commit suicide. When we talk about children killing themselves, we can't talk about the usual suspects, the sort we associate with adults who kill themselves."

He did not name the usual suspects leading to suicide, nor the people afflicted by them (again, the interviewer interrupted him before he had the chance), but a handful immediately came to mind: depression and the depressed, psychosis and the psychotic, addiction and the addicted, philosophy and the philosophically inclined, mistakes and the mistaken.

The interviewer, who spoke with authority and without an accent, and whose hair, teeth, and facial bone structure, according to most standards, would be described as ideal for the camera, pointed out to his expert guest that the East Side teenager who killed seven kids could hardly be called a child. He reminded the expert that the teenager was a month shy of his eighteenth birthday. "In a matter of days," the interviewer said, "this so-called *child* would have been old enough to vote, old enough to own a gun, to enlist in the armed forces, to go to war and kill the enemy. You can't call him a child." Though the interviewer had made the remark calmly, he was visibly upset, his face red and seemingly flustered, simmering with indignation or maybe annoyance. But he still looked professional in his dark blue suit, and he did not let the expert get a word in edgewise. I thought for sure the interviewer was going to say something about the East Side teen's ethnic origins, about where he or his family had come from—not the East Side, where the teen had lived all his life, but where his long-gone ancestors had come from, which wasn't *here* but *there*. I was even more certain that the interviewer would accomplish this by using vague language and making nonspecific references to those origins, so ultimately not to be accused of bias or political incorrectness or, worse, racism or xenophobia. Such a useful tactic—if he was accused of being a racist or bigot, he could then easily fall back on the imprecision of his words and claim he did not mean what people thought he meant.

How could I be so sure the interviewer would go there? Because others like him had gone there before him many times. Because when it came to people like the East Side teen (regardless of where they lived), going there was usually the first and often the last destination for people like the interviewer. Instead, the interviewer followed up his line of argument against the teenager being called a child with a rhetorical question that may or may not have qualified as racist, xenophobic, politically incorrect, or biased, and in this way, either the interviewer was a genius or just lucky.

"Are you telling me that you think someone old enough to be sent to a foreign country and trained to kill people can be considered a child?"

After asking the question, the interviewer smiled smugly, probably because he felt he had stumped the so-called expert, stunning him into submission, and as a result he appeared to expect only silence and was ready to move on, either to change the subject or cut to a commercial break. However, to the interviewer's chagrin and no doubt to the surprise of the viewers watching at home, who must have been astonished to hear what came next—I certainly was—the expert answered without the slightest bit of hesitation.

"Yes, I do. Absolutely. It's a fact."

ɞ

The next day, the temperature climbed a degree, and the humidity, a few percentage points higher. Both the AC and dehumidifier worked a while longer this day, and each day would work harder, longer, for weeks to come, raising our electricity bill. On this day, I watched TV again, a show on a different network, with three men and one woman, each with opposing viewpoints and known for expressing firm, uncompromising beliefs. They sat around a gleaming wood table to argue with each other. Near the end of the segment on the East Side child suicides, one of the men began making the case that children had indeed killed themselves before. "In every era, and everywhere on the earth, children have killed themselves." Over the past century, according to a source he did not cite, one in every 100,000 children gave up on the thing done time and again and which some people called a life. While not a percentage that would induce sleeplessness in parents the world over (more children die annually from the flu), the point being made was the existence of child suicide.

One of the other men, a columnist for a large national newspaper, nodded in agreement but called attention to the fact that the number just cited, one in every 100,000, paled in comparison to the number of grown men and women who shot, hanged, poisoned, and overdosed themselves—to name the most common approaches to self-death. The columnist, who had also won a coveted prize, lending his opinion greater weight and authority, supported his point with statistics of his own: every forty seconds, he said, a man or woman—usually a man—kills himself. "Mostly, people shoot themselves," he said. "Last year alone, more than 21,000 people shot themselves to death."

While not described as an expert or specialist of any kind but doubtlessly assumed to be one, though what he did outside of such news programs I did not know, the third man objected to the comparisons being made between men and the children of men. With a hint of indignation and a lively but tactful banging of his clenched fist against the mahogany tabletop, he said, "Come on, now. A child is not a man. A child is a child is a child."

After this, the woman on the panel, also the moderator, interrupted the men to change the direction the conversation had taken. In doing so, she broached the subject the expert from the day before seemed on the verge of speaking about before being cut off. The woman said, "We may have to agree to disagree, but before we do that, let me be the voice of reason here. Children don't simply commit suicide out of the blue. There must be an explanation for why this has happened—why any child, any family, goes through such a horrible, unimaginable tragedy. I think we—not just us at this table, but the public and politicians, plus doctors and psychologists—all need to discuss why young people—children—would choose death over life. What's fueling the crisis—if it's indeed a crisis? Are these kids worried about climate change? Do they think the world they're inheriting, with its rising sea levels, rising global temperatures, its dramatic and catastrophic weather events, is doomed? And as such, they're doomed? Do they see only a bleak future? Maybe they're so worried about social injustices that they can't see themselves making it in the world? Maybe we need to be having more conversations—in the nation's capital and around our own dinner tables—about the impact of technology on the lives of children, about their addiction to screens and social media."

None of the men on the panel seemed to take her very seriously. It's possible I was only imagining that. In fact, in an unusual moment in the lives of men, none of them were given much of a chance to respond. No sooner had the female interlocutor ended her commentary, she repeated the remark about the need to agree to disagree, at which point, the men all smiled. Only the prize-winning columnist said something, but he directed his comment not at the so-called voice of reason in the room but rather at the guests at odds with each other.

"I would have it no other way," he said. "You're my favorite people to argue with."

Genuinely or not, they all reacted accordingly: a smile, a chuckle, and audible laughter.

The TV switched from the panelists sitting around the table and the moderator's sincere and disarming voice to another voice even more disarming and sincere, that of an award-winning actor doing the voiceover for a commercial featuring a luxury sports sedan. The car was being driven at speeds that would be considered illegal, if not categorically reckless, through oddly deserted streets of what otherwise should have been a very busy downtown in a heavily populated urban center. Given the presence of palm trees at nearly every turn the speeding sedan made, I assumed the city was somewhere out West, probably California. Around this time, M was beginning to disagree with me more than usual. She always had, but her tone used to be less derisive, her intent not to win or put down but simply to do as the panelists had: to disagree for the sake of disagreeing. Or else it was me who couldn't agree with her as often as I used to or would have liked, especially because I had told myself I would try to think more like her, a task that was turning out to be harder than I had assumed. Either way, about where I thought the car commercial had been shot, I said, "Looks like Los Angeles." Sure enough, without even looking at me, M said, "I'm pretty sure that's Miami."

A very old movie star, who lived a long, good life, died the next day. The day after that, a famous, good-looking athlete cheated on his slightly less-famous but equally attractive wife. And less than twenty-four hours later, a wildly popular singer said something publicly that no one expected or wanted singers to say, and for a day or part of a day, a sizable portion of the public lost its mind over the singer's opinion.

For these three days and the better part of a fourth, we had gone without news of suicide. No children killed themselves, and if any men or women had done themselves in, no one reported it to the news, or else the news decided against airing these stories, letting the dead be dead. Tragedy did not come to a stop—far from it. The world is not science fiction or fantasy. People continued experiencing loss, suffering, and heartache, but they were of a lesser degree, or so we believed. On the other side of the state, a weeks-old forest fire swallowed up hundreds of acres of pine, oak, farmland, and livestock. Closer to home, a retired but beloved baseball coach announced he had prostate cancer. Even closer, in the neighborhood adjacent to the East Side, a coffee factory that had been family-run since 1900 was sold to investors from California who planned to convert it into luxury condominiums. These minor misfortunes of other people had allowed us some much-needed respite from the misery of our deeply unhappy youth. But like a sudden and swift rainstorm during a drought, the hiatus was short-lived. Before the week was up, the old preacher with the beautiful blue eyes who preached at the small church on the edge of the East Side showed up at the East Side's gracefully landscaped public cemetery, which had small rolling hills even though the city was entirely flat. He did not come alone. A schoolteacher, a dentist, and a store-owner turned up at the cemetery with him with the intention of picketing the funeral of the teen who had committed murder and suicide by driving his mother's stolen SUV into a classroom teeming with kids.

Most everyone remembers only the old preacher being at the cemetery, an easy-to-understand omission in memory given that most people are accustomed to seeing clergy perform funerals, not protest them. The incongruity of his role as a preacher and the role he took on that day (not to preside over but picket a funeral) must have impressed itself so fully, so emphatically in the public's otherwise short-term memory that they simply blotted out the others with him. That, plus the protest sign the preacher held close to his chest similarly ran counter to the message most people expected from an old man (a man of God, no less) who could have easily been cast in the part of a sweet old grandpa. The sign, white with black lettering, read,

GOD HATES YOU AND YOUR DEAD CHILD.

All the signs held up that day, not just the preacher's, did their best to insult and hurt. They were awful. They were hard to forget.

The sign carried by the teacher, who had on khaki pants, a blue Oxford shirt (the top button unbuttoned, the sleeves rolled up to the elbow), a pair of brown leather boat shoes with white soles, and dark sunglasses, read,

HOPE YOUR KID ENJOYS HELL.

The dentist wore a strapless white summer dress that made me think of a town I had seen in more than one magazine and ad and movie, Santorini, the Mediterranean coastal town that rises above the sea on steep cliffs, famous for its white-washed, blue-domed buildings. The dentist also had on sunglasses and an oversized straw fedora sunhat a few shades darker than her blond hair. She looked ready to spend the day in the sun, poolside, sipping cocktails in a lounge chair. Instead, she was at the cemetery, proudly holding up a sign that read,

THANK GOD YOUR SON IS DEAD.

The storeowner was a shabby, disheveled man. His jeans were either twenty years old, or else he only wore them to do dirty work. He had clearly outgrown the tight-fitting polo shirt he had on, too, its faded black barely hiding the sweat stains under his arms. He carried a sign that read,

GOD IS LAUGHING AT YOU.

M says I often overindulge in particulars that most people would not bother with or could not care less about. How people dress, for instance. She's not wrong, but I take her point *not* to be that appearances don't matter or that meaningfulness cannot be gleaned from the outward display a person puts together for others to see. Our exterior, after all, hides the interior, literally and otherwise, and how we choose to cover ourselves reveals a lot about us and about what lies underneath. Rather, I take M's point about my so-called overindulgence to mean that what the picketers wore to the cemetery that day mattered much less than the words on their picket signs. I will concede the argument, but only partially, and will meet M halfway—three-quarters of the way, to be exact. So, once more: God hates you and your dead child, Hope your kid enjoys hell, Thank God your son is dead, and God is laughing at you. But, as I said, M and I were disagreeing a good deal around this time, and while it may not ultimately make a difference what the schoolteacher, dentist, and storeowner wore to picket the teen's funeral, the old preacher's appearance did in fact matter.

He was wearing a gray suit jacket at least one to two sizes too large, making his shoulders appear broader than they were while at the same time, especially given his age and thin frame, making him seem even more frail than he might have been. Why did his jacket fit so loosely? Was he once a larger man with a larger frame? Or was he merely a man with a proclivity for ill-fitting suits? Why would a grown man intentionally put on clothes far too big for his frame? Many reasons exist for why men dress badly. Poverty being one, ignorance another, lack of concern or good taste being two more. But no one in the media bothered to ask the old preacher or to speculate a cause, probably because such questions never occurred to them or because most journalists and TV news personalities would deem asking questions about appearances not newsworthy and not attention grabbing. I don't believe this to be true, either. On

TV, appearance is everything, and the old preacher would soon enough be on TV plenty. People must have wondered why the news left the old preacher's appearance unattended. I certainly did, and wasn't the rule of thumb true that if one person thought something, a thousand others must be thinking the same thing? Don't you have to admit that a person's appearance does indeed influence the way you see that person, one way or another? Oddly enough, the old preacher's trousers, a slightly lighter shade of gray that almost but not quite matched the color of his suit jacket, fit him just right. They were properly hemmed, not too long or too short, and they appeared perfectly pressed, with a visible crease running down the center of each pant leg. In every single image I saw of the old preacher, on the Internet, TV, or in print, he completed the outfit with a dark red tie and a white dress shirt. In this way, among others, he came off as a down-home politician. Only missing from his look was a flag pinned to the lapel of his jacket.

Given she had known about him much longer than I did, I asked M about the old preacher's attire, if he had always been so fixed in his choices. For as long as she could remember, he had had that look about him. A look of solemnity, the honest-to-goodness kind. Complementing it, conveying hard-earned dignity and upstanding moral character, was his seemingly perfect posture: his shoulders always square and never slumped, his back always straight and never slouched, his head held high and his chin up. At some point earlier in his life, the first time he put on the gray jacket and pants, the red tie and white shirt, he must have beheld himself before a mirror and recognized in its reflection the effect of his appearance and from that moment forward decided not to deviate from the image, ever. The old preacher was the only one among the picketers that day who was not wearing glasses of any kind. This might explain why, when

I picture him, even now, the first image to materialize in my mind's eye are his brilliant blue eyes, which, that day, matched the blue of the sky. Maybe this also explains why people remember him more than the others, or why they believe, incorrectly, that the old preacher protested the teen's funeral all by himself.

A friend of the teen's family, an average-sized man wearing a dark gray shirt, trousers, and light jacket, walked from the burial site to where the picketers had gathered. When he reached the protesters, the friend of the family stood face to face with the old preacher and, without a word of warning, spit on him. The old preacher drew a white handkerchief from his pants pocket and wiped the spit off his face.

In response to this act of contempt against the old preacher, the others, as if prepared for such a happening—indeed anticipating it—did nothing. With a self-possessed placidity that reminded me of the rare but enduring activists from decades past and present who set themselves on fire, they stood immobilized, holding their signs up, aiming their messages at the mourners across the way, and did nothing else, not even turn their heads toward the old preacher or the family friend who spat on him. I imagined that, inwardly, the old preacher's companions must have been experiencing storms of doubt and apprehension. Given what I know about them now, they must have hoped and prayed that the man would not take turns spitting on each of them, and not for anything would they have turned themselves into charred martyrs.

By the time the old preacher had folded his handkerchief and put it back in his pants pocket, someone else from the funeral party joined the family friend—the teen's uncle. He did not spit on anyone. He did not pull the family friend back, either. Instead, he shoved the schoolteacher, who was next in line beside the old preacher, nearly knocking the teacher over. Remarkably, the schoolteacher readjusted his stance and simply stood there—again, doing, saying nothing. This only enraged the uncle, who upped his antagonism by snatching the sunglasses from the schoolteacher's face and flinging them over his head. For this, it seems, the schoolteacher had not been prepared. He took the bait, and then he took what could only be interpreted as either a defensive or a threatening stance, or both: He dropped his picket sign to the ground, raised his hands, and clenched his fists.

The old preacher finally made a move. He stepped between the two men on the verge of fisticuffs. At that very moment, the third and last member of the funeral party approached the picketers. The dead teenager's mother grabbed the uncle by the arm, whispered something into his ear, words that no one else heard, and hearing them, the dead teen's uncle lowered his hands and backed off. So, too, did the family friend, though his retreat did not require a word from the dead teen's mother. Then the three of them— uncle, family friend, and mother—walked back to the gravesite to finish laying their dearly departed to rest.

At about this time, a local television news crew arrived in a van equipped with a satellite dish on its roof, ready, if necessary, to broadcast live from the cemetery. A few minutes later, without fanfare—no flashing lights, no menacing siren—a police car pulled up, and two officers got out and made their way, casually, from the gravel road to the picketers. After conferring with the old preacher, one of the police officers, who was male and wearing mirrored sunglasses, informed the teen's grieving mother that in protesting the funeral, the old preacher and his picketers had not violated any existing laws. The old preacher had produced for the officer a permit from the inside pocket of his ill-fitting jacket. Had the teen's mother chosen to bury her son in a private cemetery, the police could have asked the old preacher and the picketers to leave, but the cemetery where her son was being buried was public, owned by the city. The policeman also let the teen's mother know that the old preacher had refused to leave the grounds, as a matter of principle. After some cajoling by the second police officer, who was female and wearing reflective sunglasses, the old preacher finally acquiesced, but to a limited extent. While he would not agree to leave the grounds entirely, he and the schoolteacher, dentist, and storeowner did relocate further from the teen's casket, a distance from which the mourners could still make out the words on their signs if they squinted but, no matter how hard they strained to hear them, not the words they were chanting. If, however, anyone in the funeral party ended up watching the five o'clock news later that day, they would have heard the chant the TV news crew caught on tape:

"You animals, you, God hates you."

I had so many opinions about the picketers and the signs they carried, but M wouldn't let me share any of them with her.

"I don't want to talk about them," she said. "It makes me feel awful, and that's bad for the baby."

Because the news story about the funeral and the picketing was so riveting *and* in our own backyard, I had nearly forgotten that she was pregnant.

"Sure," I said, and I kept my opinions about the old preacher and the signs to myself. I had other judgments I also kept quiet about, including whether at this point in the pregnancy we should even call the baby a baby. Naturally, though, because of the TV news coverage at the cemetery, a lot of other people did share their two cents' worth, which I read online. Not surprising, I came across as many opinions about the picketers and their signs as I did about the deceased East Side teen. For the most part, opinions on the teen and his family and friends, and the people like him—people like M and me—could be divided into two categories that happened to be, also for the most part, diametrically opposed: those expressing bigotry and those expressing indignation over the bigotry. The people accused of being bigots could be further divided into two camps. The first believed that while it might have been deplorable for the picketers to disgrace the sanctity of a sacred rite, they generally forgave the picketers for the transgression because they found what the teen had done much more deplorable—he had murdered children, by way of suicide, and as such, he had asked for it. The second camp simply dispensed with decorum and empathy entirely. Their opinions, which I read on a wildly popular online community forum, echoed the old preacher's sentiments. They wanted the people of the East Side, those who looked like the dead teen or his mother or his uncle, to go back from where they came. They wanted East Side parents to stop teaching their children to kill. People like the teen, his mother, his uncle, the family friend, or people like M and her father and his father before him, and people like me—they insisted that before we had come to the East Side, it was a great place to live and raise children, but we had ruined it for them.

M declined every effort on my part to get her to join me in ranting and raving about these opinions. We didn't need to talk about it, though. We had had that conversation already, dozens of times. Hundreds, maybe. We knew that all the facts in the world, those that undeniably and incontrovertibly contradicted "You animals, you" and "Stop teaching your children to kill," would do nothing to change the mind of someone like the old preacher. The problem wasn't facts.

The problem was belief. The old preacher insisted that East Siders like us were influencing children to kill themselves—that the reason they were killing themselves had nothing to do with depression, bullying, the Internet, peer pressure, or any psychological or medical explanation. They were suicidal because they belonged to a particular community—ours. To me, this was the stupidest, most unbelievable thing I'd heard. But that did not make it go away. The preacher said it, and others believed. Probably because they wanted to believe. Probably because it made them feel good to believe we were so terrible. As for the preacher, he must have understood that his preaching and protest instilled fear in the community, and that would incite fear among us, too. And with fear comes opportunity.

M might have been right not to engage. Maybe it was better to leave other people's opinions to other people, to ignore them, to leave the people voicing them be. But maybe it was also dangerous to look the other way. And so, I kept reading opinions, and of the various ones put into words about the picketers and their signs, one breed stood out: that which mingled harsh judgments with the threat of death. While all the picketers (the teacher, dentist, storeowner, and preacher) each received one or more death threats (some by phone, a few by mail, the majority via email), the bulk of them went to the old preacher. In turn, he and his fellow picketers, and his congregation at the small church, made a lot of noise about the death threats. Much of it was some version of "I told you so" and "See, they are menacing." Occasionally, I came across a version of "They're not helping the cause." Which cause? Against whom or what? All these outcries against the preacher's message and method inevitably led to considerably more attention, the consequence of which was that their ideas ended up being amplified and repeated, not silenced or stifled. And because not everyone believed that the old preacher was wrong (whereas the teen and people like him must be), the threats to do harm against him, an old man with beautiful blue eyes, often gave way to sympathy. And where there is sympathy, invariably there are sympathizers.

In addition to the schoolteacher, dentist, and store-owner, the old preacher's cause was joined by a nurse, a retired police officer, a certified master plumber, and a personal injury lawyer. It's not clear if at this point it makes sense to call these people a movement. More properly, they might have been only a group. Let's say that's what they were, a group. To be sure, while the group's number had, almost overnight, literally doubled in size, they still constituted a relatively small number of individuals. The congregation at the small church itself numbered only in the dozens. Adding in the congregants, the group remained relatively small. However, the number was still large enough for the old preacher to feel that the group needed a name. He named them The Good Neighbors.

The Good Neighbors should have been shunned, ridiculed, chastised, and castigated as a bunch of crazies. In fact, that was precisely what happened. The news media went out of its way to disparage the old preacher. Journalists, especially those on TV, reported on the picket signs *with* bias. Newscasters offered not just the who, what, when, why, and where of the old preacher's picketing, but also their opinion of him and his signs. And their opinions leaned toward the side of righteousness and indignation. However, an unexpected consequence of the press coverage, one that would ultimately play a much more pivotal role in the trajectory of our story, was a sudden influx of donations to the old preacher's church. The day before the picketing, donations to the small church could be reliably described as practically nothing. They amounted to no more than the pittance ordinarily collected in wicker baskets during church services. Within a few days of the picketing—of its news coverage—the amount had grown to such an abundance that the old preacher was able to lure back into the fold his only son, a handsome, well-spoken man who had been making his way in the world as an upwardly mobile entrepreneur. He would return to the family business, which had, overnight, become lucrative.

At the time that all this happened, I did not understand why. Why weren't The Good Neighbors *only* shunned, ridiculed, chastised, and castigated? Why did people send them money? Why would anyone do such a thing? Now I know. It was a confluence of two things: One, the media initially went out of its way *not* to identify the ethnic or racial makeup of the East Side teenager, and two, The Good Neighbors did the exact opposite.

Plenty of people had wanted to name names and call people out, to name a people collectively and associate them, unapologetically, with the worst of humanity's ills. Plenty of people were willing to give up money to ensure that men like the old preacher got to do that indefinitely. Much later, after the old preacher was dead and gone, an online magazine ran a short video documentary on The Good Neighbors, interviewing some of the group's supporters. One man said of the old preacher, "At least he wasn't afraid to say what a lot of people were thinking," and another offered the following bit of posthumous praise: "He didn't care one bit about being politically correct." Neither of these men, nor others featured in the documentary, lived in the East Side. Neither of the two men just quoted lived in the state—one hailed from Oregon, the other Wisconsin. Which is to say, donations poured in from across the country. It's hard to say exactly how much money came their way. Only the preacher's son knows, and he has never disclosed the information, despite requests to do so. No one other than the preacher's son knows whether the donors were many (lots of people sending $10 here, $20 there, whatever they could afford) or few (one or two people writing checks with enough zeroes on them to allow The Good Neighbors, despite what anyone thought of them or anything they did, to keep doing what they wanted no matter what anyone said or thought about them). Whichever way the donations came, the fear of kids killing themselves wasn't behind them, not really. I didn't think so, at least. The fear that fueled The Good Neighbors was the men who looked like the kids. Men who could've passed as their fathers, uncles, or older brothers. Men who had already done worse, far worse. An infinitesimally small number of men who, nevertheless, were more feared than heart attacks, cancer, car crashes, viruses, mass shooters, angry husbands, and short-tempered coworkers, all of which were more likely to cause death than a suicidal teen. If they had once taken for granted that the children of the East Side would grow up to be like those men, those who supported the old preacher and his cause now believed that these children had already become the men they feared. And people who could afford to do so, and for that matter even people who could not, gave and gave and gave.

With him, the preacher's son brought certain skills and talents to the group, not the least of which was the gift of speech. With his talent for words—the best ones in the best order—the old preacher's son took The Good Neighbors and their message from the fringes to the center, from grossly unapologetic to barely controversial, from appalling to acceptable.

He began the journey on a syndicated radio show. Asked about the "despicable and grotesque" protest at the cemetery, the preacher's son said, "The last thing anyone wants is more tragedy. The signs were meant to grab attention, and since there's so much fuss being made these days about this, that, and the other, it's easy for people to lose sight of what's right before their eyes."

"And what's that?" the radio show host asked him.

"Our freedom," the preacher's son said. "Freedom is under attack. The freedom to raise our children without fear, to send them to school without worrying they might not come back home. Sometimes people need to be jolted into seeing the truth."

I could just hear people responding, "Amen to that."

Not once did the preacher's son make explicit reference to the people of the East Side, those who did not look like him. He did not mention our origins, our habits, or our customs. He chose, instead, to speak about us implicitly, vaguely, allowing his listeners to think of us, and of themselves, in the ways they had already been prepared to think—to see us as us and them as them. Compared to his father, the preacher's son took a softer, gentler approach to coax the worst from people. In this way, he showed he was more talented, more sophisticated. Unlike his father, he spread fear and hate under the guise of good intentions. Given the propensity of opinions to mutate as they spread, the preacher's son did his best to guide and focus the "opinions" advocated by the group, and in doing so, he became, practically overnight, the official spokesperson of The Good Neighbors.

Why the scare quotes around *opinions*? I never got the impression that the preacher's son ever thought that he, his father, or The Good Neighbors were managing to influence others by way of opinion. The preacher's son viewed himself, no doubt, as a man who spoke in terms of truth and conviction. Those who would listen to him, he compelled into belief. Strictly speaking, belief is a kind of opinion, and vice versa. The preacher's son must have known this. He knew something else, too. That meaning depended as much on what we called something as it did on what that something in fact was. Opinions could be dismissed more readily than beliefs. More importantly, people argued over opinions, but they died for beliefs, actually and figuratively. Worse—or better, depending on which side you're on—for a belief, people would not only sacrifice themselves but others. The preacher's son understood very well that with or without evidence, it would take only time and effort to establish in the minds of those who wanted to believe in something sinister that, yes, indeed, there was something sinister going on.

How did he go about doing this?

He took the more the broadly accepted notion that the East Side suicides were a coincidence and twisted it around. He evolved it into speculation that the children born, raised, and dwelling in the East Side—those he and his father had in their own ways identified as a part of *them*—were prone to suicide, to violence in general, and not just against themselves but against others. This notion, which is utterly ridiculous from our point of view yet completely acceptable from theirs, he shared repeatedly, deliberately, indiscriminately, all with the intention of propagating the notion far and wide. The goal: The notion would travel so far and wide it would ultimately be regarded by enough people as a taken-for-granted fact of life, what most of us call common knowledge. And as we all know, across every culture in every era, common knowledge has often been confused with undeniable fact. How often in the long, troubled, uninterrupted history of bad ideas has a lie become a truth? Exact numbers are not available. Suffice it to say, a lot.

Reared by a man who always carried a Bible, the preacher's son knew something about indisputable truths, but his greatest insight was recognizing that most people hardly cared if children were going the way of Ophelia. They cared infinitely more if their own children were going to kill themselves. They cared to an even greater extent if children other than their own were going around killing other children, especially innocent children, particularly their own innocent children. Like his father had before him, the preacher's son had—again in his own way—referred to the East Side as a threat, and its children, both those already here and those yet to come, he had also judged to be extremely dangerous. However, unlike his father, the preacher's son avoided the use of debauched slogans, which had the effect of pissing people off and undermining his message. By contrast, he stuck to facts. For example, he reminded the syndicated radio show host, and everyone listening, that *all* the children who had killed themselves had hailed from the East Side. "Every single one." And although so, too, did his children, he knew—and we knew—he meant *our* children, not his. He also warned the radio show host and the listening audience that the threat posed by the East Side's children went beyond harm to the body. "They threaten the very fabric of our lives." This, too, was code, but even if it hadn't been, who could argue with it? Not even the dead teen's mother would have. After all, the fabric of her life had come undone by her son's actions. And those mothers and fathers whose children were killed by the teen, hadn't the threads holding their lives together been pulled apart? Even the East Side parents the preacher was really talking about, those who might have looked like M and me, like the child we were going to have, those who were now being forced to defend the viability and tranquility of their children, wouldn't they also have to agree with the preacher's son that the teen who killed seven first-graders had fucked things up?

Yes, yes, they would.

The preacher's son accomplished a lot in that first interview, and had it ended with him imploring us to see the suicides as amounting to a major breech of the social contract, he could have left the recording studio and congratulated himself on a job well done. It didn't end there. He went further. Even though the teen was the only suicide who had killed anyone other than himself, and even though nothing about his suicide could be described as remotely political, the preacher's son called the suicides (that of the first girl, her parents, and the teen) "acts of terror."

The back-and-forth between the host and preacher's son came to a halt. A short pause, lasting only a few seconds. Two or three at most. But because it was radio, the silence seemed epic. After clearing his throat, the radio host asked, "What do you hope to gain by calling a bunch of children terrorists?"

Unperturbed, the preacher's son answered without hesitation. "*You* said the word 'terrorists.' I only said that that the suicides instilled terror in the hearts and minds of people. That's a fact. If you don't like the word 'terror,' then how about 'intimidation' or 'extreme fear.' We can call it whatever you wish. The fact is that we live in bad times. Bad things are happening. We simply want to protect good people from bad people, to keep bad things from happening to good people, especially our children. My God, I would hope that no one would be against that."

M was listening to the broadcast with me. We were in the kitchen. Ordinarily, after brewing a pot of coffee, M would have taken her cup elsewhere. Upstairs, in the bedroom, usually. Sometimes on the front porch steps. Other times, in a lawn chair in the backyard. On this day, out of curiosity, I suppose, she stayed in the kitchen. But because she had taken to reading a lot of online articles about pregnancy, the most recent of which urged expectant mothers to quit caffeine immediately, M took to drinking herbal tea, not coffee. She was spooning organic cane sugar into a white porcelain mug. The interview ended, and the radio switched to a commercial about protecting ourselves from thieves who wanted to steal our identities.

About saving the good from the bad, I told M that tonally and rhetorically, the preacher's son sounded like a biblical character. Noah came to mind, probably because a seemingly ceaseless progression of storms had blitzed through the area overnight, waking me up (M had managed to sleep through the lightning and thunder), and it was still raining. Also, Noah had been tasked with warning the children of men to change their ways—or else.

I expected M to push back, to remind me not to fill the house with negativity, to keep the atmosphere healthy and wholesome for the baby growing inside her. Ever since the two red lines, she picked up recommendations about being pregnant from blogs and forums by and about pregnant women. Every day, before going to sleep, she read an article about pregnancy and told me about it. Every day, after getting out of bed, she practiced this or that habit encouraged by expectant mothers the world over. These included adding more lentils and asparagus to her diet, taking a daily dose of prenatal vitamins, and writing a birth plan. On this day, the day the preacher's son made the case that the East Side suicides were terrorizing us, M filled a heavy-duty trash bag with household products she deemed to be harsh and toxic. Windex, Pledge, Drano, Scotchgard, Formula 409, and the like. Of course, she asked me to throw the bag out. Then she jotted down a grocery list of safe and natural ingredients we would use from here on out. I can say with some certainty it was around this time M began obsessively preparing for the baby's arrival. Nesting is the term I would come across, and it fit. Early on, M's nesting manifested it-self in the form of spring cleaning, but given that the pregnancy forums warned against heavy lifting and overex-ertion, almost every day I was dusting or mopping or rearranging furniture or taking more of our belongings to the trash or donating them to Goodwill. My own descents down the rabbit holes of online pregnancy sites led to the following discovery: Most women did not begin nesting un-til the last two weeks of their pregnancy. M had flipped the timetable, nesting right from the start. I kept this to myself. The chores gave me something to do. More crucially, they made M need me, a feature of our marriage long missing.

About the preacher's son sounding like Noah, I said to M, "He's talking about the suicide of one girl and one teen-ager like they're the raindrops before the flood."

As a rule, after saying something like that, I awaited M's judgment.

"Raindrops before the flood, huh?" She set the white porcelain mug on the kitchen table and pulled up a chair. "That's clever."

The compliment was wholly unexpected. I tried but failed to suppress a smile.

Schools closed for summer. The temperatures climbed. Sprinklers arched intermittent sprays across growing lawns. Louds lawnmowers cut the growth. Birds chirped. Ants marched. Mosquito eggs hatched. Honeybees made honeycombs and honey. Crickets and grasshoppers pro-duced music. Cicadas rose from the ground. Trees filled with noise. Dogs added to the clamor by barking at cats and squirrels. Cats lounged under parked cars, and squirrels dug holes in front yards and backyards. Under mostly cloudless skies, gleaming suns, and waning moons, snakes slithered through flower beds, lizards stood perfectly still, bugs crawled in the dirt, possums crossed fence lines, owls hooted, and every other living thing in the East Side went on living, including its children, who, in spite of everything supposed and believed about them, carried on with their waking, stretching, eating, drinking, playing, running, hiding, jumping, falling, eating, drinking, whining, yelling, laughing, crying, yawning, sleeping, dreaming, waking, and doing it all over again.

Throughout the first few weeks of summer, despite the upright nature of the East Side's kids, the TV and Internet also did something repeatedly and continuously: They emphasized that over a period lasting one month, more East Side children had self-induced their demise than had any other concentrated group of youth during the same timespan anywhere else on earth. The number was two. Two East Side children dead by their own hands. While I want to avoid callousness, I must stress that there were *only* two. Yet this represented, somehow, more child suicides than anywhere else on earth. Incredulous as it was, no one disputed the claim, and like the children of the East Side, the claim about them also continued living and breathing unabated.

In other places around the world, because children did die for all sorts of reasons, the makers of very small coffins carried on with their sad craft as the lost children of their cities and towns wreaked irreparable hardship and unending agony upon their mothers and fathers, siblings and cousins, aunts, uncles, friends, and neighbors. The parents occupied my imagination. The deaths of their children forced them to put together one last outfit. Which pair of shoes would they choose? Which shirt? Which dress? The choices must have left the pitiable shells of their former selves bereft of true happiness and with little to no hope for the future. But because these other children had roots elsewhere, in countries far, far away, their deaths came and went with hardly a drop of ink spilled or a pixel illuminated or a sound bite captured or a stranger aware. For these dear departed and those survived by their untimely departures, life, death, and life after death carried on as usual.

Not here.

For at least a full month, people waited and waited for the deaths of East Side children by their own hands. During that lunar cycle, which coincided with the passing of one season and the advent of another, something even more curious than the waiting occurred. The child suicides in the East Side came to a full stop.

Ever since the tragedy on the West Side involving the teenager, his mother's SUV, and seven first-graders, not a single girl or boy, tween, teen, or young adult—healthy, depressed, bullied, or beloved—had attempted to cut short their already short lives. Nor, for that matter, had any East Side kids attempted to end anyone else's tenure on earth. Nevertheless, the radio, the Internet, the print news, and the TV resolutely stood by for the suicides to start up again, and in the wings, The Good Neighbors waited.

THREE

EXACTLY THIRTY-ONE DAYS and nights after the tragedy at the grade school, M turned to me and said, "It's been a month. The baby's sex is already decided."

I opened my eyes and saw her face lit up by words and images on the laptop. She was reading about the stages of pregnancy, the screen's diffused blue glow the only light source in the bedroom. Not a full minute before she spoke to me about the baby's sex, I had switched off the lamp on my bedside table. Tired, my mind had been gradually slipping into its other world, but the fact about her being a month pregnant, stated out loud in near pitch-darkness, brought me right back into this one.

Without checking to make sure I was awake and listening, M kept talking.

"Our child is just an egg right now. Growing and growing inside a watertight sac, and soon—if not already—the baby's face is beginning to take shape, and its eyes, too." She was practically giddy about the details, the facts of the baby's emerging existence. "Can you imagine," she said, "eyes coming into being right now, eyes so small they're no more than tiny circles, black dots no bigger than pin pricks?"

Finally, she looked away from the laptop and sideways at me, and when her eyes met mine, I smiled for her. She smiled back and returned to the pregnancy website. I adjusted my eyesight to the light, faint as it was. Glancing up,

I noticed a crack almost exactly down the center of the ceiling. In all the years I had lived in the blue bungalow with M, lying in the bed beside her, staring up at the ceiling while she slept or read a book or surfed the Internet, I hadn't caught sight of it before. Was the crack new? Was the foundation shifting? Or was it a trick of the eye, a shadow or the natural consequence of coming to light after a period of darkness? Given my age—I wasn't old, but I was hardly young anymore—it could have been blurred vision.

M kept talking.

"The first thing our child will see in this world will be you and me."

Babies are born blind. That was my immediate thought, which might have been true. I didn't know. I couldn't even remember if I had read that somewhere or heard it from someone. Hasty, possibly false, and likely completely fabricated, I decided to let the image of blind newborns die in my head. Without replying to M, I decided instead to listen and only listen. She continued to read aloud about our baby's development in her womb. She kept reading and talking. For how long, either a few more seconds or minutes, I was in the wrong state of mind for judging subtleties like the passage of time. The last thing I remember before everything went dark and I slipped back into that other world was M saying that our baby, in that moment, was smaller than a grain of rice.

The next day was a Saturday. I know this for a fact because on the first Saturday of each new month I headed out to collect rent payments from the tenants living in the white, yellow, and pink bungalows. Just as I had so many previous Saturdays, I left the house early in the morning and left M sleeping in bed.

Of all the bungalows M had inherited, she wanted the pink one for us, even though it was the smallest of the lot.

On his deathbed, though, her father made M promise she would take up residence in the family home, the blue bungalow. While the world over dying parents expected their children to keep unreasonable promises (quit smoking, stop being gay, always be good, vote Republican), I never understood why anyone obliged them. Worrying about promises is a concern for the living. Once dead, the dead simply cannot give a damn.

Either way, I didn't care which bungalow we would live in. Any of them would have been fine with me: blue, yellow, white, pink, the smallest, the largest, the one with a back porch, the one with a wrap-around front porch, the one closer to the grocery store, the one a short walk to the park. What I cared about infinitely more than which bungalow we called ours was that we no longer had to pay rent. All the bungalows had long been paid off, and as much as it must have irked her father, who regarded me with contempt, the bungalows provided not just M, but me, too, with a steady source of income, which we didn't have and badly needed. The lack of income had become a strain on our marriage after I lost my job at the college when a committee of my peers recommended my dismissal due to moral turpitude. My firing must have given the old man a taste of joy right before his death. In the long run, bearing in mind that I not only outlived him and went on to live in his home, but also, since his death, collected a good amount of money every single month from the properties he worked his whole life to finance, there's no doubt that I one-upped him.

I hardly saw our tenants. Only now and then did they get in touch. When they did, usually they only called to tell me that their worlds were crashing down because of a blown fuse, a clogged sink, or a critter in the attic. Several years back, a single mother renting out the yellow bungalow phoned me panic-stricken. She had inadvertently locked her two-year-old boy in the bathroom. I tried explaining how to pick the lock open, a simple task, but rather than listen, she yelled and screamed into the receiver, "Mister, mister, he's in the tub, he's drowning." I hung up and bolted out the door barefoot, sprinted the three blocks down and three streets over to the house. I pictured myself crashing through the bathroom door, knocking it off its hinges, and finding the toddler floating face down in soapy bathwater. I reached the yellow bungalow with my lungs on fire, a piercing pain in my abdomen, and my heart ready to explode. The single mother, whose name was Janet or Janice—honestly, I can't remember, and I didn't bother looking her name up on the old lease because she's simply not that important to the story—she wasn't there, waiting for me. Not by the front gate or on the front porch or at the front door, which was still locked. The kid must have died already, I thought. Or the mother is in the bathroom on her knees hopelessly administering CPR. Instantly, I doubted that. She couldn't figure out how to unlock the bathroom door— she wasn't about to save a life. I was sure to find her weeping like a forsaken mother in an ancient Greek tragedy.

I banged on the front door with so much force that I was one hundred percent sure that I fractured a bone in my wrist. Hard as I pounded, no answer. Fortunately, I had grabbed my keys on the way out—a force of habit—and the master key to each bungalow was on the ring. I fumbled a bit for the key, but in retrospect I realize that under the circumstances I managed to unlock the door relatively quickly. Then I did what I had imagined myself doing: I burst into the house, dashed down the hallway, and though I could see that the bathroom door was slightly ajar, I threw it wide open the way heroic men do in Hollywood blockbusters. The doorknob slammed into the mother, and she yelped. To my astonishment, she was on her knees, next to the tub, but the boy was not floating face down in the water or resting limp and lifeless in her arms. He was upright, his mother toweling him dry.

"Jesus Christ!" I screamed.

The outburst stunned the mother into speechlessness. And as for the boy, I'm frankly amazed he didn't piss himself. He did start crying, but that didn't keep me from yelling at Janet or Janice.

"What the fuck," I said, or "Fucking unbelievable." Something along those lines.

She covered the boy's ears.

"I tried calling you back," she said. "You didn't pick up."

"Because I ran here—because you left your kid in a running tub and somehow locked him in the bathroom—because I thought the little shit was about to be dead."

I wanted to keep berating her, but the boy's crying went from mild to severe, from manageable to inconsolable, and to make matters worse, his mother joined him. As soon as she started sobbing, the boy took the cue and completely lost it. He bawled uncontrollably—eyes slammed shut, cheeks bright red, snot draining from his nose. He was barely breathing.

"No, no, no, no, no," I said. "Don't do that. Never mind. It's okay. He's okay. He's okay, right?"

She nodded yes.

"That's all that matters," I said. "He's okay. Don't worry about it. It's okay. It's fine."

But it wasn't fine or okay.

"The important thing is that no one got hurt," I told her. Except I had hurt my right hand banging on the front door. Not badly, no broken bones, just a bruise, but I had hurt myself, nonetheless. And running to the yellow bungalow, to save her boy's life, I had stepped on something sharp, a rusty nail, a screw, or a shard of glass, and I cut the heel on my left foot, which I only realized after Janet or Janice pointed it out to me. The blood, my blood, my bloody footprints on the floor tiles in her bathroom. In *my* bathroom. In the house she was paying *me* to live in.

I tried my best to calm down, and to calm her down and reassure her. Two, three times, I said, "Don't worry about it" or "Everyone makes mistakes" and "It's understandable." Something like that.

The next month, I raised her rent. By a lot.

The month after that, just as I had expected her to do, she moved out.

I ended up leasing the yellow bungalow to a childless, middle-aged widower who doesn't have pets and spends half the year traveling around the world with his old but active mother. He leaves his rent checks in the mailbox, sealed in an envelope, so I never have to knock on his door or make idle chitchat. In the years he's been renting the yellow bungalow, he hasn't asked me for anything, and I leave him alone. We have a perfect relationship.

Most of the time the tenants didn't bother me, and I let them be. I never showed up uninvited, either, except on the first Saturday of every month, when I came for rent. For a while now, the last year or so, I had been saving the pink bungalow for last. The tenant was a college student, a pretty girl with short hair who wore tortoiseshell eyeglasses and, like me, liked to drink coffee and talk. I rang the doorbell. Waiting for her to answer, I noticed the sign staked on the lawn across the street:

BE A GOOD NEIGHBOR.

The girl with tortoiseshell eyeglasses and short hair opened the door.

"Hey," she said.

"Hey," I said back, and then, looking over my shoulder at her neighbor's lawn sign, I asked, "Are they?"

"Are they what?"

"Good neighbors."

She shrugged her shoulders, a gesture of profound indifference, and invited me in.

She was barefoot. On her toenails, glossy black polish, and on her left pinkie toe, a silver toe ring. She was wearing skinny blue jeans with a tear in the right knee. I wondered if she had bought the jeans that way or if time and wear had made them fashionably distressed. Up top, she wore a white T-shirt with a low-cut V-neck, the fabric thin, almost see-through. She was not wearing a bra. I could make out her nipples. I tried looking away. Mostly, I focused on her face. Mostly, her eyes and forehead. The goal was to fix my attention on anything but her chest. Mostly, I failed.

She led me to the kitchen, nearly identical in layout to the one in the blue bungalow. Sink, countertops, stove, and fridge in the same spots. Even the white tile matched. M's father must have cut a deal on building supplies when he had the bungalows built. Or else the world had become more opulent, with more choices than necessary. Obviously, the kitchens were not identical. Our table was rectangular and sat four comfortably; hers was round and sat three, and only three, no matter the chair arrangement. Lots of stuff cluttered our countertops: toaster; coffee maker; sugar bowl; utility bills; saltshaker; pepper grinder; paper towel rack; bowls filled with bananas, tomatoes, garlic cloves, lemons, avocados; a bottle of olive oil; a bottle of balsamic vinegar; a drying rack; and a row of plants on the windowsill: aloe vera, a fuzzy cactus, a tall prickly cactus, and mint. The girl with tortoiseshell eyeglasses and short hair kept her countertops practically bare.

Even though by now she must have known what my answer would be because it was always the same, she asked if I wanted coffee.

"Yes."

And even though she attended the college where I used to teach, she had no idea what subjects I had taught or for how long I worked there or why I stopped teaching. The one time she had asked why I left the college, I didn't say a word about being terminated on account of my moral character or supposed lack thereof. I gave her instead the explanation I had rehearsed and memorized for precisely such instances. "For years, I'd been going in at the same hour, every morning, doing the same things throughout the day, same times, same buildings, same classrooms, and at the end of each day, at the same time, just before rush hour, I'd head home, taking the exact same route back. I'd been doing this circle of life day in, day out, for so long that I was sure one of these days, while driving into campus, I would see myself driving out. I had to get out before that happened."

She had asked me if I meant that one day I would see my doppelgänger.

"Something like that," I replied, to which she said, "Uh-huh. Okay. Isn't that just called life?"

Then and there, I knew we would get along fine.

On this Saturday morning, though the temperature outside hadn't yet reached an unbearable number, which it would in a few hours, the house was still warm. The college girl either didn't like air conditioning or couldn't afford to run it all day, the way M did. In the kitchen, the coolest room in the house on account of the tiled floor and open windows that allowed a cross-breeze, I grabbed a seat at the small white table, and she poured two cups of coffee. I took the room in once more. The kitchen sink, a mirror image of ours. The fridge, too, except that ours, like our countertops, looked more cluttered on account of M posting clippings from the Internet on its doors—about pregnancy, of course.

Everyone, everywhere, is living only a slightly different version of the same life, I told myself.

Most months I got our conversation going by asking what she was reading at the college. Because it was summer and school was out, I had some anxiety about what we would talk about. Luckily, and unsolicited, she told me right away that she was taking a summer course and was reading the Book of Genesis.

"I've been thinking a lot about Eve," she said. "Growing up, I took Eve to be awful because, you know, she gave in to the Devil's trickery and ate the apple from the tree in the garden, which the Lord told her not to eat."

She sipped her coffee. The steam rising from the porcelain cup fogged over her tortoiseshell glasses. I tried hard not to look at her T-shirt, at what the almost see-through fabric revealed.

"I blamed Eve for giving us original sin," she went on, "and for tricking Adam into taking a bite of the apple and for the fall of mankind. That's the story I heard growing up. I heard it at home, church, in Sunday school. The Devil fooled Eve, Eve deceived Adam, and because they both turned their backs on God and on Paradise, the Lord banished them, cursing them with work, pain, and death. Blah, blah, blah."

I laughed.

She didn't.

"I believed every bit of the story," she said.

Her eyes widened, and she leaned back in her chair, the way I used to when teaching, when I was about to say something that I thought my students had never heard before. The gesture, the couple of seconds it took to pull off, added gravitas. Or so I believed. Whether the move ever accomplished what I hoped, I can't say, but it worked for her. Intrigued, I leaned forward. She took the cue and pulled both her chair and herself closer to the table. She also leaned forward, her body touching the table's edge, her chest leaning over the top, which made it easier for me to peek down her T-shirt, which I did.

"Did you know there's no apple?" she asked.

I drank from my coffee cup.

"There's fruit on a tree," she said. "Just fruit. There's no apple mentioned in Genesis. My professor says the fruit in the story is probably a pomegranate or a quince. I know what pomegranates are. I've seen pictures but have never eaten one. I've never heard of a quince and don't have a clue what one looks or tastes like. How is it that I've gone my whole life never hearing of or seeing the fruit Adam and Eve supposedly ate? If you showed me a quince right now, I wouldn't know it from Adam. Maybe that's where the saying comes from, not knowing something from Adam. My professor also says that the Tree of Knowledge of Good and Evil could've been a pear tree. He says it's also possible Adam and Eve didn't eat fruit at all. That the so-called fruit could've been wheat or mushrooms. That's what grows in that part of the world. And if Adam and Eve were eating mushrooms, the magic kind, that would explain a lot."

She laughed, and I laughed with her.

By most standards, the joke was mediocre at best and only original to someone as young as she was. I laughed because I wanted her to feel heard, recognized, and liked. If laughing made these goals achievable, then I would laugh until my face hurt.

"By the way," she said, "I looked long and hard in Genesis for the Devil, but just like the apple, the Devil isn't there. There's a serpent, but no Devil. There's no 'Adam' or 'Eve,' either. Not right away, not in the beginning. There's just a man and a woman, and they don't have names. If you ask me, the serpent isn't deceptive, either. He tells Eve the truth." She made air quotes when saying Eve's name. "The serpent tells Eve that she'll gain knowledge if she eats from the tree, and that's exactly what happens. She eats from the tree and gets knowledge."

I loved what she was saying, how she was thinking. It reminded me of my days as a professor. Coincidentally, I found myself much less distracted by what I could and could not see through her thin V-neck T-shirt.

"Imagine eating something that opens your eyes to the whole world, to the truth," she said. "The fruit must've tasted delicious. Adam and Eve must have craved the taste for the rest of their lives."

She bit her lower lip.

I can tell you—because I have long since moved past the shame and embarrassment of it all—that the sight of her doing that stirred something in me.

"What I don't get is why the Lord puts the tree in the garden in the first place," she said. "That's like putting a gun in the middle of a room full of games and toys and telling a bunch of kids they can play with *everything* in the room. Except the gun. How fucked up is the Lord to do a thing like that, to his own creations? Eve, she eats the fruit because she's got desire. I can appreciate that. Who doesn't desire things they can't have? Everybody. Eve's not a sinner. She's just human. She's a rebel, too. She's the world's first freethinker."

She went on and on like that, waxing philosophically about the human condition. To every bit of it I listened, unabated in the conviction that my interest in her equaled hers in mine. If you're thinking that I wanted to have sex with her, a student, at least half my age, who happened also to be my tenant, living in the house my wife loved, then you're right—I did—but not just because she was pretty, which she was, but as is so often the case with the beautiful people whom we ruin our lives over, there was much more to her than looks. Something about her reminded me of myself. She brought back my previous life, a life that suffered the revisions of nostalgia, true, but more determinatively, a life that I had presumed to be gone for good. She called to mind those students who I had wished for every semester, those who eventually saw the old books I assigned them not as relics from the past but monuments in the present. Not dead, but alive and well. Living and breathing every time we opened them up.

The sentences she doled out in that small kitchen nearly identical to ours, she might not have said them exactly as I have typed them out, but what you're reading reflects just how I heard them. Her words here are exactly how I remembered them then, and how, today, they still exist in my imagination, the place where stories are made, where the fact and fantasy hash it out, and where the college girl, with her tortoiseshell eyeglasses, her thin T-shirt, and distressed jeans, even the glossy black polish on her toenails, continues to astound me. In all these places (past, present, actual, imagined), she took another sip of coffee, leaned forward even farther, closer both literally and metaphorically, and in that unguarded instant I knew, with complete and utter certainty, a line would be crossed. Which line exactly? I hoped for several, prayed for one, and waited to find out.

For what could not have been more than a few seconds but felt infinitely longer, we sat at the white round table looking at each other without speaking. She gave me a sideways glance (I'm sure of it), and she raised her right hand and ran her fingers through her hair (that's how I remember it), and she took what must have been long, deep, exaggerated breaths (if her feelings remotely mirrored mine, how could she not?), and in that split second or two, I entertained two divergent but not entirely incompatible thoughts. The first was corporeal and set in the future: to see and touch her body. The second was cerebral and located in the past: the last time I had gone off on a tangent to a less-than-captivated audience of first-year students. "A hundred or so years from today," I had said to them, "every single human being alive right now will be gone. Every single one of us will be wiped clean from existence. If you're lucky, you will write a story or a poem or come up with an idea or notion that outlives you. Unfortunately, the odds of that happening aren't in your favor. Living and dead, around 108 billion people have populated the earth. How many of those billions do you suppose wrote something so special or had an idea that mattered so much in the history of civilization that we still talk about it or are even remotely affected by it today?" Half the students no doubt didn't give a rat's ass—they only wanted the hour to end. The other half, I'm sure, cared even less and wanted only to die on the spot, so I answered my question for them: "A thousand people, maybe. Two thousand. Let's be generous and say ten thousand people have accomplished something we end up calling 'great'—inventing a god, establishing a myth, telling the rest of humanity that everything it believes is bunk and then convincing them. Out of 108 billion people, what percentage is that?" While my speech might have sounded spontaneous to the students, it was anything but. I had already done the math. Some of the students would be guessing a number. Most of them clearly didn't care who left what behind, and they slouched in their chairs, their eyes rolling in their heads. Before anyone could blurt out a number, I would write the percentage on the board and, for effect, add the decimal point last: 0.00000926%.

"The odds are not good. Not at all."

I missed those days so much. She may or may not have realized it, but once a month, when I came to collect rent and drink coffee with her and listen to her talk, the college girl brought those bygone days back to life.

She leaned so close now, her arms rested on the table, her upper body nearly entirely over it.

I have no clue what I'm doing, I thought.

I also thought, she knows exactly what she's doing.

Nervously, I sipped from my coffee mug. She seemed apprehensive, too. Though given the vibe, it must have been something else. Anticipation, I hoped. Then she made what I took be a flirtatious gesture. She began playing with the silver chain around her neck, on the end of which was a crucifix.

"Can I see?" I asked.

She came closer. To do so, she had to lift herself up off the chair and stretch her body toward me. I mimicked her, and when I got close enough to see the details on the crucifix, she took a deep breath and held it—that's what I still tell myself she did. The silver Christ's body was smooth and polished. On his head, a lustrous crown of thorns. I inched closer. She remained motionless. We were almost touching. The Christ's hands and feet had spikes driven though them, smaller than mustard seeds.

While I had told myself that I had no idea what I was doing, in my imagination I knew exactly what to do. There, I could do and say things much more easily, with greater confidence, without fear of failure or embarrassment. There, we touched. But in the actual world, I pulled back.

I said, "Do you still believe in God?"

She pulled away after that, and the crucifix fell against her chest. She sat back in the chair and tucked the dangling Christ underneath her shirt. Obviously, the gesture indicated a degree of disappointment.

"Yeah," she said. "I do."

The sound of her voice, the tone she took, confirmed my suspicion. If not disappointment, then she must have felt annoyance. Or worse, relief.

"What about all the problems with Eve's story? It's clearly not a true story."

She stood up, took both mugs from the table, and set them in the sink.

"Every story is true," she said. "You just have to read it the right way."

She was young. In her early twenties. Twenty-one or twenty-two. But she was more than just youthful in age. She was young in the way she saw the world and herself in it. Brimming with exuberance and innocence, she lived her life, and talked and thought about it, as if anything were possible. She possessed what every person her age should: certainty unburdened by doubt, worry, or contradiction. Whether or not she understood, and whether you or I or the whole of humanity gave a damn, she let her life twist and turn and followed it every step of the way. And in this way, she reminded me of M when M was still a student at the college—when she was my student.

"The rent's in the bedroom. Be right back."

I blew my chance—if I even had one to begin with. I immediately felt a sense of loss, even though what I presumed to have been taken from me I never possessed in the first place. Waiting for her to come back, I looked around and wondered what her life was like when I wasn't there. Did she read at the small table? Did she always walk around the house barefoot? Did she drink coffee with other men? Younger men? Who weren't like me? No signs in the kitchen offered up clues. There was little evidence that she even used the kitchen. In the sink, only the two coffee mugs she had just set down. Out of curiosity, I opened a couple cabinet doors. The first contained only a handful of mismatched plates, and the other, bare, only dust. I checked the refrigerator. I saw a half-gallon of milk, a carton of eggs, a take-out container. Here, too, there were not enough signs for me to interpret.

On the fridge door, a single magnet. I knew the image: a painting, a masterpiece. Goya's drowning dog. The dog treading the surface of a brown sea. If you saw it differently, had a perspective other than mine, then you saw the dog buried in dirt or maybe mud. It could have been any of these or even something else. The dog was lost in an unidentifiable mass. Ears drooped and snout raised above the dark mass submerging it, the dog gazed upward and outward, its eyes focused on something or someone out of sight, outside the frame. There, where we could not see, was the someone or something that could come to its rescue, save it from drowning or sinking, from being swallowed up. A still life, the dog existed like that always and forever. Always alone, forever on the verge of slipping beneath the surface. Always, someone or something nearby to witness the vanishing that awaited.

This must have been a sign. But of what, I couldn't tell.

From the living room, the college girl called for me. Like the contents of the fridge, the kitchen cupboards, and the kitchen itself, the living room was also mostly bare. In the center, a coffee table with nothing on it but a thin film of dust. Next to the table, a small gray couch, no pillows, no throw, no rug underneath. The walls were also unadorned except for bands of sunlight cutting through the blinds. She was standing by the front door, her hand on the doorknob. When I entered the living room from the kitchen, she turned the knob and opened the door. On my way out, she handed me an envelope stuffed with cash.

"You can count it if you want."

"I know where you live."

"Funny," she said, but she didn't laugh.

"You know, we almost ended up living here."

"I know. You told me before."

"Oh, yeah? I must've forgotten."

"Your wife, she wanted the pink house, but her daddy wanted her to live in the blue one, so you guys live in the blue one."

She opened the door wider and stepped out onto the porch, leading me out behind her. She said, "It's a good thing you didn't end up here. You wouldn't want to live across the street from that prick."

She gestured toward the house with the BE A GOOD NEIGHBOR lawn sign.

"I guess he's *not* a good neighbor after all."

"He goes up to people who walk past his house—they're walking their dogs or just strolling—and he turns his camera phone on and interrogates them. 'Are you with us or against us?' That's his favorite line. Such a douchebag."

"That's a classic line," I joked.

She didn't laugh.

"Does he do that with everyone? Has he interrogated you?"

She shook her head no. "He better not screw with me."

"I guess he wouldn't. You're not..."

I stopped myself.

She waited.

"You know," I said. "You don't really fit the profile. Besides which, you're not a kid. They're worried about kids, right? And you don't have kids. Even if you did, they wouldn't be...well...I guess...I guess they could be..."

I stopped myself once more. I was saying things I didn't want to say. She laughed a little, which made me feel better. Instead of changing the subject or saying goodbye, which I didn't want to do, I made joke, insinuating a nonexistent condition: "You're not renting for two, are you?"

"I may not look like the people they hate—like you, like your wife..." Then, with a smirk, she added, "And no, I'm not pregnant, but I can get pregnant. I could easily get pregnant. By someone who does look like..." She paused. It's possible she purposefully hesitated. Then she said, "I could get pregnant by someone who looks like you."

I let the words take hold.

"Me getting pregnant by someone like you, that's enough for them to worry about me the way they worry about you or you wife. I'm not afraid. He can shoot his mouth off all he wants. The guy people should be worried about is the preacher's son. He's not so in-your-face. He's softer, gentler. If you're not listening carefully, you won't realize just how dangerous he is. His threats may not be full of bluster like his dad's, but they're threats all the same. And people like the piece of crap across the street, he hears the dog whistle the preacher's son is blowing just as loudly and clearly as when the old preacher blows on it. Trust me, they'll be coming out of the woodwork soon enough."

"You really believe that?"

She darted her eyes across the street and shook her head disapprovingly.

"Hold on," she said, went back inside, and left me staring across the street.

With its modest but welcoming covered front porch, its gradually pitched gabled roof, cedar shingle siding, exposed rafters, and grouped windows, the guy's house could have been my house. Most of the East Side houses resembled each other, all Arts and Crafts–style homes built at the turn of the century, within a few years of each other. Except for minor differences—the color scheme, the chimney placement, stucco siding instead of wood—they stood as monuments to an early era of mass reproduction and con-formity: This house is every house, this neighborhood is every neighborhood, we aren't so different from each other. For a brief dumb moment, I was awash in the American myth of sameness.

She came back.

"Guys like my shithead neighbor," she said, "and like the old preacher and his son, they've always believed that peo-ple like you are trouble. They just kept their prejudiced bullshit to themselves, behind closed doors. Now the preacher and his son are giving people like Mr. Are-You-With-Us-Or-Against-Us the green light to take his private thoughts public. Only thing I don't know is who's more dan-gerous, the preacher or his son. The preacher's son, he could just be doing it for money, or maybe he wants to go into pol-itics. The old preacher, he believes he's doing God's work. There's no reasoning with people like that."

That was when she touched me for the first time. She placed her left hand on my arm and said, "I grew up with people like that. They make your hair stand on end." Then she let go and said, "One day, sooner than later, the shit's going to hit the fan." Then she brought her right hand from around her back, and I saw a small pistol. "When it does," she said, "I'll be ready."

She drew the pistol up and away from her body and showed it to me. It was a .38, the grip, mother-of-pearl. I reached out, and my fingertips touched hers.

❧

I knew what I wanted, but under no circumstances—no way, no how—would M allow a gun in the house. She would give me all kinds of grief for asking. This was a great big problem, which I would solve by wheedling my way into get-ting my wife to say yes. That's what I told myself on the drive from the pink to the blue bungalow. No matter how vehemently she refused me or how many times she said no, I made a pact with myself to keep at M, to persist, to keep twisting her arm, putting the screws on, and browbeating until her will broke, until—if only to make the pestering stop—the final no was followed by a yes.

On the drive back, I concocted a plan.

To start, I would plant the seed straight away, within a day or two, if not as early as dinnertime. I would say, "I should buy a gun." Immediately, I revised my approach. Include her in it, I told myself. "*We* should buy a gun." Yes, yes. That would be more persuasive. Either or, whether my word choice expressed inclusivity or self-absorption, I knew M would still outright reject the idea. I would keep stirring the pot. Or, to stick with the original seed-planting metaphor, keep tilling the soil. I could give reverse psychology a try, which until that morning I had believed only worked on children, never adults, and certainly not M. Wishful thinking has a way of making even the most ridiculous notion appear logical and right. I would act as if the idea of owning a gun had only come to me as a passing thought. "Never mind," I would say. "We don't need a gun. It's a dumb idea. Forget I said anything." But a week or two later, I would casually mention the gun again. "Did I ever tell you about my father's guns?" M knew the story by heart. If I asked her to, she could tell it for me. Regardless, I would tell it to her again. When I was ten years old, at exactly midnight, New Year's Eve, the air cold, the night dark, my father let me fire his Colt 45. I took aim at the biggest, brightest object in the sky and, after hesitating, pulled the trigger. I would leave the story at that, an image of a boy shooting at the moon. It would speak to her viscerally, emotionally, carrying extra-semantic meaning. After the story, I would drop the subject. Let the image live a while in her mind. Go a few days, a week even, without saying another word about guns. Then, over dinner or coffee or during a TV commercial break, I would ask M if she felt safe in the house. Why, she would ask in return, why would I ask her that? Did she have reason not to be? she would wonder. Did I know something she didn't? Was I hiding from her a terrible fact? I would say, "Would you feel safer if we had some kind of protection?" She might say yes. Who doesn't want to be safer? If she said no, I would begin with the badgering. Day after day, relentlessly. If my continual hounding did not break her will, then, to make it appear that I was appeasing her, I would agree to concessions and offer compromises. We'll keep the gun locked up and store the bullets separately. We could sign up for gun safety lessons and take them together, as a couple. "It'll be fun," I would say. "We can bond."

She would have to say yes.

Full of optimism, I walked up the porch steps two at a time. Self-assured about the plan, I unlocked the door and entered the house impressed with myself. I might have even said, "It's brilliant" or, worse, "You're brilliant." I was so lost in self-congratulatory notions that I barely noticed the smell of freshly brewed coffee, and I didn't register the scent as a bad sign. After all, M had stopped drinking coffee because an article on pregnancy told her to quit, but I seemed to be under the impression that, while I was out collecting rent, purposefully spending an inordinate amount of time with the college girl who lived in the pink bungalow, M had made a batch just for me, which is something she had never ever done before.

I found her in the kitchen. She was holding a mug. I smiled and reached out to take it from her, but she pulled the mug away and drank from it.

"Are you drinking coffee?"

"Just a little. To calm my nerves."

Coffee had the opposite effect, but I decided to keep the fact buried. I had a plan to stick to. Besides which, I was hardly one to talk when it came to quitting vices.

M took a big gulp, and asked, "What took you so long?"

"Was I gone a long time?"

"Longer than it takes."

"I didn't think I was gone very long. Anyhow, you were sleeping when I left. You can't exactly say how long I've been gone, can you?"

"Did you see the college girl?"

"I went out to collect rent, and she pays rent. So, yes, I saw her."

I immediately regretted taking a combative tone. Not because it was wrong or unnecessary, which it might have been, but because M had been gifted with, and over the years honed, a better-than-average ability at reading outward signs, at deciphering the meaning hidden beneath them, and for some time, I'd had more than a sneaking suspicion that she suspected irregularities, a lack of propriety, between me and the college girl. Taking a pugnacious stance would only confirm her misgivings.

Though I knew the answer, I asked anyhow.

"Is everything okay?"

No. Everything was not okay.

"What's wrong?"

Again, she didn't answer, but her silence spoke volumes about her displeasure and her wariness. The room was so quiet I could hear the ceiling fan whirring above our heads and a dog barking next door. I could have asked again, a tact I had taken in the past, knowing full well she would inevitably admit to what was bothering her. And though she had every reason to be inclined toward suspicion, as well as to its maidservants (uneasiness, resentment, annoyance), the fact was that I hadn't done anything wrong. Not yet. As such, I didn't feel the need to get M talking just so she could unburden herself of the doubts she harbored.

Another fact of the occasion: Although the duration of her muted reply seemed interminable and its weight unbearable, both making me want an antacid more than a coffee, the exchange lasted no more than a few seconds. Guilt will do that to our sense of time, warping it against our better judgment, not to mention our wishes. To say, then, that "She didn't answer" is not entirely accurate. "She paused" is truer. Another fact: Her silence didn't speak volumes. The cliché attested not to an abundance of worries but to a single, unsubstantiated lack of faith: my lack of fidelity.

"Look," she said finally.

I took the word *Look* to be an exclamation, a call to attention. I believed that M was going to accuse me of having an itch because she believed I had already scratched it. I was only partially right. She was calling attention, but not to my indiscretions—rather, to a yellow piece of paper.

"When you were gone, someone rang the doorbell. I didn't answer right way because I assumed you were home. You weren't. So I came downstairs to check, but no one was there. There was only this. Taped to the door"

She handed me the paper, and I read it.

Some of you are responsible for the recent acts of violence. You know who you are. We know who you are. Your children are murderers. Or they will be. This makes you both guilty. The fruit does not fall far from the tree. You and your children put the rest of us in danger, and when those who are supposed to be in charge don't do anything about the danger in our midst, then it becomes the responsibility of ordinary citizens to keep people safe. Most citizens are lazy and cowardly, but not us. We take our responsibility seriously. We will root out and eliminate threats to our safety, our freedoms, and our existence. You are the threat, you and your children. Good mothers and fathers don't teach their children to murder; they don't let their children go on suicide missions. Those who give birth to killers are worse than the killers themselves because you breed violence and you allow it to spread like a cancer on society and on the future. This is a warning. Take it seriously. You must leave. We do not care where you go, but you need to go. You are not welcome here. We won't allow wolves into our homes. If you ignore us, you will pay the price.

The warning wasn't signed, but both M and I agreed The Good Neighbors must have written it. Maybe not the preacher or the preacher's son, but the sentiment belonged to them. We stood there, in the foyer, staring at the yellow paper, half-expecting it to speak, to reveal more than its words already had. I puzzled over the warning the way I used to do with a badly written college essay. The logic didn't make sense.

"They're talking about the kids like they're terrorists," I told M. "As if the girl who killed herself and the teenager were suicide bombers. The first girl, she was probably troubled, and she didn't kill anyone. The teen who stole his mother's SUV did, but he wasn't a terrorist, he didn't have political aims—he was just a screwed-up teenager. The East Side isn't a hotbed of terrorism. Do they really believe that kids are terrorists?"

M shook her head no.

"Why say it then?"

"Because if they keep saying it, people will believe them."

"Really?"

"Yes, really. That's how a lie becomes the truth—repetition by many."

"But to what end?"

"This isn't the first time someone's pointed a finger at us and called us violent, dangerous, a threat to society. Enough people already believed that about us from movies, TV, politicians, the news. What the teen did, even if his actions weren't exactly what they're insinuating, it was all the confirmation they needed. The old preacher, I'm one hundred percent sure he thinks we're evil because he calls his God by a different name. The preacher's son, his motivations are somewhat harder to pin down. Money, attention, power. He's clearly inciting fear and hatred, and he doesn't have to believe that we're inherently evil. He only needs others to believe. And if enough do, we're screwed."

It all seemed too much, too close to home, too real. I searched for a reason to convince M that her concerns were probably overblown. I might have been trying to convince myself of the same.

"Maybe it wasn't them. This could be a prank."

"What makes you say that?"

"The warning wasn't signed. Not by the old preacher, not by the preacher's son, and not by The Good Neighbors. It's anonymous. They showed their faces at the teen's funeral, and the preacher's son gives interviews on TV and radio, and now they're hiding behind a nameless, faceless flyer? Why would they take credit for all that but not this?"

M provided an answer without hesitation, suggesting she had already thought about this.

"There's a notable difference. Before, The Good Neighbors were just protesting, speaking publicly. Those are rights, guaranteed by law and tradition. They're entitled to voice their opinions publicly. Now, though, with this piece of paper, they're threatening violence. They can't go around threatening people—not legally, not..."

I interrupted her. Apparently, I was a serial interrupter, always succumbing to the urge to put in my two cents' worth. I've thought about this moment more than most. In retrospect, I've wished for the impossible—to travel through time to the past, to this moment, and stop myself. I've come to believe that among the many contenders for the instant when everything changed, this one wins. I cut my wife off with a question, and in doing so, the seeds of doubt and worry finally took root and eventually took over.

"Does this mean they know you're pregnant?"

The question paralyzed her.

Awful as it is to admit, I thought of the college girl. Did she also receive a yellow flyer? There wasn't one on her door. It was possible she had already taken it down. But she would have mentioned it. She wouldn't have kept something like that from me.

M just stood there, looking detached and afraid, so I said something to snap her out of it.

"Getting the rent, I saw a lawn sign. It said, 'Be a good neighbor.'"

My comment had the desired effect.

"What does that mean?" she asked.

"I don't know exactly. It's a vague sentence."

"Was the sign hand-lettered or professionally printed?"

"What difference does it make?"

"A professionally printed sign would demonstrate commitment and seriousness."

I sighed and then asked, "Is there more coffee?"

M nodded yes, and I followed her into the kitchen. She poured me a cup. We didn't speak, and the silence became uncomfortable. I looked around the room, deliberately checking out details. There were crumbs under the toaster, the white tiles on our countertop were whiter than those in the pink bungalow's kitchen, and we had a ceiling fan over the table; the college girl didn't. Our kitchen did not resemble hers as much as I had presumed. I wondered to myself, "How can we be sure of anything?" Right then, M placed her palms over her belly, presumably to protect the child within, to keep it from hearing, seeing, feeling, or knowing what was happening in the outside world.

What an impossible burden to carry.

"Look," I said, setting the yellow warning on the kitchen table. "I'm sure it's nothing."

"How can you say that?"

"They're just trying to scare us."

"It's working."

"They're not going to do anything."

"You don't know that."

"It's all for show."

"Your saying so doesn't make it true. It doesn't make me feel safer, and it's not just *me* that I'm worried about."

I sat down, sipped from the coffee she had poured for me, and reread the warning one more time. What a simple ploy. The easiest way to get rid of people without putting your hands on them was to make them *want* to leave—to make staying put unpleasant and, ultimately, unthinkable. That was the tactic used, against me, by the other professors in my department—men and women I'd considered not just colleagues and peers but neighbors. They quit talking to me at meetings. They ignored me at official college functions. If they saw me at the end of a hallway, they turned around. If they spotted me heading toward them on campus, they bee-lined into the nearest building. Even the staff took part. The advisors discouraged students from taking my courses. The person in charge of putting together the course schedule "accidentally" forgot to list my classes. The following semester, which would be my last, none of my courses met the minimum enrollment requirement, about which the dean scheduled a meeting to tell that he might have to deduct my salary. "It's only fair," he told me. "We can't pay you for *not* teaching." "Come on, it's not my fault." "My hands are tied." "This is bullshit." "There are rules, and you broke a big one." "Jesus Christ, Bill. We're friends. Who took you to the ER when you buckled over trying to pass a kidney stone? Who got you drunk when your ex-wife ran off with a foreign exchange student who barely spoke English? Who kept quiet about every underqualified, incompetent, big-titty assistant you've hired over the years?" I expected him to throw me out of his office, but instead he brought up M's father, who had contacted him and the department chair and the provost, threatening to go public about the college knowingly allowing a professor (me) to continue teaching after having an inappropriate relationship with a student (M). Before the semester even got going, I received a memo on college letterhead, signed by a committee of my peers. They recommended revoking my tenure. I would have fought the college for as long as I could—until a security guard or police officer ushered me off campus—if not for M begging me (after a yelling match about her father's intervention) to accept the decision, to give up my job, find another, and avoid her public humiliation. "Then your father wins," I told her. "No," she said, "he doesn't—he wants to split us up, and I'm not leaving you." But I won't be a professor anymore, I told her, and she told me she didn't care. "Your father will hate us if we stay together," I said, and she said, "He'll hate you, not me." I asked, "And if we got married?" and she replied, "It would kill him." So I asked her, "Will you marry me then?"

I could be so easily gripped by the past, mesmerized by nostalgia for what was—even for what never had been—but it took only looking up from the yellow flyer to be thrust back into the present. M beside me. Waiting. For me to say something, anything, that could save us. Those days were terrible, I thought, but the days to come could be worse.

Before the old preacher had given them a name, The Good Neighbors were just neighbors. People with umpteen opinions about everyone and everything under the sun, some of which were about people like us. But they were also neighbors we could ignore. They were people who had kept to themselves, who, like the guy who lived across the street from the pink bungalow, had kept their opinions locked behind the four walls of their houses. They might have whispered their discontent and unfounded fears out in the open, but either out of embarrassment, shame, or ridicule, they did so behind our backs. Just as we had done with unsolicited opinions about them. They stayed on their proverbial side of the fence, and we stayed on ours. Isn't that what it means to be a good neighbor? Isn't that why people build fences in the first place? You might disagree with your neighbor, hate him, be suspicious of him, but if he's there and stays there, you let him be. Isn't that the rule of a well-ordered society, what we call tolerance?

That was before. When they were just neighbors. Neighbors we could shut out and who had shut us out. We both liked and wanted it that way. Now they were willing and able to say out loud what they had to whisper for so long. Now radio hosts were setting up microphones before them, TV crews were focusing cameras on them, and journalists were copying and preserving their opinions and ideas. Rather than leave them be, now people were asking The Good Neighbors questions. Rather than ignore them, people wanted to hear what they had to say. Their two cents had gone up in value. No longer embarrassed or afraid, they talked openly. No longer ashamed, they translated their zeal into action. They typed out their threats on yellow pieces of paper and posted them on our front doors. Did they see themselves walking in the footsteps of Martin Luther? Did they think of themselves as reformers? Did any of that even matter? Unlike before, what mattered now was that their words and ideas stopped living on the edge of acceptable speech. Their visions, judgments, and convictions radiated not only from a bully pulpit on the outskirts of the East Side but from radios, TVs, and newspapers. The Good Neighbors, before anyone called them that, used to occupy a minuscule spot on the periphery. Now they took up residence in the most coveted of spaces—smack dab in the center. Furnished with this newfound leverage, the more The Good Neighbors talked, the more people listened, and the worst possible consequence gradually became a reality: Once associated with the lunatic fringe, their diatribes now swam in the same sea of normality as every other mainstream idea.

M didn't say it, but I could hear the words coming from her. "If you ask me," she would have said, "The Good Neighbors think we've destroyed their way of life, tainted it, stained and corrupted it. They've thought this for so long it doesn't occur to them to think anything else, much less question whether there's any truth to the belief. With that kind of conviction, facts become irrelevant. What's worse, they've deluded themselves into believing a legitimate reason backs up their convictions: the suicides. Every time a kid sneezes—so long as the kid is one of ours, not theirs—they're going to claim he's going to kill himself and take innocents with him. That's their logic, their article of faith. They'll keep pressing it upon everyone who will listen, every which way they know how, until those who don't believe it finally start saying it. Even if we both know it's a crock of shit, what difference does the truth make when the lie is what people want?"

"Okay," I said to M. "Let's say they mean to do us harm. The warning does explicitly say so. There's a simple solution. We call the police."

"And tell them what?"

"We show them the warning. It's evidence. It's proof."

"No," she said. "It isn't. For all they care, you could've written it. You could've taped it to the door on your way out to collect rent. Maybe there was never a knock on the door. Maybe I made that detail up. Why not? Why wouldn't the police think I dictated the letter, you typed up it, then photocopied it on yellow paper, and either last night or just before the crack of dawn, the two of us snuck out and plastered the neighborhood?"

"The police aren't going to think that."

"If they can believe that an old preacher would do it, why not you and me?"

"Why would we do anything like that?"

"Because we want to discredit The Good Neighbors, or because we crave attention, or we're dying to get on TV, or we're batshit crazy. That's why."

"We're not crazy."

"That's not the point."

"What is your point?"

"We don't know who is and who isn't a Good Neighbor. Some of them are out of the closet, but not all, not most. This flyer wasn't signed, right? Anyone could've written it. What if the cops are Good Neighbors? What if the police chief is a Good Neighbor? What good would it do to show this warning to a man who may have helped write it?"

"How can you claim that without a single shred of evidence?"

"You don't have evidence that the police chief *didn't* write this, that he's *not* a Good Neighbor."

I threw my hands up. "What are the chances?"

Unperturbed by my skepticism, she said, "In all likelihood, they're probably better than the chances of me getting pregnant. But here I am, pregnant."

She snatched the yellow paper from my hands.

"They're not going away," she said, "and I'm not going to wait for something bad to happen before I do something about it."

"Like what?"

The trembling of her hands transferred to the yellow paper. She looked it over once more, though I don't think she reread it or even skimmed it. The message had already done its job, its impression already made. What happened, I have no doubt about. She glanced down at the paper, and a handful of words emerged from the surface: terror, terrorists, violence, eliminate, children, mother, you will pay the price. In an instant, my concern for M, and for the dread welling up inside her, which was bound to erupt at any moment, grew larger and more menacing. I could see she was trying to steady her hands. She took several long, deep breaths, then she looked straight at me. Here it comes, I thought to myself, but just what "it" was, I couldn't have predicted.

"Listen to me," she said. "Listen carefully. This child is coming into the world. No one—I mean no one—is stopping that from happening, especially not a garbage preacher and his scum-of-the-earth followers. Do you understand?"

I understood.

"Is that clear enough, professor?"

It was, in every respect, not open to interpretation.

"Here and at the other bungalows, I'm going to have security cameras installed," she said. "I'll make the calls and set up the appointments, and you'll meet with them when they come out to do the work—I don't want anyone outside of you seeing me pregnant. We should put up a fence, too, out front, with a gate that locks. Again, I'll make the arrangements, you deal with whoever shows up."

I was witnessing a metamorphosis right before my eyes. M suddenly looked and sounded better. Her hands stopped shaking, color returned to her face, and she was breathing normally. I don't think it is physically possible for all that to happen in a flash, but that's exactly how I remember it happening. In this way, truth is sometimes like fiction, where anything is possible. And yet, I could hardly believe what M said next.

Calmly and with more restraint than I have ever seen her practice in our entire life together, M said, "First, before anything else, you go out and get us some protection, and so there's no confusion about my meaning, I am telling you to go get a gun. On second thought, just to be on the safe side, get a pair—one gun for me, one gun for you."

Without push coming to shove, I got a gun. I should have felt proud and triumphant for having won an argument without having to argue. However, without realizing it, M had snatched from me the sense of accomplishment that comes with persuading someone to act against their better judgment, their self-interest, or a gut feeling. Instead of pride or pleasure, I felt the emotional equivalent of a shrug.

A few hours later, I put an end to this minor disappointment by handling several firearms at a sporting goods store. There, I relived the euphoria of touching the college girl's gun, and though exciting, the experience at the gun counter obviously fell short of the height reached with the college girl. The clerk talked up gun ownership, and I took his words to heart. I should handle the guns with care, he told me, and only occasionally take them out of their hiding place, for which he recommended a biometric pistol safe. He tried selling me a model that held up to forty unique fingerprints. Why allow so many people access to a gun, I had asked. "It's so you can input multiple fingers or multiple fingerprint angles, ensuring you have quick, reliable access when you need it. If you're doing guesswork about which fingerprint on which finger on which hand while an intruder is coming at you, well, you don't want that, do you?" No. No, I didn't. While he finalized the sale, I wondered if M and I would ever need to use the guns. I thought about the most roundabout way to ask the clerk his opinion. I came up with the following: "What are the chances a gun like this gets used to kill someone?" The sentence never left my head. Even as inner monologue, it sounded like I was thinking about murder. Instead of his opinion, I relied on my imagination for the answer. Only under the rarest of circumstances, if ever, would I use the gun for its intended purpose.

I left the sporting goods store believing I would feel good about having become a first-time gun owner. To the contrary, I spent the following week or two racked with worry. I doubted if I could ever use the gun against another person, and not just any person but someone who likely lived nearby, a neighbor who I might have stood in line with at the grocery store or the post office, a man who believed, incontrovertibly, that M was carrying in her womb a menace to society.

The girl living in the pink bungalow seemed so self-assured. She held her .38 with ease and confidence, the way, in a classroom, I might have held a book I had read and taught a dozen times. I envied her self-assurance. I wanted to talk to her. Maybe she could help me gain insight into the comfort and familiarity with which she handled her gun. In lacking fear and anxiety over using a deadly weapon, she wielded power. She would not be intimidated or challenged. Just the opposite. She would be the one doing the challenging and the intimidating. Rent wasn't due for a couple weeks, though, and I didn't have a good enough excuse for showing up unannounced, not one that wouldn't expose my motives for wanting to see her outside of our landlord-tenant relationship. So I went to the Internet. Rather than allying my concerns, the plethora of opinions I came across, most of which were contradictory and almost all heavily biased one way or the other, only amplified my trepidation. For instance, in crimes committed against people who owned a firearm, only 0.9 percent of them had successfully defended themselves with a gun. Somewhat reluctantly, I showed the statistic to M.

"What's the point of having a gun if the success rate is practically zero?"

She answered me resolutely. "The minuscule percentage doesn't matter. What matters is that people *feel* safer owning a gun. I bet that *that* percentage is closer to one hundred."

"Then safety, by way of gun ownership, is just an illusion."

"The feeling of safety is very real," she said.

"But feeling safe and being safe aren't the same thing. People who *feel* perfectly healthy often get diagnosed with a terminal illness. A husband, or wife for that matter, who *feels* confident in the strength of his marriage will often be asked to sign divorce papers."

I could have and would have kept going, but M interrupted me.

"I'm keeping my gun. You can do what you want with yours."

I decided not to give up on being a gun owner, not yet. I would live with mine a while longer to wait and see. I was biding my time, but hopefully not for the unexpected and unimaginable to happen, which, day by day, in my excessively industrious imagination, grew more expected and imaginable. Nights, after closing a book and turning out the lamp on my bedside table, I stayed awake long past the hour I usually fell asleep, my senses lively, anticipating a loud, crashing noise to rouse me straight out of bed. That noise never came. Those that did, without fail, were never loud or crashing. Just the usual disturbances: the house settling, the refrigerator making ice, a squirrel dropping off a tree limb onto the rooftop and scurrying across the shingles. Yet every time I heard a sound, be it the air conditioner starting up or the leaky toilet in our bathroom refilling its tank, I bolted upright, secured the gun, waited for my vision to adjust to the darkness, and then scanned the room for the peril that wasn't there. On these nights, M slept through every terrifying minute.

Before receiving the warning from The Good Neighbors, I wouldn't have abandoned the comfort of my bed, blanket, and pillow over something so slight as a creaking, groaning, or thumping in the night. If M had pleaded with me to get up and check out whatever it was that had disturbed her slumber, I would have mumbled a complaint under my breath, to which she would have replied with a swift elbow to my side. Then and only then would I have picked myself up and out of bed, yawned, stretched, rubbed my eyes, and half-asleep shuffled my way across the bedroom to the hallway, and peeked down the hall. If I was feeling generous, I would have taken a couple steps down the stairwell and with bleary eyes glanced in the general direction of the first floor, not really paying much attention to anything down there. Not one iota wiser about who or what might have been lurking on the other side of our four walls, or inside of them, I would have headed back to the bedroom, crawled into bed, and mumbled, "It's nothing, go back to sleep," and I would have sunk my head into my pillow entirely certain, without any certainty at all, that I was right. It's also possible that having gone back to sleep without a single disconcerting thought, I would have dreamed a good dream: driving a convertible on a road next to the ocean, having sex with someone I didn't know.

Instead of dreams about cars and women, or no dreams at all, I began having nightmares about strangers, of me fighting bigger, stronger, merciless men. I saw more violence in my dreams than on TV, and there with me, in bed, within arm's reach, in the top drawer of my nightstand, was a .38 caliber, identical to M's.

It took a while to realize what was happening. I made the discovery while writing this down, several months after I had started waking up in the middle of the night, long after the threat stopped being omnipresent. I discovered that despite the thoughts my subconscious told me, I might not have been as convinced as M of the threat The Good Neighbors posed. In retrospect, I should have known this. The signs were available to read, in plain sight. While my fitful nights indicated the hold The Good Neighbors had had on me, during the day I still went about my routine normally. I stepped out of the house without fear or anxiety. I drove to the grocery store, the mall, the gas station, the bank, and regardless of everything The Good Neighbors had said and done, or that we believed they would do, I still felt safe. Safe enough, at least. So, too, did many of our neighbors. For all I knew, they all believed themselves to be out of harm's way. The front yards, streets, and stores never once emptied of people—not those who looked like The Good Neighbors nor those who looked like us. On the surface, nothing had changed. People seemingly went about their days as usual.

Except for M.

Her fears worsened, her anxieties deepened, her composure deteriorated. She went from willing to leave the house so long as I accompanied her to outright refusing to step past the front door except for emergencies. I witnessed the first sign of a major escalation (from understandable apprehension to unhealthy phobia) the last time we grocery shopped together. We were in the bulk food aisle, standing in front of the dried fruits, trying to decide between apricots and banana slices. M wanted both; I wanted neither. An elderly woman barely able to push her cart turned into the aisle, and M immediately checked to see if the other end was unobstructed, free of people, in case she needed to retreat or escape. She didn't admit any of this to me, but her jerky movements and shallow breaths all but disclosed the particulars of her distress. If I had had doubts about my suspicions—I didn't—M confirmed them less than ten minutes later in the checkout lane, where the relative openness of the supermarket's shopping aisles narrowed down to a small, enclosed space only wide enough to fit a grocery cart. Visibly panicked by the sudden confinement of paying for our groceries, M dropped her bag in the cart, blurted out "I can't" or else "I won't," and left the store. "It's nothing," I told the cashier and finished checking out. I found M sitting against the rear bumper of our car, hyperventilating.

We exchanged weary glances. I urged her to take deep breaths. She asked me why I didn't immediately follow her out of the supermarket.

"Please," I said, "let's just go."

She got into the car, I loaded the groceries into trunk, and we drove home without speaking about the incident. An hour or so later, we finally talked, albeit briefly—one sentence apiece.

"Don't worry, everything will be okay," I said.

She said, "There's always the chance it will not."

It was either that night or the next that M told me she would no longer leave the house.

"No one can find out I'm pregnant."

I thought she was overreacting and told her so. It was true that the ideology subscribed to by The Good Neighbors, delivered as sermons by the old preacher, disseminated as newsworthy opinion by his son, was wrong. No ifs, ands, or buts about it. But it was an outlier position, counteracted by voices of reason. For every letter to the editor that suspected villainy in the East Side, another argued our inherit goodness. Whenever the preacher's son got on TV to speak about the threat our children posed, some other guest took up airtime advocating tolerance and acceptance. More than one talking head had called the phobia of people who are different, and the us-versus-them mentality it gave rise to, as unequivocally un-American.

"You're right," M told me. "But these so-called voices of reason are making relatively weak arguments. It's obviously not right to stereotype others or to view them as intrinsically different than everyone else simply because of this, that, or the other. That's a low bar. We learn that in first grade. We're talking about a society of adults here. The stakes are higher, so the principles should be, too. Also, it's not entirely true that the reasonable voices out there are doing much to counter The Good Neighbors. In fact, they're kind of helping them. When these voices of reason come to our rescue, they usually insist on separating us from them, and we're the ones who get cast as 'them.' And yes, someone will say that we must have a conversation about *why* these kids would want to die in the first place—someone who isn't worried about the terrorists in our midst but who is more concerned about what leads children, not just in the East Side but everywhere, to kill themselves—these people want to understand the phenomenon so to keep it from happening to their children, to other children. That's good. That's great. When that gets said, you see a lot of heads nod in agreement, but that's also where the conversation comes to a stop."

Was she overreacting? Was the threat as real as she had imagined? Did she need to quarantine herself? To hide her body from the world outside the four walls of the blue bungalow? Did we need a gun? Two guns? Whatever doubts and hesitations I had, M convinced me to have misgivings about them, to believe that my doubts were not only misplaced and wrong but dangerous. She accomplished this by simply being afraid. Wouldn't I have been a terrible husband to tell her, repeatedly, not to worry, to ignore the intimidation, to go out in public, to show herself, to say to herself, "Oh, you're scared—just don't be"?

She resorted to more than sympathy to bring me around. She also reminded me this wasn't the first time that people like The Good Neighbors called people like us terrorists and then attacked them. In Palos Heights, Illinois, a man struck a gas station attendant with the blunt end of a machete, and in Gary, Indiana, a man wearing a ski mask fired a high-powered assault rifle at a clerk who survived only because of the bulletproof glass behind which he worked, and in Salt Lake City, Utah, a man tried to set fire to a family business because he believed they had to be terrorists, and in San Gabriel, California, a 48-year-old was shot and killed for the same reason, and that same day, in Mesa, Arizona, a gas station owner was gunned down because the man who shot him had mistaken him for being a terrorist, and also on that day, in Dallas, Texas, a man was found shot to death in his grocery store, and a restaurant in Encino, California was set on fire because someone called the owners terrorists, and south of San Francisco, in Fremont, another restaurant was pelted with bottles and rocks, and farther south, on a Los Angeles freeway, someone displayed a sign that advocated killing everyone who looked like a terrorist, and several days later another grocer was killed—he looked like a younger version of M's father.

"There are people like that everywhere," M told me. "Always have been. And they don't just target people like us. They're the kind who think that plagues are caused by sin. Some of them think that the mass shootings at schools are hoaxes—they send death threats to the mothers and fathers of first- and second-graders. The difference now, and here: It isn't some isolated crazy who's threatening us. It's a bunch of them, and they're organized. They've got a man of God and wannabe politician leading them, and they're our neighbors."

Was she right? Was it different now? Was the threat more real than imagined? Did she really need to stay home? And again, did we really need guns? All these questions, I put to M, and she put them to rest.

"Do you think I'm crazy?"

Knowing better, I didn't answer.

"Let me show you something."

We watched a documentary online. In the Midwest, an entire neighborhood, very much like ours, had talked itself into believing they were being followed, watched, listened to by government agents. Every sedan that stopped too long at a traffic light, every service van that parked outside a neighbor's house, every new face at the supermarket, every dropped phone call, every telemarketer who called in the middle of dinner, they took as evidence of spies among them. Did these Midwesterners change their ways, or adjust their habits, or alter their thinking? Yes, yes, yes. Did they look over their shoulders walking in and out of doors? All the time. Did they suspect everyone? Neighbors, coworkers, acquaintances, friends, and even family. Did they lose sleep? Every night. Were they delusional? Not in the slightest. They *were* being surveilled. Some of those strangers in the dairy aisle at the supermarket were CIA agents. A few of the AC-repair vehicles parked outside their homes were loaded with surveillance equipment. Their phone calls were being recorded, transcribed, and interpreted.

"Do you still think I'm crazy?"

Some days, yes. Others, no. Most days, I knew the threat was both real and imagined. We felt it, day in, day out, awake, and asleep. It didn't matter whether it was more real in our minds than outside of them. What I finally realized, and this may have come too late: While the threat resided in the present moment, its most felt presence was in the future—not in what was, but in what could be.

❧

Nearly a month after I brought the guns home (twenty-three days, to be precise, twenty-three days and nights of racing thoughts, night sweats, irritability, and hypervigilance), I woke up at about half-past three in the morning. I had heard a loud thud, or thought I had, but once upright, I only heard M snoring. I got out of bed, left M to dream of whatever she dreamed about those nights (babies, no doubt), and with a flashlight in one hand and the gun in the other, I crept downstairs. The thud had come from the room with the TV, or so I thought. I had no evidence to guide me, only intuition, and because I had seen it done on television shows and in suspenseful movies, I called out, "I have a gun" when I reached the bottom of the stairwell. No one answered. But I knew exactly what to do next—the entertainment industry had prepared me well. I flashed the light at the windows, sweeping the beam back and forth. All the windowpanes appeared intact, and I saw no sign of anyone or anything behind them. I flashed the room itself, right to left, left to right, twice to make sure I hadn't missed something. Before we owned guns—before the yellow flyer warning us to leave or else pay the price—I wouldn't have done any of this, and I wouldn't have done what I did next: I walked into the living room, tiptoed the perimeter of its walls, and then slinked into the kitchen to make sure that it, too, was free and clear of danger. After that, I checked the locks and deadbolts on both doors, front and back, and I checked to make sure that each of the blue bungalow's window frames was securely locked. Midway through inspecting the window in the sitting room, which faced the street, I spotted something that hadn't been there before: a mark on the glass.

I inched closer. I saw my reflection in the window: the flashlight in one hand, the gun in the other, the TV behind me. I looked ridiculous. I brought my face right up to the glass so I could see past myself, outside. Nothing but the front porch, the front yard, the new eight-foot cedar privacy fence, the sidewalk, an empty street, a streetlamp. Then I looked down, and there it was. On the porch floor, a bird, lying perfectly motionless. The bird was the thud. It had flown into the window, made a sound and a smudge, and died on impact or soon after. I shined light on the dead bird. Small body, brown feathers. Probably a sparrow.

I would deal with the bird in the morning. I headed back upstairs and into bed, where I tried but failed to fall back asleep. I put on headphones and plugged them into the laptop. For five minutes or so, I listened to a stand-up comedian rant and rave about eating, drinking, walking, talking, smoking, and taking a shit like a man. M was still dead to the world. She hadn't heard the bird crash or felt me leave the bed or get back into it. I never told her about the bird.

In the morning, I started the coffee maker, and while waiting for it to finish brewing a fresh pot, I went out to dispose of the dead sparrow. At night, with only the flashlight illuminating its feathers, the bird had appeared brown. Daylight revealed more colors. Shades of orange, deep reds, hints of gray. It was either a robin or a wood thrush. I used a broom to sweep away the ants making fuel of its body. Then I placed the bird, which I thought was beautiful and might have been instead a flycatcher or a towhee, into a disposable grocery bag, and I threw the bag into the trash can behind the garage where M would never see because she had stopped going outside.

For the next few hours, before M finally dragged herself out of bed and ambled downstairs, by which time the official morning hours were nearly over, I drank more coffee than I should have. On an empty stomach, this turned out to be a bad idea. I was jittery and sleep-deprived before the first cup, and even without stimulants, I had already permitted my mind to unburden itself of one absurdity after another. The side effects of huge amounts of caffeine must have made it that much easier for me to throw the doors wide open, letting the madman escape the asylum. One of those inmates told me how it would play out, my first encounter with The Good Neighbors:

In front of your house, people both strange and familiar will congregate—not suddenly but one at a time, a gradual build-up, men and women converging on the sidewalk, by the lone tree alongside the curb. Easily, they get past the fence—the first few climb over and let the others in—and they all make their way onto the grass, the front steps, the porch. In what will seem like no time at all, which is often the way of fantasy and nightmare, the large and antagonistic crowd will turn more restless, more daring. They will take to shouting, pounding on the door, demanding that you come out, that you bring the woman out with you. "Tell your wife we want her." "Bring her to us." "Give the child up." Then, the way it ordinarily goes with every story of a crowd amassing outside a locked door, they will turn into a mob. Louder and more earnest, their taunts will transform into threats. The threats will be propelled toward action by the burgeoning eagerness to do what they had come promising to do. With gun in hand, you will wait. For the door to be kicked down. For the windows to be shattered. For hands to reach ominously through broken shards of glass and splintered wood.

"Good morning," I heard M say.

The fact that she greeted me surprised me. She hadn't wished me a good morning or a good night in weeks. Something in her voice, a perkiness or vigor, helped me to close and lock the madhouse doors, for the time being at least.

"Did you sleep okay?"

I lied and said yes.

"I'm in the mood for a fried egg and pancakes, with loads of maple syrup."

I asked, "Did you hear something last night?"

"No. Why? Did you?"

I thought about it briefly.

"No."

"Will you make me breakfast?" M asked.

Over the next couple months, I spent a considerable amount of time imagining and reimagining this other world, which belonged solely to me, and which only I knew about because I had created it. My imagination proved to be less than inventive, though. My world looked a lot like the one everyone else inhabited. Sometimes it was a little bit stranger or else slightly more severe, but not always, and not by much. The more I reflect on it, especially now, long after everything has already happened, the more I am convinced that this other world, of my own invention, is no less genuine than the one we all share. Sometimes it seems more real than real. There and back, for much of the summer, I went. And I went often. During that time, the world did its thing, too, moving closer to the sun, and then, predictably, beginning its turn away. During the same period, I collected rent twice. Both times, the college girl with short hair and eyeglasses who lived in the pink bungalow had left a check taped to the door. M's pregnant body grew and grew.

FOUR

A CHANGING SEASON serves as one of the most overt and clichéd reminders of time's passage. Yet no one has ever accused nature of being a hack, and so I have no problem relying on nature to do just that. Besides which, the fact was that one season was passing from our lives and another coming to birth: shadows lengthening, light diminishing, temperatures dropping, leaves falling, trees baring themselves, and at their roots, bit by bit and then all of sudden, the grass losing its color, turning yellow and brittle, then the soil drying, hardening, and cracking, the earth below turning cold and gray, and the same with the skies above. Everything around us was a reminder that we were surrounded by change and bound by the rules of eventuality.

One fact, however, had remained constant. Ever since the day she showed me two red lines on the pregnancy test, I had been urging M to get a checkup, to see her gynecologist, to see a doctor, any doctor. Every time, she refused. No matter when or how I brought up the subject, she shut it down. This time was no different.

"We have to talk about this," I said.

"No, we don't."

"Why not?"

"Because."

"Because why?"

"Please, stop."

"Look, you've had me buy two guns, you've had an alarm system installed, an eight-foot fence put up around the house. You've had security cameras installed. Not just here but at all the other bungalows. You've done all sorts of things to make sure the house is safe, that we're safe in it, but you haven't seen a doctor to make sure the baby inside of you is safe."

M was refilling an ice tray with water. The refrigerator produced ice, but M insisted that the cubes from the ice maker had an aftertaste, one that, for the life of me, I couldn't taste.

"Well?" I asked.

"Well, what?"

"We need to talk about this."

"No, we don't."

"There's hardly a bump there now. It's not noticeable. But soon enough there won't be any hiding the fact that you're pregnant."

She returned the ice tray to the freezer. Her hands weren't as steady as they needed to be, probably on account of our conversation. Water spilled out of the tray and onto the floor.

"Did you hear what I said?"

She was ignoring me.

"Well?"

"Not now."

"When then?"

"Not now."

"A tiny life is growing inside you, and you..."

"A tiny life? No. That's not the way *they* see it. Not a tiny life. To them, because of who I am and where I live, and because of the minute, minute and a half, tops, that you spent inside me, all they see is a ticking time bomb."

"First of all, that's absurd. All I'm asking you to do is see a doctor, not attend their church. And I last more than a minute."

"You should've dropped the subject."

"Fine, fine. I relent. You're right. I'm bad at sex, and you're the mother of a future killer. Regardless, you still need to see a doctor."

"Quit telling me what I need. I've told you, I won't. We don't know who's who anymore. Anyone could be a Good Neighbor. They're not just a bunch of unemployed, got-nothing-to-do halfwits, you know. They're like us, like you and me—teachers, students, homeowners, lawyers, accountants. They can be doctors, too. And there's more of them than us. They're everywhere."

"Can't you see what's happening? They're nothing like you and me, not in the least. But they want you to believe they are. That way, you go around thinking they're watching you, all the time, anywhere, and everywhere. It's working. They've got you thinking exactly how they want you to think."

"Now you're finally making sense," she said. "They *are* anywhere and everywhere."

"That's not what I meant. You're twisting my words around. Listen to me."

"No, you listen. I'm tired of listening to you talk. I won't take the risk."

"What you're worried about isn't going to happen."

"How do you know?"

"We've known our doctor for years. We trust her. That's how I know."

"How can we tell whose trustworthy anymore? I feel like I don't know who anyone is anymore."

"You trust me, don't you?"

She didn't answer, and it upset me that she had indicated, by way of silence, her mistrust, her misgivings about relying on me. But I'd be hiding the truth if I didn't admit that it also pleased me to no end that she could not say she trusted me. She was right, but that's not why I felt good. Her silent vote of no confidence gave me the green light, I believed, to get into a full-fledged fight.

"Give me a break, will you. We can't live like this. I can't live like this. We can't go on like every single person outside this house, or even in it, might be the enemy. The fact is we need to see a doctor. We have to."

"You mean I have to see a doctor. Not we. Not you."

"I'm not trying to pull a man-versus-woman thing. I'm aware of the fact that you're the one who's pregnant. I'm saying that we'll go together. I'll go with you when *you* see our doctor, or a doctor, any doctor. I'll even set up the appointment."

Deep sighs of exasperation, eye rolls of resentment, clenched teeth of anger.

M seized one and all of these, and embodying the accompanying sentiment she said, "You want to talk about this, then we'll talk about this. In fact, I've been thinking about it. I don't see the point of a doctor."

"You don't?"

"I don't see the need."

"You're pregnant, and you haven't seen a doctor about being pregnant, and you won't see one because *there's no need?*"

"Stop interrupting me."

"And you arrived at this conclusion by *thinking?*"

I could see the muscles in her jaw tightening around the bone.

"Honey," I said. "Baby cakes, sweetie pie, love of my life, please, you're not doing this for me. You don't have to do diddly-squat for me. You would be doing this for you and for the baby. You need, need, need to see a doctor. You need to make sure everything goes right."

"I don't need a doctor to make sure it goes right."

"Yes, you do."

"No woman needs anyone but herself. We've been giving birth to babies all by ourselves since the beginning of time—before doctors or hospitals even existed. My body knows when and how."

"You need someone there. You need someone to pull the baby out."

"You can do that."

"What the hell do I know about delivering a newborn? That's a totally unhinged idea. Do you know that women used to make out their wills the instant they discovered they were pregnant? Did you know that?"

"When was that?"

I hesitated in providing details. I wasn't sure about when. I might have made this fact up.

"The point isn't when. The point is that they did, and for good reason. Until physicians and nurses got involved, a lot of women died during childbirth, and their children died with them."

True or not, the claim sounded plausible. Had I been in M's place, I would have believed every word I was saying.

"Let me ask you," I went on. "Who's going to make sure everything is sterilized?"

"I will."

"With what?"

"Bacterial soap. Rubbing alcohol. Hydrogen peroxide. It's all under the bathroom sink."

"What about antibiotics and anesthesia?"

"We've got antibiotics in the medicine cabinet, and I don't need anesthesia. Anesthesia wasn't invented until the

1800s. That's a fact. Look it up, professor. Women were giving birth without anesthesia for much longer than with it."

"What are you going to do, bite down on a stick?"

"I'll survive."

"What if something goes wrong?"

"If it becomes manifestly clear that we need help, or if a complication arises, one that we simply don't have the means or know-how or tools to deal with, then we can take the risk and go to an ER as a last resort."

If this was a battle, it was Waterloo, and I was Napoleon. It was Little Bighorn, and I was Custer. It was the Battle of Stalingrad, and I was a poor nameless bastard caught up in the annals of history.

I raised my voice.

"Women barely survived pregnancies back in the good old days of I don't know when the fuck you're fantasizing about, and their newborns died with them. *You* look that up, Miss Pioneer Medicine Woman. We live in the here and now, and in the present moment, women see doctors when they get pregnant. Women who don't are nuts. Here's another fact: You. Are. Pregnant. That's all there is to it. You can't hide this. Not for long. I'm not about to cut your umbilical cord with a kitchen knife, and unless you plan on never ever leaving the house again, I suggest you make a doctor's appointment, sooner rather than later. It's irresponsible otherwise. It's selfish. It's probably unethical. So, please, for God's sake, stop being a shitty mother."

"Are you finished?"

"I am."

"Thank you very much. Now do me a favor. Fuck off, why don't you."

❧

Another day, a Sunday morning.

I was in the living room watching the preacher's son on TV. He was the guest on a show featuring long-form interviews. M was in the kitchen, probably making herself something to eat. I had heard her run the faucet, turn on an oven burner, and open the refrigerator door. We had made up since our argument. Or else we had taken a break from fighting. One or the other felt the same. If the history of our domestic disputes were a foreign conflict, we were currently in a state of relative calm. No insults, yelling, or screaming, but no peace talks, either. No negotiations or compromises, handshakes or treaties. Which is why, when M showed no interest in watching the preacher's son on TV, and rather than go around the sofa to get to the kitchen, she walked right in front of me, blocking my view for a fraction of a second. I took it as a sign of bad faith. I retaliated by turning up the volume, forcing her to hear the preacher's son speak even from the kitchen.

"The problem with children killing themselves is that we don't think of them as having the intellectual or emotional capacity to make decisions on their own," he said. "We could not be more wrong."

M promptly appeared at the threshold between the kitchen and the room with the TV. In her left hand, a boiled egg with red stuff on top. Ketchup, probably, but given the range and intensity of her cravings over the past few weeks, it could have been something less obvious. Strawberry jam, barbecue sauce, hot sauce, chili paste. She was wearing the T-shirt she had slept in and underwear. Nothing else. The T-shirt still fit loosely around her belly.

The preacher's son told the interviewer, "We think that a child doesn't know the difference between right and wrong. We think children need people like you and me—

grownups—telling them the difference between right and wrong, good and bad."

"Don't they?" asked the interviewer.

"Sure, they do, and we spend years pointing out to children what's good and bad, almost from the day they're born. A three-month-old pulls at her mother's hair, and the mother says, 'No, we don't do that.' A one-year-old picks up pebbles and hurls them, we say no to that. The average toddler hears the word 'no' about four hundred times a day. You'd think that some of that would sink in, right?"

The interviewer did, and he nodded to show that he agreed.

"Most of it sinks in," said the preacher's son about the morality children learn from us. "If we pay attention to what they say, then we see that children understand a lot more than we give them credit for. In fact, children often think the way you and I think. Take my son, for example."

The interviewer raised his eyebrows, demonstrating attention and curiosity.

"He's five. Like every kid his age, he loves candy."

"What five-year-old doesn't?"

The preacher's son laughed at the interviewer's quip but did not miss a step. "Not too long ago," he went on, "my son asked why I keep telling him that candy is bad for him. I could tell by the way he asked me and the tone in his voice, he'd been thinking long and hard about the question, like a philosopher might."

At this remark, the interviewer chuckled, which was appropriate because no matter how intuitive or curious a five-year-old child may be, he is no Aristotle. Rather than dismiss the interviewer's chuckle, the preacher's son mirrored it, which made his comparison between a five-year-old and a philosopher come off not as outlandish, which might have been what the interviewer had implied, but amusingly ironic. Then, in a swift and spontaneous act of a self-deprecation, which endeared him to the interviewer and to who knows how many others watching him on TV, the preacher's son said, "Believe me, my son's no Plato. He does dumb things all the time. But he really, truly wanted to know why candy is bad for him. It might seem like a simple question, but it's not."

The preacher's son paused momentarily to allow the interviewer to react, which he did, the same way he had earlier, lifting his eyebrows. The interviewer also mumbled an exclamation, "Hmm," conveying to his guest and to the viewing audience that the seeming simplicity of the child's question, and the implications it carried, had deepened his attentiveness.

"To ask why candy is bad for you, that's a logical question," the preacher's son said. "My son eats candy. Candy tastes good. The taste pleases him, and that makes him feel good. There's logic at work, you see. The logical question that follows, then, is why would something that makes a person feel good be bad?"

The preacher's son smiled and raised his eyebrows, indicating a light-bulb moment. On cue, the interviewer followed suit, leaning in. The camera zoomed in ever so slightly on the preacher's son. I know this because I've watched the interview a dozen times, pausing, stopping, rewinding, taking notice each time of the deliberate and subtle techniques used by the preacher's son to lure the interviewer to his way of thinking. To my surprise, M took a seat beside me. Though she had vowed not to pay attention to any of The Good Neighbors, the preacher's son had managed to pique her interest.

At this point in the interview, the preacher's son posed a series of rhetorical questions, all of which amounted to a reiteration of the same one: "How many times have we justified an action or a thought just because it gave us happiness or satisfaction—because it felt good? An extra slice of pizza, a new pair of shoes you don't need. Or, to put it another way, how often have we decided that something is bad, even though, deep down, we know it's good for us? Haven't we all rationalized that something is bad because, instead of pleasure, it produces pain? Exercise, for example, or abstinence?"

"A lot of times," the interviewer said, laughing nervously.

"Yes, a lot of times. That's because it's rational to conclude that what pleases us must also be good. That's the conclusion most adults arrive at, and it's the one my five-year-old also came to." He paused for effect. On the third or fourth viewing of the interview, I deemed the effect to be conveying intellectual probity. Then he said, "Sometimes, children don't think so differently from adults. If I have a good day at work, I tell myself that I have a good job. If a customer is rude to me or my boss overlooks the effort I put into a project, I think to myself I have a bad job. This happens from one day to the next. The problem is, that's flawed logic. Ask any addict if his drug of choice makes him feel good, and he'll say yes. Is heroin good for him? Is methamphetamine good for him? Would you ever teach a child that drugs are good because they make people feel good?"

"I hope not," the interviewer said.

"Never," the preacher's son corrected him. "I'm only saying that children can think for themselves. Sometimes they get it right. Sometimes they don't."

The preacher's son looked ready to smile again, but instead he furrowed his brow and put his palms together, the way his father must have done before making a fervent prayer. Fingertips touching, he brought his hands close to his mouth, a sign of both seriousness and contemplation, and said, "It's not easy explaining to a five-year-old that what feels good may not be good, but do you know what's even harder?"

The interviewer did not know, and he shook his head accordingly.

"Explaining the exact same thing to an adult."

"Amazing," I said with an incredulous gasp. "Do you see what he's doing?"

"He's right," M said.

"I know he's right, but what he's talking about is wrong. He's telling people that children use logic the way adults do. If you take what he's saying at face value and apply it to the kids who killed themselves, he makes them out to be kids who *wanted* to kill themselves because, deep down, they relish death the way other kids would the taste of bubblegum and lollipops. He's suggesting that they won't stop killing themselves or, worse than that, killing other kids, because, well, it's like telling kids they can never eat candy again. On top of that, he's saying we're deaf, dumb, and blind to it all."

M hadn't yet taken a bite out of the boiled egg, which she was still holding between her fingers. She looked at me sideways, titled her head slightly, arched her eyebrows, and then went back to the preacher's son. Combined, the gestures communicated a clear message: She did not care what I thought.

That did not keep me from telling her:

"The teenager who drove the SUV into the grade school, he was taking antidepressants. Every day, there's a news story about the side of effects of these medications, and suicidal ideation is one of them. The preacher's son isn't mentioning that, is he? The interviewer isn't pushing back, is he?"

M shushed me without looking away from the TV.

"I only want what's best for our children," the preacher's son said.

"Did you hear that? He said *our* children, not all children."

M shushed me again.

"He doesn't even have to say 'East Side' or name us—everyone already knows *who* he means when he talks about kids who kill. He means us. He means people like us. He means people like you and—"

"Oh, my God," M interrupted me. "Will you please shut up?"

"I want what all parents want," the preacher's son said. "I want what teachers want—what good leaders want. You'd think everyone would be okay with that. Unfortunately, not everyone is. There are people out there who don't want the truth to get out, who want to shut it down. They want to silence us. That's the sad part."

"People are nervous about your father's group," the interviewer said. "They're worried about what he's been saying. That his message—your message—crosses a line. How do you respond to accusations that you are fomenting divisions? That your us-versus-them attitude is not only dangerous and offensive but, frankly, un-American?"

"I'm glad you asked that," said the preacher's son.

"Me, too," I blurted out.

M glanced in my direction but because she was either too tired to keep arguing or realized it would not have made a difference, she didn't shush me.

"I know what my father feels on the inside, in his heart," the preacher's son said. "He's a good man, and he's a simple man. He may not choose his words carefully, but he means well. We shouldn't confuse what's on the tongue with what's in the heart, which is good and right."

A moment passed before I realized that M's demeanor had undergone a transformation, from deeply interested to deadly serious. She set the boiled egg, still uneaten, on the coffee table. The egg rolled a few inches across the tabletop, smearing the path it took with the red stuff: French dressing, salsa, marinara sauce, or sriracha.

"There are people who feel an urge, a need, to call us hateful and bigoted, but I'm one hundred percent positive that if the people saying these things—it's a very small group of people who are worried about us, by the way, a very small number—if they could just sit with my family, eat dinner with my wife and kids, and talk to us—not scream or hurl insults but actually have a decent, civilized, meaningful conversation—I'm sure they'd see us in a different light."

I tried to imagine M and I having dinner with the preacher's son and his family. I would have bet money that for dinner she would have put on her favorite dress, high heels, and a pearl necklace. I could see her walking out of the kitchen wearing an apron over her dress, carrying a roast turkey or, better yet, a baked ham on a silver platter. She would have asked the preacher's son, who she referred to as "Honey" or "Dear," to carve and serve, but before he did that, all of them, husband, wife, and children—a girl, a boy, wearing the same outfits they would to church—would bow their heads, offer God a prayer of thanks, and in those prayers, the parts we weren't meant to hear, which they would have uttered silently, they would have asked their God to save our heretical souls from eternal damnation.

I knew for sure, was one hundred percent positive, everything I had imagined about them I had seen in a movie or a TV show, which is no doubt how the preacher's son knew what he did about people like M and me.

"If they just gave people like us a chance," the preacher's son said, "they'd come to understand that we're not so different from each other, that we're in the same boat, and that we all want what's best for our children—to love and protect them, to keep our community safe."

To my surprise, the interviewer pushed back.

"That's all well and good, but your father has said certain things about certain people, and he's accused of being...of being a troublemaker, of being..." He struggled to say the word—no one liked to throw it around, even if it was clearly the right word to use. "Some people think that he is a..."

The preacher's son interrupted him: "You know, every time I hear that, I can't help but think of Socrates."

The reference to the ancient Athenian philosopher caught the interviewer off guard. In retrospect, it was a brilliant rhetorical gesture on the part of the preacher's son. Not only had he changed the subject away from a disparaging comment about his father, but he also forced the interviewer to follow his lead and discuss whatever he had in mind on his own terms.

"Over two thousand years ago, Socrates spent his whole life advocating for what was best and good. Basically, for the truth, for the pursuit of wisdom and knowledge. And his fellow citizens called him a troublemaker, too. Not only that, but they charged him with causing trouble, and they put him on trial, which was a miscarriage of justice because he wasn't guilty of the accusations brought against him. He was guilty of telling the truth, which a lot of people didn't appreciate. Not much has changed. People still feel threatened by the truth. What scares me the most is when people are more afraid of the truth than they are of actual living, breathing dangers."

"Is he seriously comparing that old preacher to Socrates?"

M said, "He's calling our kids living, breathing threats."

"In the end," the preacher's son went on, "we know what a jury of his peers did to Socrates."

"He was sentenced to death, right?" the interviewer said.

"They killed him," the preacher's son said.

"Oh, this is just perfect," I said.

"You know who else got sentenced to death for being a troublemaker?" the preacher's son asked the interviewer.

I glanced at M. She looked troubled, as she should have been.

"Our Lord and savior, Jesus Christ," the preacher's son said.

"Is he saying that his father is like Jesus?"

M sat amazed, stunned, distraught, baffled, worried, quiet.

I grabbed the remote control, turned the power off, and stomped into the kitchen, leaving M alone in the room with the TV. I grabbed a beer from the fridge, pried the cap off, and took a swig. I considered going back to M but went outside instead, into the backyard, and plopped down on a plastic lounge chair. I waited a few minutes for M to join me. When she didn't come out, I peeked through the kitchen window. She wasn't in the kitchen or the room with the TV. She must have gone upstairs. Whenever something upset her, M went upstairs, shut herself in the bedroom, sometimes for ten or fifteen minutes, sometimes for hours. If it happened to be dark out, sometimes she didn't come back down until the morning.

I went into the garage. There, hidden from M in a toolbox, I kept cigarettes and a pack of gum. I checked my watch. Usually, I gave myself seven minutes to finish the cigarette, the same amount of time I had arbitrarily arrived at to produce a sperm sample during my infertility tests. I smoked the cigarette in less than five. I felt lightheaded. It had been a while since I last snuck a cigarette. To hide the smoke smell on my breath, I swirled the rest of the beer in my mouth and chewed the stick of gum. Then I went back inside, and over the kitchen sink, I washed my face with dish soap to get rid of any lingering scent. The egg M had boiled but didn't eat was still on the coffee table. I ate it and wiped the table clean of the red smear, which was harissa. Upstairs, I found M napping, the blanket pulled entirely over her head.

🔥

The following weekend, on Saturday, the preacher's son turned up on TV again, on a daily morning news talk program, though he wasn't speaking but being spoken about. Following a brief video montage of the preacher's son talking to a small crowd and shaking hands with businesspeople, the hosts heaped praise.

"Really knows his stuff," one of the three cohosts put forward, looking directly into the camera.

"I'm really impressed with his calm demeanor," said the second cohost. "He's even-keeled, don't you think? It's refreshing."

The third host, a man, was clearly the oldest of the three, but also evident was the fact that he must have dyed his hair regularly, as a man his age would have white or gray hair, a lot of it, whereas not a single strand on his head was either of those colors. He agreed with the others, saying about the preacher's son, "He's a voice of reason in the debate over the murder-suicides," to which all three cohosts nodded in unison.

All three had flawless TV hair, the men with severe parts, which must have taken considerable time, effort, and product to create and maintain, and the woman—who actually might have been the oldest among them but because she benefited from good DNA and a professional makeup artist, looked younger than the others—her hairstyle, like that of almost every other female news anchor I had ever watched, was straight and fell just below her chin but not past her collarbone. Out of curiosity, I went online and searched "do women news anchors have the same hair." The top search results reported that 95.8 percent of female news broadcasters did in fact wear the same style. According to a TV news veteran, who also happened to be an image consultant for on-air talent, TV news programs conform to strict hair guidelines to keep audiences focused on the news, not on hairstyle. Hair, the image consultant said, should be under control, look great, and be consistent. "If you're telling a story, you don't want people looking at your bangs."

For a few minutes, the three hosts bantered with each other about the preacher's son, making claims that were hard to argue with ("He's a smart guy") or were simply not true ("I heard he's a Rhodes Scholar"), and those that were wholly beside the point ("I wonder if he plays golf").

M was still sleeping when I left the house to pick up rent.

Outside, tucked under the car's windshield wiper, I found another leaflet warning us to leave or else. The day before, I'd gone to the grocery store around 6 p.m.—M had a craving for dill pickles spears and chocolate ice cream—and the warning wasn't there. The Good Neighbors must have canvassed the neighborhood overnight while we slept, when as few of us as possible could catch them in the act. I looked around and saw leaflets on all the other vehicles on the street. The message on this one duplicated the first issued, except this time around The Good Neighbors had photocopied the warning on orange paper.

On the way to the pink bungalow, I counted more than two dozen BE A GOOD NEIGHBOR lawn signs, an exponential increase from the previous month. I would mention this to the college student. If she was home. If she would talk to me. Two months in a row, she had left the rent check taped to the front door and didn't answer my knocking. I can't say that I was missing her or suffering from withdrawal—that would be an overstatement—but I did look forward to seeing her again, which was closer to the truth. Even a step closer is to say I sought distraction from my own discontent. When I pulled up to the pink bungalow, I couldn't tell if she had left the check on the door again. I walked up, and not seeing a check or envelope anywhere in sight, I knocked on the door enthusiastically.

She answered.

Her hair was still short but longer than when I saw her last. She wasn't wearing glasses, either, which brought attention to her eyes, which appeared greener than usual. I wondered if she was wearing tinted contacts.

She invited me in. As usual, I took a seat at the small table in the kitchen. She went to the counter, poured coffee grinds into the coffee maker, and stood beside it after pressing start. We were picking up where we left off. True or not, that's what I told myself. She stood with her back against the counter, facing me. I could not stop looking at her eyes.

"What color are your eyes?"

She squinted at me but didn't answer.

"What happened to your eyeglasses?"

"Let me ask you something," she said. "Have you ever been to the preacher's church?"

It probably should have bothered me that she ignored my questions, but it had the opposite effect, inspiring even more attraction. She had on skinny blue jeans, and she was barefoot again. This time her toenails were painted red, not black. Just like the last time, she was wearing a V-neck T-shirt, though the shirt was black, not white. Its fabric was not thin or see-through, which mildly disappointed me.

"I've never been to his church, but I've seen him and his son on TV."

"I went to the church," she said.

"When?"

"Last night. It's a small church. Really small. I was expecting it to be much bigger on account of how popular it is."

"It's popular?"

"More than it ever has been."

"What happened?"

"To make it popular?"

"No, at the church."

"A sermon."

"About?"

"God, right, wrong, fear."

"The usual stuff, huh."

"At one point, the old preacher said, 'Will you give a thief the keys to your house?'"

"Did you answer?"

"Everybody said no, obviously."

"Obviously."

"Everyone there was looking up at him like he was Moses. He has beautiful eyes, you know, and where he stands when he preaches, it's elevated, a step up from everyone else. Even though I didn't have to, I was looking *up* at him. Ever notice how a church is set up like a courtroom or a stage? A man up front, the rest down below, facing him?"

"Like a lecture hall," I said. "Or a classroom."

"I managed to get a seat in the front row. From there, I could really see just how beautiful his eyes are. He was looking out like he could see all of us at once. Like we were all one person, one body. I kept checking out the people next to me, on either side. All the faces I saw looked totally calm and content, but at the same time they seemed worried and afraid. I can't explain it."

"What do you think they're afraid of?"

"Thieves in their house, I guess. I got the impression they'd been hearing about that from the old preacher for a long time. They were already initiated. He said things that didn't always make sense to me, things that could've been about anyone, anything. Like 'thieves in your house.' The others there, the congregation, they understood exactly who and what he meant. 'Beware the lies outside these walls'— he said that, too, and they all knew exactly which lies he meant, without him having to explain or elaborate. He went on for a while about Judgment Day. That it'd been coming for some time, and for us not to expect the earth to crack open or for devils and demons to rise from the ground or even to hear angels singing or trumpets blowing or horse- men riding on the horizon—none of that nonsense. The end, he said, would look, sound, and feel exactly like every other day. Like today, like right now."

When the coffee maker beeped, she turned around to take the pot out, and with her back turned to me, she said, "We're living the end times. That's what he was saying." She faced me again. "Everyone who wasn't in that small church under his watchful eye, his widening spell, they ought to be shaking in their boots."

I laughed a little.

I could tell she didn't think what she had said was funny, but she forced a laugh anyhow.

"But there, with him talking, watching over us, he made the congregation feel that even though the end was at hand, we would be okay."

"You're speaking in the first-person plural—*we* and *us*. Did you join the church?"

"No," she laughed—this time it was genuine, her voice infectious and sprightly. "But I did feel safe. I haven't felt like that since I was a little girl, when it'd be storming at night, lightning and thunder, and my dad would hold me and tell me, 'There, there, now, now, it's all right, everything's okay,' and he'd keep saying it until I closed my eyes and fell asleep."

"Sounds like you had a good father."

"What I know now that I didn't know then: He was telling lies."

"The old preacher?"

She set two mugs on the small table. She filled hers up first, then mine.

"No. My dad. Everything was *not* all right or okay."

"Some lies are necessary," I said.

"That might be true. But they're still lies."

She grabbed milk from the refrigerator, and after closing the fridge door, I noticed that the magnet with the famous painting of the dog was no longer there. I asked myself if this was symbolic.

She added milk and sugar to our coffees, and while stirring hers, she said, "At the end of the sermon, the old preacher said that the day's going to come when our sons and daughters will know us as heroes."

She sat down at the table and said nothing else. In that brief instant, I could hear the house itself, the low but audible buzz of lights, the whir of the ceiling fan, the hum of the refrigerator.

"It's never really totally quiet," I said.

She just sat there, leaning, listening, looking.

"So," I said.

"So," she said.

I searched for something to say. The difficulty, the discomfort, unnerved me. I relied on a usual subject.

"Are you still reading more of the Bible for your class?"

She thought about it a second or two, which struck me as unnecessary.

"The semester's done, the class is over with," she said. "But yes, I'm still reading the Bible. I'm in a group. Three of us, me and two other girls. I met them in the class. Wait here a minute. I want to show you something."

Waiting, I remembered that I hadn't yet told her about buying a gun. She returned with a leather-bound Bible.

"What do you think about Exodus?" she asked.

"I don't think about Exodus."

She set the Bible on the table in front of me. The chair she'd been sitting in, on the other side of the table, she slid around next to me. She took a seat and opened the Bible to a bookmarked page.

"This is where the Lord instructs Moses to stretch his hand out over the sea so the waters fall back onto the Egyptians and drown them."

She reached for her coffee. The length of her arm touched mine. The touch gave me goose bumps. She must have felt them against her skin. She must have, but she didn't let on. She then read out loud from the bookmarked page.

"'Then the Lord said to Moses, "Hold out your arm over the sea, that the waters may come back upon the Egyptians and upon their chariots and upon their horsemen." Moses held out his arm over the sea, and at daybreak the sea returned to its normal state, and the Egyptians fled at its approach. But the Lord hurled the Egyptians into the sea. The waters turned back and covered the chariots and the horsemen. Pharaoh's entire army that followed them into the sea; not one of them remained. But the Israelites had marched through the sea on dry ground, the waters forming a wall for them on their right and on their left. Thus the Lord delivered Israel that day from the Egyptians. Israel saw the Egyptians dead on the shore of the sea. And when Israel saw the wondrous power which the Lord had wielded against the Egyptians, the people feared the Lord; they had faith in the Lord and His servant Moses.'"

She returned the ribbon to the Bible's gutter and closed the cover.

Could she tell by the way I was looking at her what I was thinking? On the one hand, more than anything, I wanted her to know those thoughts. On the other hand, equally as much, I wanted her never to find out.

"You can read this and think God is all powerful because by parting the Red Sea, he defies the laws of gravity, and you can call it a miracle," she said. "Or you can believe that miracles don't exist, that splitting the Red Sea in two is only an exaggeration of a less spectacular natural event, like a low tide. Or you can say that God doesn't perform miracles because the laws of physics are themselves miracles—God's miracles—and the laws of physics obey rules, God's rules. Einstein said something about that. God doesn't play dice."

"Something like that."

"So how does the sea get parted? The answer is easy. Someone imagined it being parted and then wrote a story about it. That's how. God as an ancient comic book hero, bigger, faster, and stronger than all the other gods."

I laughed a little bit, and this time she laughed a little more than me.

"One of the girls in the group—she's nice but kind of timid, which is weird because she's tall—you kind of expect someone as tall as she is to be bolder—she says it's messed up that God expects everyone to obey him. If you obey God, like the Israelites, you go free. If you don't obey God, like the Egyptians, you get killed. The other girl in the group, she's shorter—she's a talker, super sassy, too, and she can't keep her mouth closed—she says the best part of Exodus isn't at the Red Sea. It's on Mount Sinai with the molten calf."

"You mean golden calf?"

"No, it's molten, not golden."

"Are you sure?"

"One hundred percent."

"I believe you then."

Looking at me slantwise, she went on. "The girl who's the talker, the short one, she says that when Moses comes down holding the Ten Commandments and finds the Israelites worshipping a *molten* calf, it goes to show how fickle people can be, how easily they shift allegiances. As for the Israelites who lost their way while Moses was up on the mountain, they got right back in line and not because of the Ten Commandments or because of faith. They turned into believers again because of fear. God ordered Moses to slaughter the Israelites who worshipped the calf—three thousand people executed—and that, that's what terrified the rest into worshipping God all over again."

She shifted her chair so it butted up against mine, and she turned toward me, her eyes lining up with mine. They were so green, I thought to myself.

"Listening to the old preacher, I felt that kind of fear," she said. "I'm betting that everyone in that small church was gripped by it, and near the end of his sermon, he lifted his arms up, like Moses must've done standing at the edge of the Red Sea or up on Mount Sinai."

It was then that she laid her hand on top of mine. The goose bumps returned, and my heart rate jumped, but I kept perfectly still, except to look down at her hand and mine underneath it.

"He put the fear of God into that church," she said.

She covered more of my hand with hers and applied more pressure against it.

"If he does the same with enough people outside of the church, people like you and your wife, you're screwed," she said.

Then she let go.

I breathed deeply and asked, "What about people like you?"

She thought about it a few seconds and said, "I don't know yet." Then she reached into the back pocket of her jeans and pulled out a pack of cigarettes.

"I didn't you know you smoked."

"It's a new habit."

She tapped out a disposable lighter from inside the pack, lit up, and offered me a cigarette.

"No thanks," I said and then told a lie. "I don't smoke."

"I can put it out if it bothers you."

"It doesn't bother me."

She blew smoke in my direction.

"I used to smoke," I said. "I loved smoking. I would set my alarm for three in the morning just to wake up for a cigarette. Every now and then, I still have dreams in which I'm smoking. Sometimes I wake up from those dreams feeling guilty about having smoked a cigarette. The guilty feeling goes away quickly, but I'll admit this: Those are my favorite kinds of dreams, the ones where I get to do things that I'm not allowed to do in my waking life."

She took a long drag and said, "Why would you give up something you love?"

I had quit smoking—tried, at least—because M had asked me to quit. She wanted me to give up smoking because she wanted to rule out every possible explanation for why she wasn't getting pregnant, or why I wasn't getting her pregnant, one of which might have been low sperm on account of my nicotine habit.

"Just because," I told the girl.

I watched her smoke. Her hands looked like a child's, smooth, not yet marked by age or labor. She had painted her fingernails with the same glossy red polish on her toenails. She exhaled. Smoke swirled about her face, hair, and neck, a few wisps drifting toward me. The expression on her face changed, matching (I hoped) my own transformation—from unassuming to willing. By the second, it seemed to me, she turned redder. I wondered if she could tell that I was also blushing.

"You can't put it on me," she said.

I pretended not to understand.

"It's not right for me to be the one who takes the first step," she said.

"What do you mean?"

"You know what I mean. You know. You have to say what you want—to say what you want from me—what you want to do with me. You've got to ask for it. You're the professor, after all, and I'm the student."

"I'm not a professor anymore, and you were never a student of mine."

"You mean like your wife was?"

"How did you know that?"

She put the cigarette out in her coffee mug and placed her hand back on top of mine. "If you want something from me, you must ask. If you ask, I'll let you know if you can have it."

I asked, and she let me know.

FIVE

FOR AS LONG as possible, I kept what happened between me and the college student to myself. As the journalists say, I killed the story. Or, as most people would put it, I cheated on my wife and kept it secret. Was it a fling or an affair? It wasn't romance; I knew that. Whatever it should be called, I confined it to memory and interminable silences. To M, these moments must have appeared as displays of thoughtfulness, introspection, boredom, or blameless distraction. Once, and only once, did she ever question me during a guilt-ridden episode.

"Are you okay?"

I told her I was.

"Well, you look like you're about to drool. Snap out of it."

Of the choices available to me (to pretend innocence or to fess up), I chose the more fantastical of the two because, like all cheaters, I did not want to get caught. There was another reason, though, and it happened to be a cliché: The truth hurts. The world is full of useful platitudes. They are unoriginal, but they work, they have staying power, and I made good use of them. I kept up a façade of innocence to spare M the consequences of my actions. Given that I cheated, I told myself, the truth would hurt her more than it would me. I told myself what millions before me had told themselves: What she doesn't know can't hurt her. Make no mistake, I wasn't patting myself on the back for keeping my secret a secret. I was choosing harmony, or a cheap imitation of it, over the truth, which I wholeheartedly believed to be necessary.

If you happen to be a righteous, morally inclined reader, do not get your panties in a knot. A few months after that Saturday morning in the pink bungalow, an unanticipated but wholly probable thing cropped up, and depending on who you are and what you believe, you would call it karma, comeuppance, or a miracle. Regardless, it compelled me to admit the truth. When I did eventually confess to M, I divulged only the bare minimum. She did not need or want specifics. Had she wanted them, her imagination would do the work. At a much later date, however, I did ask if she wanted to read—for herself and before anyone else—what I had written about that morning with the girl. Pages in hand, I prompted her to view the scene not as confession, or even reminiscence, but as a piece of fiction. I encouraged her to take to heart the disclaimer found in the front matter of so many novels: to read the names, characters, and incidents she would come across as imaginary, to trick herself into believing that the people, places, and events she recognized from her own life were in fact being used fictitiously, that any resemblance they bore to actual experiences, locales, or persons, dead or alive (herself and myself included) was entirely coincidental. To put it succinctly, I was asking M to read her own story—set in my words, not hers—with disinterest and detachment, to judge not *what* I had done but *how* I had described it. I was asking her to be my reader, not my wife.

Although I had hesitated for months and months to share this part of the story, M was not the least bit tentative in expressing how she felt about me finally doing so. "Fuck you," or something to that effect, was how she put it. Then, rightly so, she took the pages from me and read them anyway.

❧

One more disclosure about the girl: Alone with her, on the edge of her bed, putting my clothes back on, was the last time I saw her face to face. A month later, when I drove to the pink bungalow to collect rent again, it didn't really come as a shock to find that she had taped a check to the front door. No note, no explanation. Neither of which she owed me. She owed me rent, that's all, and that was all she left.

Regardless, I knocked several times and rang the bell, and even though she was in all likelihood inside ignoring me—standing with her back against a wall so I wouldn't be able to spot her though a window, or else completely hidden from view behind a closed door in her bedroom—I milled about on the porch for a few minutes, in the off chance that she would change her mind about not wanting to see me.

That did not happen.

It did not surprise me, either.

Maybe next month, I thought. But like I've said, I know now—and so do you—what I couldn't have known then. There would be no next time.

❧

A Sunday. The daily temperatures milder, the plants and trees readying themselves for dormancy, the animals harvesting for the coming cold, the birds fleeing south, the children returning to school. Cats woke me early. I heard them fighting or mating. It's possible they were doing both. Lust and violence: such human urges, we deceive ourselves into believing. Whatever the cats were doing, they were nearby. Had someone asked me how close, I would have guessed the front porch. I got out of bed and went downstairs and opened the door to find out.

I didn't see cats. On our doorstep, however, I found a flyer. This time, The Good Neighbors used white paper, patriotically adorned with red and blue trim. In lieu of laying down an ultimatum or issuing a threat, the flyer invited us to a rally being held the following Sunday at 9 a.m., at the East Side Civic Center.

BE A GOOD NEIGHBOR!
Join Us!
Come Listen!
Be Heard!
Show You Care!
Show Your Pride!

I checked the houses on either side of ours and across the street. The flyers had been delivered to them all.

The number of people who showed up outside the civic center on the day of the rally impressed me. How many people attended, M and I each guessed. As a sign of how far apart we had drifted in such a short amount of time, her estimate did not even come close to mine. Not the same ballpark. Not the same game. As we made our way through the throng, I judged the crowd to be at most a few hundred people strong. M figured on at least three and up to four times that many. She insisted that the headcount should be in the thousands, not hundreds. I supposed, but kept to myself, that she was demonstrating an error of judgment rooted in a desire to confirm a bias—specifically, that the threat posed by The Good Neighbors had become pervasive and was on the rise.

While the headcount might have been debatable, I was absolutely sure of one thing: Of all the people who had come to the rally (those who gathered on the grounds of the civic center, on its spacious lawn, and its unnecessarily oversized parking lot, as well as those meandering on the adjacent sidewalks and walkways who may or may not have been there for the rally, who may have come to protest or else to show support), none struck me as blatantly threatening or menacing. Some of them even looked like us. And those who looked nothing like us, they made no sign of displeasure or discomfort by our presence. Maybe not everyone came here for the same reason, or they were ignorant. Or maybe we had been overthinking everything. It's possible that we had allowed for reality to get too mixed up with imagination.

I shared my opinion with M.

"Don't be fooled by your impressions," she said. "What seems is not the same as what is."

That sounded exactly like something I would have said. In fact, I have no doubt that I had at one point communicated that very sentiment to M—that very sentence, verbatim. I am practically one hundred percent sure I said it to her when she was my student, during a discussion about Shakespeare's Venetian Moor or else the wretched Caliban. All the same, it bugged me that she had used my words to dissuade me of my opinion. She looked nice saying it, though. She was wearing a brand-new outfit, which she had ordered entirely online. By now, M had all but stopped leaving the house. She only occasionally ventured into the backyard. The fact that we had left the blue bungalow and made our way to the rally constituted a minor miracle. Her new white sneakers were scuff-free, the pink and blue stripes, still vivid, standing out against her black leggings, which had an embroidered pattern made of velvet. On top, she wore a thin heather gray pullover V-neck sweater, cashmere-blend, with long sleeves and gunmetal beaded trim. Over the sweater, a waffle-knit cardigan with an open front and a shawl collar, also long-sleeved. The cardigan was a lighter shade of gray than the sweater, except for the cuffs and the front patch pockets, which were black. She looked like a picture in a magazine. The colors, textures, and fit made it nearly impossible for anyone to recognize M's body as pregnant.

Some at the rally were talking loudly about safety, freedom, and vigilance. Some were holding up signs with printed and handwritten slogans about the same themes. Neither the signs nor the boisterous chatter of the people we walked past echoed the two-fisted belligerence of the yellow and orange warnings with which The Good Neighbors had canvassed the East Side. Not a single sign or person we walked past made use of the words "terror," "terrorism," or "terrorist." If anyone said those words, we were not within earshot. If anyone had written them on poster board, we did not see them. We stopped for M to rest her feet. The bench was on the perimeter of the rally, which was also where the manicured, impossibly green civic center lawn ended and where a long, newly paved sidewalk began. The sidewalk ran alongside a narrow one-lane two-way street separating the civic center from a line of retail shops, including a Bohemian-inspired coffeehouse, a dive bar, a Mexican bakery, a family-style restaurant, a Greek diner, a fast-food chain, a donut shop, another fast-food chain restaurant, and a 24-hour pharmacy. On this day, at the time of day we were there resting, people-watching, eavesdropping, I saw no indication whatsoever that God hated children or wanted them dead or banished from the neighborhood.

"None of this used to be here," M said to me.

By here, she meant the civic center. It didn't exist when she was younger. By here, she also meant the shops and restaurants in the general vicinity of the civic center. When M was a small girl, rows and rows of warehouses dominated the main thoroughfare. Here, where there used to be nothing but three-, four-, and five-story red-brick buildings, busy loading docks, and a labyrinth of screeching railroad tracks, people were now milling, mingling, chatting, joking, and laughing. I saw men and women of every age. Some had children at their side. The children, like the men and women they would eventually become, were also of every age a child could be, either too young to walk, too young to walk without holding a hand, too old to be carried, or old enough to wander about unsupervised. We were surrounded by the past, present, and future. A feeling of incomprehensible optimism swept over me. But this was immediately followed by a feeling of acute anxiety and a question: Why would any parent bring their child to a rally organized by a religious zealot who became famous for picketing the funeral of a dead boy?

I wanted M's opinion. More accurately, I wanted to share my opinion with M.

"Let me ask you something," I said.

She stood up, and I stood up with her.

"We should get closer to the stage," she said.

Before I had the chance to criticize the mothers and fathers who had brought their children to the rally, a couple approached us, a man and woman. Like me, the man had on slightly worn blue jeans, sneakers, and a plain white T-shirt. Unlike me, over the T-shirt he wore a brown leather bomber jacket, whereas on the way out of the bungalow, I had chosen a green hoodie, which M had insisted was not green but a shade of blue. The other half of the couple, the woman, was also wearing a slightly worn pair of jeans, black not blue, and a T-shirt, not white but gray, light not dark, and a leather jacket, not brown but black, and instead of sneakers, she had on shiny yellow rubber rain boots, even though the area hadn't seen rain in a month. Officially, we might have been in a drought, and the weather forecast called for mostly clear skies with the chance of rain at zero percent. About the woman wearing rain boots, I guessed that she was likely a healthy woman, probably in her late twenties, and no doubt childless. I presumed this not because she had tried, tried, tried, and failed, failed, failed (like M) but because she merely did not wish to suffer the burden of children. Not just yet. Not until she knew without a doubt that she was ready to give up the habits she had grown accustomed to, about which I also hazarded a guess: The habits she enjoyed consisted of staying up late, sleeping in late, and not having another living being of the same species be totally dependent on her for its survival. She was a stereotype of my own making, and I envied her.

With a cheerful voice, smiling at both of us—though clearly directing her attention at M—the woman said, "What's going on here? A street festival?"

"Festival?"

Let's stop here for a moment.

Let me tell you something else that I am categorically, unequivocally certain about: I know M. While I may be wrong half the time about half the judgments I arrive at, I can interpret her mood better than anyone else on the face of the earth. The woman, a stranger, and therefore ignorant, could not—would not—have been able to sense M's indignation. Neither would the man she was with, not from a single word, phrased as a question. The couple must have interpreted M asking "Festival?" as my wife not having heard them, which, given the clamor surrounding us, was not an unreasonable verdict on M's response to the woman's inquiry into what was happening at the civic center. Given my intimacy with M, I knew otherwise. She was not the least bit unsure or confused about the woman's question. M had heard it perfectly, and she was on the verge of incredulousness.

"There's no festival here," M said. "There's no music, no games, no rides, no carnival food. This is a rally, and the people who organized it want our children dead."

The woman flinched. "Who wants children dead?"

"They do," M said.

"They who?"

Though he was looking right at M, apparently listening, the man with the woman didn't seem to care. Either he wasn't really paying attention to M (but merely looking at her), or else he was hearing her but simply didn't give a shit about dead children or the people who wanted them dead. Unlike the woman he came with, nothing M said caused him to flinch or blink or balk. A part of me admired his indifference. On the other hand, M's remark about dead children perturbed the woman. Just as I had done only minutes earlier, she also surveyed the amassing crowd, and like me, she did not detect anything about the people milling, mingling, chatting, joking, laughing that gave the impression they harbored an urge or need to murder children. How could I have known this about her appraisal of the crowd? First, she shook her head. Second, she furrowed her brow. Third, she squinted her eyes. All together, these gestures expressed confusion and bewilderment over the discrepancy between what she had heard (people want children dead) and what she saw with her own two eyes (people in a crowd, none of whom were advocating murder, and some with children, none of whom were being murdered). Each gesture, by each part of her face, pleaded with us not so subtly to point out who among the crowd was a child killer. So much so, she asked, "Who wants your kids dead?"

"The Good Neighbors," M said.

"Your *neighbors* want your children dead?"

Just as a part of me admired her man's indifference, a part of me also coveted the woman's special breed of ignorance, an innate ability to live in the same world as others but to exist entirely in another that was much, much better. She lived in a world where children did not kill themselves, old men did not open the Bible and openly pray for death, and the sons of preachers did not speak eloquently and obliquely about purging people.

M is going to punch her in the mouth, I thought. I stood back to let M handle her, and I was startled to hear M's response, for which she tempered the disapproval in her voice.

"No," M said. "I mean, yes. I mean, The Good Neighbors. The group. The people who picketed. You *must* know who they are."

"Oh," the woman said.

I wasn't sure if she suddenly remembered or if she was simply placating M. Either way, M must have felt pity for the woman, or else her sense of indignation had reached a saturation point or, conversely, had exhausted itself into reluctant patience. I say this because of the way M spoke to her, which was how I imagined she would one day speak with our child—gently, carefully, compassionately.

"It's hard to tell who's a Good Neighbor anymore. At least it used to be harder to tell. That's all changed now. They used to threaten us with anonymous warnings. But they've since gotten comfortable attaching their names to their opinions and sharing them openly. Now, they're holding public events on city property. Do you know what that means? It means they had to apply for a permit. It means a city official approved the paperwork. It means a government institution gave their stamp of approval to a group of people making illicit threats of violence against another group of people. Is that okay? Is that right? I'm all for freedom of conscience, but when your conscience compels you to see other people's children as devils in disguise, do I have to tolerate that? Or the speech that follows from it?"

The stuff M said, I still couldn't tell if the woman understood. My bet: The woman didn't have had the slightest clue. How could she not, though? The Good Neighbors had made headlines. Did she not watch TV or read the news? Maybe, on the other hand, she knew exactly what M was talking about but was too embarrassed to admit that she had mistaken the rally for a festival. Incredulous as that seemed, it was in fact possible. How often did we not realize, until a movie or a miniseries revealed it to us, that these or those people in some place near or far had been completely fucked by this or that? No one was immune from that kind of ignorance.

The woman looked at me, presumably in the hopes that I would offer an explanation or say something to help her out, or that I would change the subject, assuage her, or minimize what M had just told her, but I only shrugged. She then glanced sideways at the man she was with, who either wasn't paying attention or else could not give a rat's ass about us, our neighbors, or our kids. He took a cue from me, or so I like to believe, and shrugged, which made me smile, which the woman might have noticed, which would have confused her even further. I could get along with her man, no doubt about it. He was the sort of guy I could disagree with vehemently, bring up religion, politics, kids these days, and be downright cantankerous about all of it, and still buy him a cold beer and laugh at his inappropriate jokes.

"Sorry," the woman said. "I just wanted to know what was going on."

"And I told you," M said.

"I just didn't know."

"Now you know."

"I still don't understand."

Around this time, whichever month of pregnancy M thought she was in, she was all over the place emotionally. One minute this, the next minute that. She had already swung from incredulous to indignant to patient. The pendulum was now swinging in the other direction. Deciphering the look on M's face after the woman said she still didn't understand required no intimate knowledge of my wife or her temperament. It was obvious, and just in case the woman was not only ignorant but also dumb, M made it clear.

"Lady, what the hell don't you understand?"

"I don't know what you mean."

"How can you not know what I mean? Clearly, you aren't blind, and you don't live under a rock. So, please, enlighten me on how it's possible that you don't know what I'm talking about?"

"I just don't."

"You don't know about the child suicides?"

The woman gasped.

To this day, I remain convinced that no matter how many times M would have told her about children killing themselves, the woman would have reacted, every time, with equal amounts of shock and horror.

"You don't know about the sons of bitches protesting the funeral of the teenager who died?"

"Who would do such a thing?"

"I told you already, The Good Neighbors. Weren't you listening? What about the signs, the threats, and the speeches? Tell me you haven't heard about those, either. What about the warnings, the leaflets? What about the old preacher? What about the preacher's son?"

"I vaguely remember something like that, but I'm not really a religious person, so I don't really follow religion or know much about churches."

M's disbelief was now anything but subtle.

"How do you not know what's happening? It's happening right now, right here, for God's sake. Here. Not on the other side of the world, but right here before your eyes."

I could have stopped M at this point and explained to her how it was indeed possible for people to remain ignorant of things, especially if those things were happening to someone other than them. My doing so would have been for the woman's benefit, not mine—for me, it would have spelled trouble. So I chose not to interrupt M.

The woman shrugged and said, "I don't know what else to tell you. Sorry."

"Oh, you're sorry, are you? You don't know what to tell me. Of course, you don't. How lucky you are. I bet, though, you know exactly when the next new phone is coming out, or what's her name's new album."

"What?"

"People like you make me sick. If it's not happening to you or if you're not being entertained, you couldn't care less."

Finally, after so much apathy, the man who hadn't been paying attention or didn't give a shit suddenly began to do one, the other, or both.

"Come on," he said to the woman. "Let's go."

He pulled at her leather jacket. When she didn't immediately follow his lead, he grabbed her by the arm, forcefully, and ushered her across the street, away from us, from the rally, from what was going on. I watched them until they blended into the scenery, ultimately vanishing from our lives. A part of me was sad to see them go.

"I need to sit down," M said. "I'm a little agitated."

"Just a little?"

She didn't laugh or acknowledge the joke. We sat back down on the bench. While M did breathing exercises to calm herself (intermittent short and long breaths, a technique she had learned from a video on the Internet), I watched the crowd.

On closer inspection, some people had come to the rally to protest. These people held up signs not only for the supporters of the rally to get worked up about, but for The Good Neighbors themselves to see, those who, in a short while, would take the stage and make passionate speeches, among them, presumably, the old preacher and the preacher's son, plus one or two of the less prominent members—maybe the dentist or the retired police officer. Whoever was going to address the crowd, I wondered if from their vantage point on stage the speechmakers would be able to make out the protest signs. They would see signs, yes, but would they be able to read their messages? And if so, would they care? M hadn't yet decompressed enough from the encounter with the woman who had pled ignorance, so I decided, again, against soliciting her opinion.

A couple times, I stood up to stretch my legs and got a wider, deeper picture of the crowd. I made out more protesters against The Good Neighbors than supporters. Unlike the signs that The Good Neighbors had used to picket at the teenager's funeral, the sentiments heralded by the rally's demonstrators could not be called deplorable, derogatory, vulgar, offensive, or nasty. These protesters had taken the moral high road. Good for them. Yet their messages lacked creativity. They were predictable, boring, and repetitive. They weren't risky, witty, or ironic. They weren't even remotely stupid enough to warrant someone spending five seconds responding to them with a sarcastic or clever retort. The signs would never go viral or make the highlights on the five o'clock news. Case in point: A woman with a beautiful smile and matching beautiful children, two of them, one child on either side of her, carried a NO HATE placard high above her head. On her left, the girl, curly hair, held up a smaller, child-sized poster with the slogan ONLY LOVE. The boy on the right, whose hair was darker and kinkier, his poster's mantra called for ONLY PEACE.

I wanted to make a snarky remark about time-traveling to the 1960s. It used to be that M would have laughed at such a jab, trite as it was. Probably, she had only been humoring me, which was what people who cared about each other sometimes did. Now I assumed that, at most, she would only smile mockingly or else accuse me of being a smart-ass, which was probably true.

A few minutes later, I saw another NO HATE message, its bearer a tall, thin man, standing by himself, reading on his phone. I guessed that he was about the same age as the beautiful woman with the beautiful children, but he was without children, and his NO HATE appeared not on a sign but across his chest in black letters on a white long-sleeve T-shirt. Within a couple minutes, NO HATE cropped up again, this time in white letters on a short-sleeve black T-shirt worn by a young man with an old man's beard. Had I pointed out the young bearded man's shirt to M, as well as the nearly identical mirror-image shirt worn by the other man, and the beautiful woman's sign with the exact same phrase on it, and said, "Hey, that's original," I'm pretty sure M would have rolled her eyes.

Another incontrovertible fact: Somewhere on the grounds of the civic center, a vendor must have been selling NO HATE merchandise: T-shirts, hats, buttons, magnets, bumper stickers, key chains, water bottles, coffee mugs. A great idea by a righteous capitalist.

M was ready to stand up again.

"Let's get closer to the stage," she said.

In front of the stage, work crews had erected a temporary barricade of interlocking galvanized steel fences, which served as a line of defense between The Good Neighbors, who would soon take the stage, and their detractors in the crowd. As a secondary measure against unruly protesters who might attempt to rush the speakers, four policemen on horseback had taken positions along the barricade, the length of the stage. In front of the mounted police, I saw a man who looked homeless. His hair was a mess (long, disheveled, and clumped at the ends), and the seams of his shirt looked ready to pull apart (only the middle two or three buttons were done, the rest either unfastened or missing), and his beard was scraggly (though it was indistinguishable from that of the young man wearing the NO HATE shirt who was still absorbed by something on his phone). I tried guessing the homeless man's age, but I couldn't tell if he was young or old, even when he smiled, and he was smiling a lot. His teeth, like his shoes, were falling apart, and though the condition of his teeth could have served as a reliable indicator of his age, his poor dental health might have been due to his derelict and destitute existence, not the passage of time. Young, old, or somewhere in between, the homeless man also carried a sign, and its message brought a smile to my face.

GOD HATES FREE SPEECH.

His sign was made from a flattened cardboard box, the flaps shorn by hand. No one in his immediate vicinity seemed to notice him or his sign, which might have been why he turned to face the four police on horses and began moving the sign up and down, side to side, hoping to grab their attention. They didn't notice him or his sign, either, or they pretended not to see him. Then he took to making a semicircle with the sign, moving it from left to right, right to left, back and forth, the arc of his movement an invisible rainbow, which to some people is a symbol for God's love and for others a symbol of another kind of love. Finally, the homeless man caught the attention of one of the policemen, the one closest to him. This policeman nodded and then must have said something to the other police because a second officer acknowledged the homeless man with a grin. Then a third police officer gave the homeless man a friendly wave. The fourth officer, the farthest away, only looked on, uninterested, unaffected.

The distance between us and the stage was only a matter of yards. Ten, twenty, I don't know or remember. However, I do remember and know that right around now, the sound system cracked. Some in the crowd cheered the amplified crackle. Some booed.

A young woman (twenties, thirties) pushing a very old man in a wheelchair (late seventies, eighties, possibly early nineties) strolled in front of us. Neither the young woman nor the elderly man was carrying a sign, and there was no telling why they were at the rally or which side they were on. The old man in the wheelchair glanced up at M as he passed us and, smiling, said, "God bless you."

M smiled back at him. Apparently, she was no longer infuriated. Seeing her smile, I sighed relief.

There was a hum in the air. Probably from the speakers. Probably also from the crowd. I felt my body vibrate. Just then, a man started speaking loudly, shouting almost. M and I both turned toward the sound of his voice, which was coming from behind us.

Ten, maybe fifteen feet away, the man paced back and forth within a circle of people slowly gathering around him.

He said to the encircling crowd, "I'm telling you, there's nothing worse than people. Nothing. Always wanting. Gimme, gimme, gimme. The minute they're born, they want air, they want mother's milk, they want to be fed, clothed, cleaned, nourished, loved. Gimme, gimme, gimme, and gimme some more. And what do they give back? First, they cry all day long, they give you that. Then they cry all night long, and they piss on you and shit on you and vomit all over your clothes. They scratch themselves and scrape their knees and get blood on your nice shirts and mud on your floors, and they dirty up all your nice furniture. Next thing you know, they've taken your time, your money, your youth, your hopes, your dreams. Then they put you in an old-folks home."

The circle of people around the man grew larger.

"After you give them everything, they put you out, they sell everything you called your own, and what they can't sell for a nickel or dime, they leave on the curb for the trash man to pick up. Your life dumped, discarded, trash, garbage, and if you're lucky, they'll visit you once a year on your birthday. They'll bring you a cake when they know damn well you like pie. Then one day they'll take away your Pall Malls because they worry you're going to set the building ablaze all because once, just that one time, you forgot your cigarette was lit, and you put it in your pants pocket because you didn't want them knowing you were still smoking, and you burned a hole right through. Then comes the day you start forgetting. You forget their names, you forget your own name, you can't remember what year it is or who's president, you can't remember if your mother and father are still alive."

He wagged his finger at the circle surrounding him. No one wagged theirs back. No one did anything but watch and wait.

"What you don't know yet is that you forgetting everything is the only mercy left in your wasted life."

The sound of a bullhorn muffled his voice, and I heard another voice in the crowd begin a chant. "No justice, no peace." A few others joined in, but the chant lasted only two or three rounds before dying out.

I listened for the man in the circle to pick up where he had left off, but he was interrupted again when a second chant got going. Its words were muffled though, and again not enough of the crowd had come together to keep it alive. It ended before getting started. Almost immediately after the second failed attempt, another rallying call rose. It came from the direction of the stage. This time the words reached the crowd loud and clear.

"No fear, no hate."

M turned her attention toward the fear, the hate—toward the stage—and added her voice to the chanting.

This third attempt took hold. The radius grew, and I gave up on the man in the circle. Loudly, the crowd chanted, "No fear, no hate, no fear, no hate."

Why not? I wondered. Shouldn't some things be feared? Shouldn't some people be hated?

As swiftly as it burst forth, the chanting dwindled and altogether disappeared when a man walked across the stage to a podium in the center. A few boos followed his appearance, and a few cheers. The man looked off to the left, nodded, and waved someone else over. Then he tapped the microphone. Loud thumps and feedback filled the air above the rally. More cheering and booing followed. Some people clapped. The man on stage, still waving someone over, spoke into the microphone.

"Please, please, let's quiet down," he told the restless and eager crowd.

Within a few seconds, he got what he had asked for—quiet.

Then shots rang out.

In the opinion of the local TV news, Channel 7, once it became clear that the noise had come from a gun—described by a rally-goer as "pop-pop-pop"—panic set upon the crowd.

From where M and I had been standing, near the man who had launched into a tirade about ungrateful children resolved to place their mothers and fathers in assisted-care facilities until they lost their minds and bodies, the successive shots were plainly audible. Both M and I also immediately recognized the sound as gunfire, a skill developed as a direct consequence of living in the East Side, some residents of which annually exhibited a penchant for celebrating the Fourth of July and the New Year by firing shots into the sky. We also concurred that mistaking the repetitive noises for anything but shots being fired would be unusual. Unless, of course, you were someone who had never heard actual gunfire. Even so, we both later agreed that in our country, in our state and city, this seemed unlikely. All this is to say we both believed that most people who heard pop-pop-pop must have understood the sound to be shots fired. And yet, contrary to the reporting on Channel 7 News, the people standing around us, five or six deep, if not a dozen, reacted to the pop-pop-pop not with panic but composure.

If I look back on the crowd and imagine it to be a body acting in unison, then I might have to concede that once the actuality of gunfire became apparent, panic did indeed characterize the state gripping its collective psyche. It was true, after all, that the crowd did become suddenly frightened and anxious, and everyone knows that fear and anxiety are hallmarks of panic. It was also true that the crowd was not in total control of its emotions, which some in the rally demonstrated by bolting from the civic center grounds in an unruly, disorderly manner. It goes without saying that confusion of this sort is also a telltale sign of panic. In these ways, I would have to allow that, yes, absolutely, panic besieged the crowd.

However, the crowd did *not* act wildly or thoughtlessly.

Overall, no one freaked out, and while many people did in fact run like mad in the opposite direction of the gunfire, who in their right mind wouldn't? Even still, nothing remotely close to a free-for-all ensued after the crowd heard shots fired. Those escaping the scene did so with relative ease and without harming anyone. They did not trample over the elderly. They did not shove the slow, disoriented, or indecisive out of the way. They did not unthinkingly abandon a child or pet. No fights broke out. No injuries to person or property were reported. No thefts, either. Under the circumstances, chaotic as they might have been, relatively speaking, the crowd revealed not a loss of control but more than a modicum of self-restraint.

It was also true that in response to the gunshots ("crash-crash, crash-crash" according to a second attendee/eyewitness), a few people pulled out their own firearms. M was among them. She snatched her .38 from her bag. However, I stopped her from bringing the gun completely out into the open, grabbing her arm just as I saw the grip reveal itself. With a measured but forceful tone, I said, "No." And just as the indifferent man who only minutes before had ushered his ignorant wife away from us, across the street, away from the rally, I did the same with M, leading her all the way back to the blue bungalow, not once stopping or looking back.

People in a crowd, strangers no less, drawing guns when someone else has already opened fire—such an occurrence should have spelled all kinds of disaster: men, woman, children writhing in pain, bleeding through clothes, screaming, agonizing, forming piles on the ground. The stuff of war, massacre, indiscriminate violence. None of that took place. On that day, despite the heavy presence of guns, ammo, and intolerance, no one, not even the police, fired a single round. No one except for the shooter, who got off either three or four shots.

With respect to how people had described the sound of the gunfire, M and I agreed that it could have been either a series of pops or a set of crashes. We saw no reason why the sound couldn't have been a combination of the two. We likened the difference between "pop-pop-pop" and "crash-crash, crash-crash" to the difference between "ruff, ruff" and "woof, woof." Both accounted for the same thing (shooting, barking). Arguing over which would have been entirely academic.

How many pops or crashes? On this point, we could not come to a consensus. Not because we opposed each other, but because the shots had been fired in such close succession that in the absence of forensic evidence and relying solely on the basic senses (in this case, hearing), it was all but impossible to say, definitively, whether the number was three or four.

Back at the blue bungalow, less than an hour after the shooting, the two of us sitting side by side on the couch in the room with the TV, the TV turned on, we waited to hear what *Eyewitness News at 11* had to say about what we had just witnessed.

"It's a miracle the rally didn't turn into a bloodbath," I said.

While she did not necessarily agree with me (she replied "I guess"), M did not technically disagree. I wondered if I should take her response as an omen. Yes, I told myself, I should. Whether I should have construed it positively or negatively, I really couldn't say at the time, not with confidence or bias. Of course, I wished for it to be good.

Eyewitness News at 11 on Channel 4 did not report the shooting at the rally. Neither did Channel 2 or Channel 11. We kept flipping between channels until each news program moved on to weather or sports, at which point I turned off the TV.

Several hours later, the anchor on *Live at 5,* a woman in a red dress who had been voted one of the nation's sexiest local TV news anchors, confirmed what we had suspected: Both the old preacher and the preacher's son had started walking across the stage just before the pop-pop-pop or crash-crash, crash-crash. They had been the people out of sight waved over by the man at the microphone telling the crowd to quiet down. Presumably they had been standing behind the three or four large speakers stacked on top of each other, on either side of the stage, which were taller and wider than the average man. Neither M nor I had been able to see the old preacher and his son—not before or after they stepped from behind the speakers to make their way to the center of the stage. The culprits obstructing our view, we both guessed, must have been either tall people in our line of sight or the policemen on horseback. I do remember telling M seconds before the pop-pop-pop or crash-crash, crash-crash, "Do you think the old preacher will speak first or last?" She shrugged, which I took to mean, "I don't know" not "I don't care." During a moment of reflection some months later, I told myself that I could count on the shrug as evidence that M and I had turned a corner, that we were slowly but surely coming together, that soon enough we would finally be on the same page.

The sexy news anchor referred to the old preacher and his son as "the speakers." She noted that the old preacher served a small, local congregation. Not once during the segment did the anchor reveal the actual names of the old preacher or his son, respecting the privacy of their identities, ensuring, too, that no harm might come to them by revealing their given names. Nor did she identify, by name, the group to which they belonged, The Good Neighbors, though we all knew, didn't we? Maybe we didn't all know. Maybe there were many people like the woman at the rally M had berated for her ignorance. The news anchor did not give out the name or the address of the small church or specify the denomination adhered to by the church's members, even though, M reminded me, people would easily have been able to guess. Both father and son had been on TV, after all, which is to say that they were already somewhat famous, at least locally. In speaking of the shooting, the sexy news anchor did not make any claims, judgments, or associations whatsoever about the faith of the old preacher or his son or the congregation. Nor did she, or anyone else on the *Live at 5* news broadcast, make sweeping generalizations about how the religious beliefs of the old preacher, his son, or the congregation might have influenced their thoughts, actions, or motivations.

"Must be nice," I said.

"Uh-huh," M agreed.

Later that night, on *News at 10,* which aired on Channel 11, the anchor, a woman with a bright smile wearing a dark brown suit with hints of red, a cream shirt with a ruffled collar, and a pearl necklace, *did* explicitly reference The Good Neighbors. She mentioned the group's name once, but she dubbed the group "a movement founded in opposition to the recent suicide attacks against children." While I can't claim those are the exact words she used—apparently, only premiere news programs offer free written transcripts, and *News at 10* did not qualify—they are a very close approximation of what she reported.

Either way, I yelled at the TV, at the Channel 11 anchor.

"Are you out of your goddamn mind?"

"She can't hear you," M told me.

I could have taken M's remark to be snide, but the impression I had then, and which I still have now, is that she wished it were possible for the anchor to hear me complain. I know for a fact that M also found fault with the anchor's choice of words. M wasn't chiding me. To the contrary, she was trying to assuage my indignation.

Regardless, I kept criticizing the news anchor.

"Attacks? How can you say attacks?"

On this point, I was entirely right. There was only one attack. Singular, not plural. Carried out by the teenager who stole his mother's car. Only one other East Side child had committed suicide, and she hadn't attacked anyone but herself.

"You can't call that an attack," I said and stood up, and then sat back down because I had nowhere to go. Turning to M, I asked, "Is she counting each first-grader killed as a separate attack? How is she even referring to it as recent? It's not recent. It happened the day you found out you were pregnant. That was months and months ago."

"Could you please shut up for one minute? I'm trying to listen to the TV, not you."

Again, I could have judged M's remark as bitchy or shrewish, but I didn't. Out of context, in and of themselves, her words might be interpreted as rude or belittling—not the way married people should speak to one another—but the tone she took uttering them was anything but. She wasn't interested in analyzing what she already knew—that the news story was being reported with bias. Rather, she wanted to know more, and my little outbursts were keeping her from that. For M to ask me to shut up seemed fair enough. She had even said "please."

The news anchor kept talking, M went on watching, and I tried to catch my breath, to quiet my mind, and to keep my opinions to myself for at least the sixty seconds M had requested. To accomplish the task, instead of watching the TV, I watched M watching the TV. Her hands were covering her mouth. Not in shock or disbelief. The gesture appeared to be more a reflection of her engagement, the seriousness of her concentration, the degree of her pensiveness. Gradually, she lowered her hands from her mouth to her chin. From there, she let them fall to her chest, where she interlaced her fingers and lifted her hands from her chest, slightly, bringing them together as if in prayer. By the time the prayer had been relinquished to a higher power, which coincided with the end of the news segment, she unclasped her hands and rested them atop her womb. In that moment, when the TV switched from an incident of gun violence to a commercial about type 2 diabetes, somehow M looked even more pregnant than she was only a minute before. While a famous old actor told us about the symptoms of diabetes, I said, "You're finally starting to show."

M let out a sigh.

Because *News at 10* did not let us know whether the shots fired at the rally had struck anyone, I changed the channel. The anchor on the *10 O'Clock Action News* was wrapping up a story on a recall of one-pound packages of ground beef and ground chuck under a handful of brand names, distributed in five states, after which she said, "We have more news about the shooting earlier today on the East Side." The screen switched from the anchor to a reporter standing in front of the civic center. His cheeks were red, and I wondered why. The weather was seasonably mild. The temperature had dropped since the morning, but only by a few degrees, not enough to flush a person's skin. I concluded that he must have been a novice when it came to live reporting, and because he hadn't yet acquired the ease that familiarity and practice engender in a person, he got red in the face when the voice in his earpiece announced, "We're live."

He greeted the anchor in the studio and went straight to the news.

"We're hearing from the police that the suspect in this morning's shooting has been identified. Police aren't releasing her name yet, and the reason is probably because she's a teenager."

"Did he say a teenager?"

"Yes, he did."

"He said *she*?"

"Yes, she."

"One man I talked to told me that as soon as he heard gunfire, he saw police rush the stage and take down the suspect and quickly disarm and handcuff her."

Please, please, I told myself, do not let it be one of ours.

The same desperate plea must have run through M's mind.

The reporter's face already looked a lot less flushed than just a moment earlier. I was probably right to attribute the redness in his cheeks to the nervousness and jitters any beginner in any endeavor is bound to experience. He was on live TV, which must be stressful, given that every mistake or misstep would be noticed by thousands of people, and though a mistake on his part might only last a split second, he would undoubtedly let it consume him for hours, perhaps days. Depending on the kind of person he was, his history, his emotional maturity or lack thereof, and any traumas he might have suffered as a child, making a small mistake on live television could have haunted him for the rest of his life. If he evidenced the least bit of nervousness, it would be understandable and forgivable. Once he got going, though, he seemed to settle into his reporting. Any fears he might have had about publicly embarrassing or humiliating himself abated, and the color in his face quickly returned to normal.

"We're still waiting to hear more details about the suspect. We're expecting the police chief and the mayor's office to make an announcement very soon. As you know, Carmen, the rally at the civic center was supposed to bring awareness to the uptick in violence at local area schools, which culminated in that horrific attack we reported on a few months ago when seven children were killed at an elementary school on the city's West Side. The attacker in that case, like the shooter at today's rally, was also a teenager. Authorities aren't saying if the suspected shooter is from the East Side or not. In fact, they seem to be going out of their way *not* to draw conclusions until they gather more information, but people I spoke to here and in the mayor's office, they tell me that they're worried. After a period of relative calm, they're concerned that today's shooting is the beginning of a new wave of violence."

The anchor, Carmen, was shaking her head. Was she doing so out of disappointment, distress, or dismay? She was an attractive woman with shoulder-length blond hair, and she was wearing a sleeveless red dress, hoop earrings, and a matching gold necklace with a glittery pendant on the end of it, hanging low. She thanked the reporter on the scene for his special report. Then, looking straight at us, she added, "We'll keep you updated as we learn more. Sonny Fields is up next with the weather forecast."

I flipped to another channel and waited for *Nightly News at 10:30* to come on. The anchor opened the newscast by wishing us a good evening and telling us that there was a significant development in the shooting at the rally, but the mention was only a teaser. "But first," he said and went on to discuss the news concerning the ongoing debate over an immigration bill that had recently stalled in Congress. The story after that was about an incident involving a hotel siege in an overseas country with which we were unofficially at war. Though people had been killed and the siege was ongoing, the anchor covered the war story quickly, without giving many details about those killed, or those doing the killing, or whose side the living and the dead were on. Presumably, we should have known, but we didn't. Then, finally, the anchor said, "We have more information about the man shot at the civic center earlier today."

I looked at my watch and did the math. It had taken the news more than twelve hours to report that someone had indeed been shot at the rally.

The anchor, a man in his mid- to late forties, his face, hairstyle, and dress nondescript, said the shooting victim, who had not yet been identified and was still in the hospital in critical condition, was a member of the organization that held the rally. I expected to see either video footage or a photograph of the old preacher or his son or one of the original protesters at the cemetery (the schoolteacher, the dentist, the storeowner), but only an image of the civic center appeared on screen. The image was obviously not taken at the time of the rally, either—on TV, the civic center grounds were empty, the makeshift stage was missing. The anchor did mention The Good Neighbors, and he also mischaracterized the group, referring to them as "a local neighborhood association." Then he told us to stay tuned for updates on the victim's condition and moved on to news of another national food product recall: eggs tainted with salmonella.

I turned to another channel.

A man wearing a tuxedo was standing face to face with a woman in an evening gown. The man's hair was shiny, the woman's done up in an elaborate bun. The man was holding the woman by the shoulders. He looked deadly serious. She looked distressed. They were in an elaborately furnished house. There were more pieces of furniture in the TV frame alone than M and I owned, and the walls were covered with oil paintings, recessed niches, and sconces. None of the sconces were lit, though, and there were no windows. The only light source was a chandelier, and yet the room was well lit. There were flowers in vases on mahogany cabinets and side tables that surrounded the couple. The flowers looked artificial—the leaves too green, the petals too bright. The woman looked ready to faint, the man ready to catch her.

I changed channels.

A family (father, mother, son, daughter, all good looking, healthy weight, blemish-free skin, well dressed, and outwardly happy) sat side by side on a comfortable-looking extra-wide sofa, in that order, right to left, father, mother, son, and daughter. They were watching TV. On their TV was a commercial reminding them to protect their family with life insurance.

I changed channels again.

A woman with long brown hair, wearing a strapless dress and large silver pendant earrings with diamonds or some other glittery gem, was lying on her stomach on a modern platform bed in a luxury penthouse suite with floor-to-ceiling windows revealing a million-dollar view of a nighttime city skyline. The city could have been Hong Kong or Shanghai or Tokyo or Singapore or Kuala Lumpur. The woman stared into our eyes. I thought of the word "ravishing." A voiceover, that of a man, told us, "About half of men over forty suffer from erectile dysfunction."

I switched back to the *Nightly News at 10:30,* which that night I discovered was the only local news program in the 10:30 p.m. time slot. After four commercials (the first for dog food; the second for car insurance; the third for a new drug treating arthritis, plaque psoriasis, axial spondyloarthritis, Crohn's disease, and ulcerative colitis; and the fourth for a drug treating restless leg syndrome), we watched a news story about the arrest of a fifty-year-old man, a high school baseball coach and gym teacher accused of sexually assaulting an untold number of students. The segment ended with the anchor giving out a web address and phone number to report sexual assaults anonymously. Then the news teased us three times. First with a story about a highly unlikely occurrence ("Find out how to survive if your car plunges into a lake"), second with a story about the president finally choosing a pet dog ("Can you guess which breed?"), and third with the weather (the cameras turned to the meteorologist, Johnny Weathers, who said, "We've got severe storms on the way, but what's right behind them could be worse. Up next, the forecast.").

After four more commercials about four things M and I did not want or need but were nonetheless intrigued by, the anchor came back on the air and said, "We have a special news bulletin about the shooting that took place at that rally earlier today." He was wearing a charcoal-colored suit, a white shirt, and a blue tie the shade of the sky in the morning on a clear day. He had great hair, too. Dark, thick, and wavy, but kempt and without a part. He told us that the police had identified the shooting victim and the shooting suspect.

"Did he say victim?"

"He said victim."

"Does victim mean dead?"

"Not always."

He described the victim as an elderly minister.

Then he changed the tone of his voice, speaking the way one does when offering condolences. "Charges against the suspect will be upgraded from attempted murder to murder."

He altered his tone again, still serious but not somber, and added that the police had also released the identity of the suspected murderer, and that a spokesperson for the police department had confirmed earlier reports that the shooter was, in fact, a teenager and female.

"I hope she's not from the East Side," I said.

"If she's one of us," M said, "we're screwed."

The anchor doled out more bad news, confirming what he had heard earlier but with more detail: The teenaged suspect was eighteen.

"God," M said. "She's so young."

"I hope she doesn't look like us."

"Me, too."

We were agreeing again.

The anchor said the suspect lived in the East Side.

"Oh, shit."

The TV screen split into two.

On the left, the news anchor, who kept talking.

On the right, a photograph of the college student who lived in the pink bungalow.

I could feel M looking at me, but I kept my eyes fixed on the television, on the image of the college student. She was wearing eyeglasses but not the tortoiseshell frames I had been using to seeing. She had on red plastic frames far too large for her face. Her hair was long but pulled back into a ponytail. She had a shine on her forehead, braces on her teeth. She looked like a high school student. A teenager. A little girl.

❧

Within a few days of her face appearing on the news, someone spray-painted on the front of the pink bungalow, in big, bold letters, the word CUNT. Most of the letter C was on a window looking into the living room, the U and N were entirely on wood siding, and the T was divided, almost perfectly in half, between the siding and the front door. Beneath CUNT, someone else added a racial epithet, half of which—the first half, the actual epithet—yet another person had covered over with more spray paint, leaving only the second half legible: LOVER. Every letter of LOVER was on the siding.

The graffiti did not make the news. It remained on the bungalow for a few more days until I got over to the paint store, bought a can of paint stripper and a gallon of pink exterior paint, removed what I could from the window and door, and painted over the rest. But because the shade of pink that I had picked out for the siding did not exactly match the bungalow's pink, and because I wasn't about to repaint the entire house, anyone giving it more than a passing glance (and who had already seen the graffiti) could still at least make out the offensive act if not the word.

About the college student, her being eighteen years old, I had to think long and hard about the possibility that I must have known her actual age but overlooked it, or else blocked it out. For all my efforts at remembering and reflecting, I could not confirm prior knowledge of her actual age. However, I did recall eagerly showing her the pink bungalow and selling M on her becoming a tenant ("She's a student, seems mature, no roommates"), and in recalling this, I had an aha moment: She must have entered her date of birth on the lease agreement. I dug up the lease to find out if she had lied about her age. That would provide me with an explanation for why I couldn't have known she was so young.

She hadn't lied. She wasn't even on the lease. Her mother and father were the signatories. I did the math and arrived at a logical reason for why this was the case: When the student became our tenant, she was still legally a minor, and when she returned the lease to me, filled out with her parents' information and not hers, I never bothered reviewing the paperwork. I simply had wanted her as a tenant, knowing I would be able to see her at least once a month. That was my error. M's mistake was trusting me.

I didn't know how to feel about all this new knowledge, so I tried hard not to think about the college girl. I tried even harder not to think about what she had done at the rally. I tried infinitely harder to dispel all thoughts of what she and I had done together in the pink bungalow—with her, to her.

Every time I tried, I failed.

The past is a strange place. The past brought into the present—revisited, relived, reimagined—is even stranger. A single moment unfolds over a long period of time. If lucky, a few minutes of real life may take an hour, or even part of day, to bring into being. If unlucky, or stubborn about getting the details just right, then weeks or even months may lapse before those few minutes materialize into words and sentences. Sometimes they never see the light of day. That unpredictable, disorderly, random phenomenon we call "a life," here translated into the written word, turned into a book, is no more than a series of infinite choices, false starts, and endless corrections. In the world where past is always past, what happened with the eighteen-year-old girl happened only once. In the world where the past has been revised countless times, it's possible that I have spent as much time with the girl as I have with my own wife. But the sole purpose of each of these encounters has almost nothing to do with desire or longing. Each return is simply another attempt at getting it right. A life of second chances, ad infinitum. How much simpler life is when it happens once and only once. No burden of perfection, no compulsion to relive experiences in any number of ways just so someone else—

not me, not M, not anyone I may have hurt, but *you*, a total stranger—may find those experiences not only authentic and worthy but satisfying, engrossing, and entertaining.

I wasn't the only one obsessed. Everyone else could not get enough of the college girl. Her face, sometimes the younger version of herself (awkward glasses and braces) and sometimes her mug shot (the face I saw last in her bedroom), showed up on TV, online, and in articles on a regular basis. For a while, this happened every single day. Every time she appeared, I wished for her to be left alone, for her story to blow over, for her name, face, and everything about her to be forgotten. Every day, everywhere, people killed other people. Given this fact, I prayed for someone else to quickly take her place among the publicly hated.

Less than a week after spending the afternoon at the pink bungalow painting over the graffiti and changing all the locks—by then investigators had already cleared her belongings from the house, presumably keeping some of it as evidence—I read about The Good Neighbors holding a private funeral for the old preacher. The small church where he had preached reached maximum capacity, something that, on any other given Sunday, hadn't happened in recent memory. Mourners had to be turned away. Some of them gathered in the parking lot and stayed there until the service ended. Some remained until sundown and held an impromptu candlelight vigil. In their coverage of the old preacher's funeral service, each of the four local TV news stations, all affiliates of the major national broadcasting companies, referred to the old preacher differently: a minister (ABC), a pastor (CBS), a man of the cloth (NBC), and man of faith (Fox).

Exactly one week after the old preacher's burial, his son gave a televised speech.

So many people wanted to hear him speak in person the event had to be relocated from its original location, the small church in the East Side, to the city's convention center. Thousands gathered. How many thousands, the news didn't say, but the convention center used to be a college basketball arena. I had watched a game there the year I began teaching at the college, and that same year M had also been to the arena on a field trip with her high school. In its original layout, for use as a sport arena, the convention center had a seating capacity of just over three thousand. If three thousand people showed up, how many more *would* have come? Did the crowd represent a small portion, most, or nearly all the people among us who supported The Good Neighbors? Did they share the same ideological hatred? Or did they simply feel so much grief for the old preacher that they wanted to pay their respects in person? I wondered if the crowd size served as an indication of what had always been there, or was it a harbinger of what was still to come? If the rule of thumb still held true—that for every person who wrote a letter of complaint to a newspaper or a TV station, a thousand others (who did *not* write) held the same view—then how many people hated us if three thousand had showered, shaved, dressed nicely, paid for parking, and filled a sports arena? Whatever the figure, the preacher's son had counted on there being a lot, and in addition to changing the venue to accommodate the sudden surge of support, he also made the event available online, free and streamed live.

M and I watched on the laptop, in the bedroom.

Cameras projected the preacher's son onto several high-definition screens set above the convention center floor. His image and his voice—amplified by more than 100,000 watts—came down from high above. Early in the speech, the preacher's son called his father "a good man," "a man of

God," "a man of conviction," "a man of unswerving commitment to truth." Above all else, he said, his father valued human decency, adding that the old preacher had been "a humble, unassuming father figure." To illustrate his father's modesty, he recalled the old preacher's ubiquitous gray suit jacket and pants. "He married my mother in that suit," the preacher's son said. At that moment, the livestream cut to a young couple, who may or may not have been married but more importantly looked married. The preacher's son said, "And he was wearing the suit when he gave my mother's eulogy." The video remained fixed on the couple long enough to capture the young woman appearing visibly pained by the revelation. When the shot cut back to the preacher's son, he reminded everyone that his father was wearing the same gray suit the day he was murdered by the college student, and then, to bring the symbolism of the old preacher's suit full circle, he told us that the old man had been buried in it.

That must have been a lie.

"I doubt it," I said.

M seemed to shrug.

First off, the suit would have been stained with the old preacher's blood. Even if I gave the preacher's son the benefit of the doubt (a dry-cleaning service might have been able to remove the bloodstains), there remained the matter of the holes and torn fabric created by the bullets that pierced the old preacher's clothes and body. The bullets went through his jacket, shirt, stomach, and left lung, in that order. The college student, getting as close to the stage as possible—the front row, right up against the galvanized steel barricade—had aimed her pearl-grip gun at the preacher and his son and discharged four times, not three. She split the shots between the two men, hitting the old preacher twice and missing the son.

Was I supposed to believe that the old preacher had been buried in a bloodstained, bullet-riddled suit?

"That pause he just took," M said of the preacher's son, "that was perfectly timed."

Lost in the forensics of the gray suit, I missed the pause, but I agreed anyhow.

"It was, wasn't it."

The livestream panned the audience. None among the three thousand or so in attendance looked curious or doubtful about anything the preacher's son was saying. Just the opposite. Hearing about the outfit in which the old preacher was laid to rest, they showed signs of sadness and distress. One woman, probably in her late forties or early fifties, appeared absolutely appalled, so much so she covered her mouth during this part of the speech. No doubt, she was holding something back. Probably not a scream. That would be too much. More likely a gasp.

"At home, at church, anywhere my father went, he behaved with decency, with the utmost propriety. I tell you again, and I'll say it over and over because it's true: He was a good man, a good father."

He paused again, and this time I was paying attention.

"But most of all, he was a good neighbor."

I rolled my eyes, but I didn't bother bringing up with M, or she with me, the picket signs with which the old preacher and the original Good Neighbors had interrupted the teen's funeral, though the question of how the signs could have possibly signified the decency and propriety that the preacher's son wanted us to remember his father by had undoubtedly run through her mind as it did mine. As for the crowd in the convention center, when they heard the preacher's son utter the phrase "a good neighbor," they did not doubt its veracity, and they demonstrated this by standing up. First, a few, and then a few more, and seeing that the audience members were getting out of their seats by twos, threes, and fours, and then in clusters too large to count, the preacher's son halted his speech once more. Just as he had responded to them, the crowd now reacted to the preacher's son. Almost immediately, they understood the intention behind his hesitation, and within a few seconds, the rest of the audience rose and gave the preacher's son, as well as what he had said about his dead father, a standing ovation.

He gave the applause a five-count. Then he raised his right hand and closed his eyes until a hush fell over the convention center. The crowd silenced itself and when the preacher lowered his hand, they sat back down. The preacher's son told the crowd that while the shooting at the rally had resulted from a failure of common sense, it had also strengthened his resolve to fight what he called "the tyranny of stupidity and foolishness infecting society." Acts of violence, he said, like the murder of his father, an old man with grandchildren, amounted to a perversion of good judgment. He told them that the goal of such disgusting, despicable behavior was not and could never be the betterment of life or progress or the good. "The true aim of violence," he said, "is nothing short of the humiliation of the most precious gift of all."

He took another skillful pause before naming this gift.

"Life."

Most everyone in the crowed illustrated their agreement by nodding their heads.

He told them, "Every day, people misuse common sense. They manipulate words and misrepresent ideas just so they can gain what they want, regardless of the consequences. Despite the consequences, in fact." He tilted his head sideways to show that the world was also askew. Raising his voice, he added, "Too often—far, far too often—people twist logic and reason to bring about harm and injury to innocent people—to good people, to innocent and good people, like you." The preacher's son swallowed his breath before continuing, and either out of pride or because he felt he would need to speak the next part of his speech in a long, single breath, he inhaled deeply, filling his lungs to capacity, which made him look bigger, stronger, and more assured. He looked not like a man delivering a memorial address but a leader speaking to his followers.

He said, "Even worse, when people like that young...radical...woman..."

The crowd booed.

"People like that," he went on, speaking over the jeers, "when they resort to violence to get what they want, when they distort reality and subvert common sense, they end up injuring the dignity and self-respect of all people—men, women, and children."

The crowd applauded.

"All his life, my father fought for good, hard-working people, like you, and I will walk in his footsteps and continue to fight—for you. The world doesn't need any more radicals. It doesn't even need one radical. What the world needs are more decent, dignified people." For added emphasis—pausing between each word, thumping his fist just above the podium but never actually touching it—he said, "We. Need. More. Good. Neighbors."

This time, without prompting, the crowd rose to its feet again, clapping, cheering, and shouting words at the preacher's son not discernible on the livestream but which must have sounded wonderful to his ears. The lights in the convention center brightened. The preacher's son stepped back from the podium. One of the cameras momentarily focused on his face, just long enough to record the warm glow coming over him as he took stock of the affair before his eyes. Then the video cut to another angle, from behind the stage, with preacher's son looking out at the arena, which allowed us at home to see what he was seeing: the crowd, euphoric.

&

When the preacher's son began giving his speech, 7 p.m., it was almost dark out, the light so faint that the leaves on the trees lining the streets of the East Side appeared more black than green. The diminishing light and color acted as signs of the seasonal shift taking hold and the calendar year coming to an end. These are symbolic of many things: birth and death, change and rebirth, beginnings and ends—their progression, their inescapability.

On one of the East Side's main thoroughfares, two people each saw something that later turned them into eyewitnesses. The first of the two, a man, noticed a car heading north on Lawndale Avenue slow down and park under a large oak with its green leaves seeming black. The man, seated in his own vehicle across the street, was waiting in the parking lot of a 24-hour pharmacy for his wife to pick up prescriptions to treat his high blood pressure, anxiety, and depression. Three men emerged from the parked car, all wearing black pants and black hoodies, and headed south by foot. They did not return until approximately seven minutes later, the man said. In that time, the color of the sky, like the color of the lobed oak leaves before it, had also begun to change, the underbelly of the clouds turning yellow, then pink, then orange, then red. By the time the three hooded men returned and drove off, the sky was nearly the color of night, which, that night, because it was cloudy, was black on the horizon and gray just above.

The second eyewitness, a woman, added a significant detail overlooked by the man waiting for his medications. She saw a fourth man exit the car, who she identified as the driver. He appeared from the vehicle a minute or two after the others, but instead of following them, he stood beside the car on a patch of grass under a large red oak tree and smoked a cigarette. He also wore black pants and a black sweatshirt but opted not to pull the hoodie over his head. "On account of the smoke from his cigarette," the woman surmised. She watched the fourth man's every move carefully, not because he appeared suspicious but because she harbored a practical concern: that when he finished smoking, the driver would not stub out his cigarette but flick it onto her front law, the embers still burning. "The grass was dry and brittle," she said, on account of a lack of rain. "Weeks and weeks, not a drop, not a one."

Vigilant but cautious, she kept an eye on the fourth man from the safety of her living room, standing behind the windows facing the street, which happened to be adorned with blinds behind which she could keep herself hidden. How did she know to look out her front windows at the exact moment the car pulled up and the driver, through negligence, threatened to set her grass on fire? "I had a feeling," she said. Some people, M among them, would have viewed this not as coincidence but rather intuition. Other people, myself among them, do not acknowledge that such a sense exists, except in the imagination. The woman also testified to seeing the three hooded men come back, at which point the man smoking dropped his cigarette to the ground and, to the woman's relief, stubbed it out with the heel of his shoe. "They hot-dogged it out of there," she said.

Neither of the two witnesses had paid attention to the make or model of the car. Except for agreeing on it being a car, not a truck or SUV, neither witness could identify any other features. Not whether it was a coupe, sedan, or hatchback. Not the color. Not whether it was old or new, or if it had tinted windows, or a crack in the windshield, or a burned-out headlight or a missing hubcap. Not the license plate number and not the state issuing the plate.

As for the time when all this took place, both witness accounts put the time at seven o'clock. The man in the parking lot had a receipt from the pharmacy with a time stamp. The woman peering out her window had missed a call from her sister, which was also time-stamped on her phone. The convergence of their accounts allowed for the actions of the hooded men and the speech given by the preacher's son to unfold in perfect unison.

So, at the same moment that three hooded men exited a parked car on Lawndale Avenue and a fourth smoked a cigarette, the preacher's son was telling the convention center crowd that while the misuse, manipulation, and misrepresentation of common sense played a role in his father's murder, it was not the only culprit. "Blame," he said, "should be spread where blame is due, not only for the death of a good man, but of goodness itself." He paused, a move he had made several times during the speech, and then added, "My father's death is emblematic of a larger crisis." If some in the audience did not know the meaning or purpose of the word *emblematic,* or its root word, *emblem,* he repeated the sentiment, using a synonym: "His death is *symbolic* of a larger crisis." He halted, this time slightly longer than any of the prior pauses. In those few extra seconds, he surveyed the people sitting in the arena and shook his head. If TV added ten pounds to a person's appearance, the few extra seconds of silence that the preacher's son took added its own weight, its own gravity, which the livestream illustrated when the cameras panned the audience held in suspense and settled on an older couple, conservatively but nicely dressed, probably a husband and wife. Like everyone else, or so it seemed, they were looking up at the preacher's son with great anticipation.

At that moment, on cue, M asked, "What's he going to say?"

I shrugged, but deep down I anticipated a sweeping but precise indictment of our times, a statement full of gravitas and so poignantly articulated it would have the effect of an earworm—for days to come, we would hear it, repeat it, and no matter our wishes otherwise, be unable to forget it.

One, two, three seconds went by.

"Things are bad," the preacher's son said. "Very, very bad."

The older couple agreed. The husband nodded, began clapping, and his wife quickly followed suit.

The camera zoomed out, bringing most of the arena back into the frame, so from the comfort of our homes we could watch the three thousand or so in attendance display their approval.

"That's it? Things are bad. Very, very bad. That's the great crisis of our age?"

"That's intentional," said M. "When he paused, he let the audience evoke which large crisis they feared the most. Each person listening inserted their own fear, creating their very own personal understanding and, ultimately, their very own personalized memory of that speech. Whatever fear or worry they filled the pause with, you can bet it was most definitely bad, very, very bad."

M was right. They would remember his speech as one that spoke directly to them, addressing their personal hopes and concerns, even though in actuality he had done no such thing. M's analysis had reminded me of when she was a student of mine, of her insightful, lively comments, so much more enjoyable to me than those of her classmates. True or not, I remembered telling myself, right then and there, that *that* was the reason I had risked my job, my reputation, and my good name to be with M.

At the same time the preacher's son was receiving praise for saying something vague and nearly impossible to disagree with (who hasn't thought that things aren't sometimes bad or very, very bad?), one of the security cameras M had had installed recorded the three hooded men walking up to the pink bungalow. As with all the images on the surveillance footage, except for light sources, which were bright white, the men appeared in shades of gray. Before reaching the front porch steps, the men stepped quickly to the right and out of view. A second camera on the right side of the house showed one of them stopping at a side window that peeked into the small dining room. He smashed the window with a crowbar. A third camera caught the other two men each smashing a window, one of which opened into the kitchen, the other into what had been the college student's bedroom.

Later, after watching this part of the footage, my memories went straight to the kitchen where, it's arguable, I drank too much coffee and listened for far too long to the college girl talk about the Bible. Soon after, of course, my memories of drinking and chatting with the girl in her kitchen brought back another, of us in her bedroom. Me taking her clothes off, and she admitting she had known for a long time that I had wanted her. "You're so obvious," she'd said and then told me that she had never thought of me in the same way. "Not at all?" I had asked, my ego bruised, even though she was naked before me. "Not even once," she replied. And, as though it were not in my mind but on the security camera footage, I pictured the diamond piercing in her belly button, and I could hear her gently scold me about my wandering eyes. "Look up here, at me," she'd said, and then, on top of me, facing me, she leaned forward, and the crucifix dangling on the end of her necklace touched my chest.

After capturing the smashing of the windows, the cameras made a record of the two men in the backyard each throwing a small canister into the house, one into the bedroom, one into the kitchen. Though not caught on camera, a third canister had been hurled into the dining room by the other hooded man. A few seconds later, all three men reappeared on the first camera, at the front of the bungalow, running away from the house back in the direction of the parked car on Lawndale Avenue.

"Look at him," I said.

The preacher's son stepped around the podium, and we saw, M and I, the thousands gathered in the convention center and the nameless masses watching him in pixels—he stood tall, proud, no slouch in his back. He was wearing a dark blue suit coat, a light blue Oxford shirt with an English spread collar. Tied in a full Windsor knot, the necktie was a shade of blue between light and dark, like the ocean in some part of the world or the sky in some other part.

"He's got a certain look," I said.

"Dignified," M said.

"Authoritative."

"Presidential."

"Made for TV."

"A TV president."

Right about then, the three canisters exploded. Within minutes, billowing flames engulfed the little pink house that M loved so much.

SIX

A WEEK LATER, M called the home security company and upgraded our plan. She paid for motion sensors to be added to
the cameras already installed at the white, yellow, and blue
bungalows, and for live video monitoring and daily on-site
drive-by visual inspections. I went along with whatever
made her feel safer. I could have pointed out that the security cams did nothing to keep the hooded men from setting
fire to the pink bungalow. At best, they merely witnessed the
danger, risk, and injury the cameras otherwise promised to
protect us from. Similarly, having a guy being paid an
hourly wage stop by the house once a day, for half a minute,
would not have prevented the firebombing, either. "There
are 2,880 half-minutes per day. What are the chances that
the security company shows up for the right one?" I could
have said that, but she did not need to hear it. Safety is an
illusion. As with any impression, its power lies in accepting
the illusion as true, even if—especially if—it is demonstrably
false.

A couple days after the motion sensors were installed at
the remaining bungalows, I arranged to meet with a fire
marshal so he could verify and evaluate the damage done to
the pink bungalow. I arrived fifteen minutes before the appointment, and I walked around the house, taking in the
extent of the damage for myself. The fire had charred every
part of the bungalow's exterior: the porch and porch steps,

the railings and tapered columns, the door trim, the windowsills, the stools and casing, the sashes and mullions, the lap siding, the gable end and overhang, the soffits, the gutters, the rooftop and ridge, the shingles and chimney, and the chimney flue. Very little of the pink bungalow remained pink. Coated with ash and soot, the fire had colored it mostly black and gray.

M stayed home. She could not bear to see what had become of the bungalow. Not yet. She also didn't want the fire marshal to see her. She did not want him, or anyone else, to know about her pregnancy. By now, her only exposure to the outside world came through word of mouth (me) or a screen (phone, TV, laptop).

Even though the damage to the pink bungalow did not require a thorough inspection—the fire had effaced even the shape of the house, much less its stability or habitability—the fire marshal performed one anyhow, taking dozens of photographs of both the scorched exterior and interior, which he would later send me via email. Otherwise, he said very little while surveying and recording the destruction. When he completed the inspection, he did ask several questions. None were about the house. He asked about the girl. If I had any worries that my answers could affect the inspection, he assured me that his inquiries about the girl stemmed from personal not official curiosity. He used the phrase "off the record" as though he were a journalist. The pink bungalow, he told me, was his first high-profile case, and the girl his first murderer. Was she this, that, or the other, he wanted me to tell him. Was there something about her that, in retrospect, I could point to and say, "Ah, that makes sense now," and could I see it coming? By "it," I took him to mean the shooting, not the house bombing. I suppose he could have meant both.

"She was just a tenant. I didn't really know her that well."

The lie dashed any hopes or expectations he might have had for gossip or anecdotes to divulge to the other inspectors at the city municipal building, or to his friends at the bar, or to a wife, a girlfriend, a husband, a boyfriend, or his mother if he still lived with her, or to his pet dog or cat.

"What next?" I asked him.

The house was not fit for human habitation, he told me. I confined a "No shit, Sherlock," among other comments, to my inner voice. I would receive an official condemnation notice in the mail, he explained. On the one front window, which did not shatter when the fire had reached more than 1,000 degrees Fahrenheit, sucking all the oxygen from the rooms, the inspector posted a notice declaring the house unsafe for human occupancy. He nailed a plywood board over the doorway, on top of which he posted another notice, a reminder that violating the notice or removing it would result in prosecution to the fullest extent of the law. From the street, the bright yellow notices looked a lot like the warnings from The Good Neighbors.

Later in the week, I filed an insurance claim, and because M did not want anyone seeing her pregnant, I met with the insurance adjuster on my own at his office. Because of my encounter with the fire marshal before him, I expected the adjuster to ask questions about the girl. At this point, M still had no knowledge of what I had done with the girl, and while it would be untrue if I said I needed to get the infidelity off my chest, I did wonder what it would feel like to tell someone that I had been involved, in that way, with the person charged with killing the founder of The Good Neighbors. I realize now how pathetic it is to seek attention on account of someone's death. But didn't it suggest something worse to seek attention by way of having committed adultery with an accused murderer, like impropriety or desperation? I acknowledged to myself that this may have been symptomatic of an inflated sense of self-importance, which is often a sign of its opposite, a profound sense of utter irrelevance. To my surprise and, surprisingly, my disappointment, the claims adjuster did not mention the girl or The Good Neighbors. However, he did bring up the surveillance footage of the arson attack.

"Have you been notified by the investigators?"

I told him about the condemnation notice from the fire marshal's office.

"No," he said. "I mean the criminal investigation."

I thought of the girl and people finding out about us. Whether or not I exhibited signs of nervousness, which included avoiding eye contact, biting my lower lip, chewing my nails, jiggling my right foot, and tugging at my shirt collar, I certainly felt nervous, and that was before the adjuster added, "A crime's been committed."

I feigned ignorance.

"They'll be in touch soon enough," he said.

Sure enough, they got in touch soon after, just as he had assured me. The two men investigating the crime at the pink bungalow would only ask me two questions. One: Did I have any suspicions about who might have wanted to bomb the house? Yes, of course I did. The Good Neighbors were behind the bombing. I told them, "Not at all." Two: How well did I know the tenant? I knew her more than most and in more ways than one. I told them what I had told the fire marshal: "She was just a tenant. I hardly knew her at all."

I never heard from them again.

At the end of my meeting with the adjuster, he told me that because of the surveillance footage, the insurance claim should settle relatively quickly. Then he asked, "Do you plan on rebuilding?"

"I haven't thought that far ahead."

"You might want to consider putting the lot up for sale. The East Side is transitioning. Property values are rising. It's a seller's market."

He told me that the lot's value was no different with or without the pink bungalow on it, a fact that M would not have appreciated. He also told me that a developer would buy the lot sight unseen. A new house would go up in less than a year, one double the size of the pink bungalow and triple, even quadruple the price of any existing properties in the neighborhood. Before the construction of the new home was even finished, a SOLD sign would be staked out front.

"Get your share now before the bubble bursts."

That night I wanted to tell M about selling the lot but chose to wait a little while longer, so that, however short-lived, she could keep intact the sentimentalities she reserved almost exclusively for the pink bungalow. It would be a time to grieve and, more important, a time to bring the grieving to an end. Having married into the property, I had none of the same attachments to the house, to any of them, and therefore, none of the grief.

That night M told me about the baby's weight. Not having had an ultrasound exam or imaging tests or, for that matter, any kind of prenatal care whatsoever because she had voluntarily immured herself to the blue bungalow, M could not positively say how far along she was in the pregnancy. Her best guess was a range. At least four months but up to five, maybe five and a half. The fact that she was counting her pregnancy in months, not weeks, attested to the lack of medical supervision she should have been receiving. Based on a mixture of guesswork and calculation, M said the baby weighed as much as a baseball or a full deck of cards.

It surprised me that playing cards and baseballs weighed the same.

I got out of bed and went downstairs. In the kitchen, I rummaged through the drawers until I found what I came looking for. Then I headed out back to the garage. I flicked the light switch on, and my eyes immediately went to the toolbox in which I hid cigarettes. I felt the urge to sneak a cigarette, something I hadn't done in a while given that M hadn't left the house in weeks, which meant I was never alone. Fortunately, the hankering subsided after spotting what I wanted, which was on a shelf lined with boxes stuffed with folders and notes from my days at the college. I grabbed what I'd come for, wiped off the dust, and hurried back to M. Two steps at a time, I ran up the stairs, and when I burst into the bedroom, M flinched.

"What's going on?"

Winded, flushed, and excited, I held my hands out and said, "Let's feel how much the baby weighs." In my left, from the kitchen drawer, a deck of playing cards. In my right, from the garage, a baseball.

M balanced the deck and baseball, one in each palm, and closed her eyes.

"The baseball is definitely heavier," she said.

"Let me try."

I did exactly as she had, even closing my eyes.

"You're right."

I opened my eyes and saw that she was smiling. I felt enormously reassured and heartened.

"So the baby weighs as much as a baseball or a deck of cards—what about its size?" I said. "How big would it be?"

"Let me check."

She typed, browsed, clicked.

"An avocado," she said.

We talked to each other for longer than we had in months. Mostly about the baby. Mostly hypothetically. We kept talking until both of us became tired, but even after yawning, we continued to chat for several minutes more, until finally, after the words we spoke to one another were interrupted by yawn after yawn after yawn, we reluctantly agreed to call it a night. I wished M a goodnight, something I hadn't done since before the two red lines, since before the first girl even. She did the same. I leaned in and kissed her on the cheek. She kissed me back on the forehead. We both secured our guns in the top drawers of our nightstands and turned out the lamps on either side of the bed.

♨

I was still expecting a group of hooded men to set fire to another one of the bungalows. That did not happen. The preacher's son did speak again, though. He gave the keynote address at a fundraising luncheon. Either an invited guest or one of the servers recorded a portion of the speech on a phone and posted the video online. Within days, the video was widely shared, even by the preacher's son himself, who had recently joined the major social media platforms and in a short amount of time garnered thousands upon thousands of followers. M and I watched the video on the laptop in bed, which had become a new shared habit.

The luncheon was held in the restaurant of an old hotel. The preacher's son spoke at a dark wood podium. Behind the podium, the walls, the parts not covered with matching wood paneling, were wallpapered, the pattern a combination of blue and purple flora, green foliage, and gold trim. On the far ends of the wall, bookending the stage, which was not a stage but a parquet dance floor, there were floor-to-ceiling drapes a shade between gold and silver. The drapes must have been weaved with metallic thread because they glimmered. Matching the wallpaper, the carpet also had a floral pattern with a variety of greens, blues, and golds. The people in attendance sat at large round tables, the chairs fitted with white slipcovers, the tables draped in matching linen. In the center of each table, a bouquet of flowers, impossible to tell if real or artificial. Above the centerpieces, the tables, chairs, and the heads of the crowd eating lunch, the ceiling must have been coffered. Hanging from it there must have been enormous chandeliers, probably gold or silver, with faux candles emitting a dim but warm incandescent light. I would have visited the old hotel to verify these descriptions, but by the time I got around to describing it, the old hotel had been shuttered and has not since reopened.

Every man and woman captured in the video was dressed in business casual attire. If the couple dozen guests within the video frame could be counted as a representative sampling of those outside of it (not seen but heard, by way of clinking cups, plates, and utensils, plus a low but audible murmur), then those who came to hear the preacher's son were mostly entrepreneurs, affluent, and likely donors.

Exactly how long the preacher's son addressed the lunch crowd, only they knew for sure. The video clip, a fragment of the whole affair, lasted only 1 minute and 57 seconds. Whoever had uploaded the video knew something about how to maintain an audience's attention. That amount of time (1:57) ensured that the average attention span would not falter (mine certainly didn't, and neither did M's). In the time it takes a person to properly brush their teeth, the preacher's son took up the following themes: "unity and determination," "shared commitments," and "a clear and purposeful vision." Quickly and succinctly, he boiled them down to a single goal, about which both M and I were of the same opinion, deeming it vague but amenable: hope. More precisely, to quote the preacher's son, "Hope for the future." Who on earth does not hold out hope for the future? Only the suicidal do not. The preacher's son never used the word "suicide" or any variation of it, not once, but how could he not have wanted us to think of those who had lost so much hopefulness in the thing called life that they chose instead to extinguish it themselves? All of which is to say that the preacher's son had infused his talk and its theme with ambiguity. He assumed his audience would draw conclusions by way of implication and suggestion, not through explicit statement. Anyone paying close attention would have recognized this as a hallmark move on his part. The things he said in under two minutes could have been expressed at any charity event or any fundraiser, political or otherwise. In the fight against terminal illness, poverty, or equality, shouldn't we be *unified and determined?* Shouldn't the *commitment* to end cancer, hunger, or discrimination be one *shared by all people?* Who would ever take *hope* away from the dying, malnourished, or oppressed?

He was not talking about any of these worries, not really. He wasn't talking about the East Side, either, or the people like us who lived there, or the suicidal-murderous tendencies of its children—not directly, not explicitly.

"He's so good at this," M said.

She was right. He knew how to manipulate language. People hung on to his words spellbound.

The video ended with an appeal to the crowd ("We can make this happen"), for which the preacher's son received a hearty round of applause. Even though there was no more to see, we were sure that immediately following the applause, the preacher's son sought donations.

"What's going on here?"

"Something sinister."

After the luncheon speech, we watched a video of a baby laughing hysterically. The baby video was 1 minute and 40 seconds in length, and it had been viewed more than 25 million times. I enjoyed it tremendously. M, too. We watched it twice. I laughed each time. I laughed more the second time. I laughed so hard, tears ran down my cheeks, and seeing me cry from laughter, M's eyes also welled up with tears of joy.

*

Days went by. A week's worth, possibly two. No hooded men firebombed more houses. Nor did they inflict harm or injury, serious or otherwise, to property or person. Not the hooded men among us, at least. There were others—like them, like us—but this is not their story. The preacher's son did speak again, though, at another luncheon, one sponsored by the East Side Chamber of Commerce. An elected official, the East Side's representative in Congress, introduced him. The congresswoman had served in the state's House of Representatives for twenty years prior to her election to Congress where she was a ranking member of a subcommittee—Homeland Security or Small Business or something I can't remember now. At the luncheon, she was wearing a green suit. I'd heard that she wore only green suits. One of the newspapers even described the color of her attire as "ubiquitous," claiming that the congresswoman stuck to green on account of her Irish heritage. However, in all her years representing the East Side, as well as a handful of other neighborhoods in the district, she never made such a claim. I didn't find evidence of her saying so, in any case. She did look good in green, which would have been reason enough never to stray from the color. She did indeed wear green frequently, but it took less than a fraction of a second to find evidence online of her also wearing red, black, white, pink, and gray. Even so, the green outfit was refreshing, on account of the drab color the grass, plants, leaves, and trees had taken due to the progression the earth made orbiting the sun.

After introducing the preacher's son, the congresswoman shook his hand. A photograph of the handshake was published on a website dedicated to the recriminalization of homosexuality, immigration bans, and the prohibition of any language other than English to be spoken or taught in the public schools. The caption referred to the preacher's son as a "rising star." The article itself was poorly written—riddled with bias and full of passive voice constructions and logical fallacies—and it more than insinuated that the congresswoman's handshake amounted to an unofficial endorsement of his political ambitions, if not also the cause with which he was associated.

Soon after another congressional representative brought unwanted attention to the photograph's publication on a fringe site, the congresswoman quickly distanced herself from the website, as well as the website's founder, a radio show host who harped night after night about several conspiracy theories growing in popularity, the most prominent among them, at the time of the handshake, the overthrow of the government—and by proxy the overtaking of the country and its values—by people who worshipped the wrong God. When reporters followed up with the congresswoman and asked her what more could she tell them about the preacher's son, she said, "You know what I know." Asked about his political aspirations, she said, "I'm not aware of any." Asked about his cause, she said, "No comment." Pressed further, she said, "It was a business luncheon. We talked about business in the East Side, not that other stuff." She was a popular congresswoman, but her reference to the suicides and the picketing by The Good Neighbors and the death of seven schoolchildren and the shooting at the rally as "other stuff" caused outrage online. Some called for the congresswoman's resignation, to which she responded by not responding at all.

During this time of speculation, M's nausea began to subside, and her middle grew rounder and fuller. One night as I was getting ready for bed, she told me, "My uterus should be the size of a grapefruit already." She also told me that the baby was now technically a fetus, and that it was anywhere between two and four inches in length. She also told me, "Its fingernails are starting to grow, and she's moving her arms and legs, or he's moving his arms or legs—we don't know if it's a girl or boy. Can you imagine a fetus moving its arms and legs?" I could not imagine that, but I nodded otherwise. She said a few other things about being pregnant, but she did not say a word about seeing a doctor or about the tests she had missed so far, one of which would have been for Down syndrome. She did tell me she suspected, now more than ever, that she might have been pregnant for a little longer than she had been estimating. "By a few weeks." She thought this might be the case because she was showing the way a woman about a month further along in her pregnancy would show. She was feeling more normal, too, another sign of someone more pregnant than M had initially believed herself to be. She was not as moody, either, also a sign of a woman more pregnant than M. Although she did not spend a lot of time talking about it, and neither did I, I had definitely picked up on the fact that M's overall temperament seemed more stable, more predictable, and she also seemed to be suffering from far fewer bouts of sudden gloominess than just a month before.

Yet another sign of a woman a few more weeks pregnant was an increase in sex drive. About feeling more urgently the need to be satisfied sexually, M did not say anything. I came across this symptom on my own, but I kept it to myself so not to make her feel pressured or resentful, which would have dashed any hope I had of having sex any time soon. Regardless, simply reading about the possibility of M's increased libido resurrected my expectations. The last time I had touched M's naked body, not a single East Side child had committed suicide.

If M was indeed more pregnant than she first believed, then the baby could be up to four inches longer than she had previously thought. She used her thumb and pointing finger to show me the length that our child had instantly grown on account of a miscalculation on her part. "Can you imagine?" she asked again, and again I could not. She said that more and more—that is, more frequently, more intensely—she was suffering from heartburn, a symptom of the uterus rising in the abdomen, another sign of a pregnancy a few weeks further along. The heartburn could easily have been caused by the food M was eating. She had intense citrus cravings and drank orange juice every single day, two to three times per day.

If M were further along in her pregnancy, then the baby could have weighed up to four ounces more than any estimate we might have had. "As much as a small apple," M told me. I wondered what kind of apple. There were so many varieties: Red Delicious, Granny Smith, Honeycrisp, Fuji, Gala. I also wondered which size apple. Some were as large as softballs, others as small as racquet or billiard balls. Naturally, thinking about apples, I also thought of Eve, and thinking of Eve, naturally, I thought of the girl. What was she doing in prison? Was she still reading the Bible? Was she talking to someone about it? Another inmate or a guard?

Like me, M must have also had thoughts that she kept to herself. Hiding ourselves from the rest of humanity is fundamentally human. It is why we wear clothes. It is no doubt the reason we dream. I took it for granted, then, that M must have read—but chose not to reveal—that at this stage in a normal pregnancy, a gynecologist would have recommended that she enroll in a prenatal class. Had she done so, she would have learned about the signs of labor, about techniques for coping with the pain of childbirth, and about the ways I might have assisted with the birthing process. She must have also read—but chose not to divulge—that at this stage in most pregnancies, a doctor should have been checking her weight and blood pressure. A doctor would have also been monitoring the size and heartbeat of the child inside her. If she had any worries, fears, or apprehensions about the baby's health because no doctor had overseen her pregnancy, M restricted such thoughts to internal monologue. Outwardly, she played dumb. At this stage, a doctor should have performed an ultrasound and tested her urine for sugar and protein and her amniotic fluid for abnormal chromosomes or neural defects—spina bifida, the main culprit—but none of this happened. Nothing that she or I knew about her pregnancy, or the life to come of it, existed in fact. All of it, speculation. Words on a page. Images on a screen.

M told me that the baby's face and heart were already fully formed. "At some point this month, the baby's eyes will open," she said. The baby would also soon feel the urge to suck. Its thumb? A nipple? She did not clarify, and I didn't ask. She also said, "My clothes are starting to feel tight. I need to buy a few things."

I agreed, but not too emphatically. I didn't want M feeling overly self-conscious about the way she looked. Also, while her clothes were in fact beginning to hug her figure more closely, the look added a sex appeal unbeknown to me. Soon enough, especially as her middle continued to grow, she would not feel comfortable wearing clothes that would have looked and felt sprayed onto her body.

"There's no hiding this anymore," I said.

She agreed with me. It felt reassuring to be on the same page.

Even though she needed and wanted to go shopping for new clothes, M still refused to leave the house. She would not sit on the front porch or even go into the backyard, just in case. She had also taken to having all the blinds drawn, day and night, so no one could catch a glimpse of her pregnant body, purposefully or inadvertently. Fortunately, everything under the sun was available for purchase online.

Packages arrived daily. I came to expect them every day, and if a day went by without a delivery, I felt anxious. Our life together was becoming more habitual by the day. I wondered if a person could become dependent on buying stuff online. Was staying home all the time addictive? Was living with someone else?

Days went by.

The hooded men who had torched the pink bungalow carried on with their own lives, unknown and unnamed. I continued to worry about when they would act again. Not if, but when. Whoever they were, and whatever they were doing, they were with me all the time.

Weeks went by.

The preacher's son continued to meet with, talk to, and solicit support from small, select, and influential groups of people, most of whom happened to be men of capital and influence, leaders of industry and community. Coincidentally, there was also an uptick in the number of reporters who followed him around. He hardly said a word to them. The few times he did, he politely ignored their questions and only occasionally offered up a smile and sometimes a laconic but civil response: "Good to see you," "Have a nice day," "Sorry, running late."

At the end of another month, news broke that the elected official who had been representing the East Side for decades, the congresswoman known for supposedly having a penchant for wearing green suits, was retiring from politics. A handful of news outlets reported on the retirement announcement, and a few of those also republished the photograph of the congresswoman shaking hands with the preacher's son after introducing him at the chamber of commerce luncheon. Only one news outlet made mention of the backlash against her "other stuff" remark. A gaggle of reporters waited for the preacher's son outside the small East Side church to question him about whether he planned to run for the congresswoman's soon-to-be empty seat in the House of Representatives. Sure enough, he exited the small church, and all at once, the reporters hurled loud and persistent questions at him, making it nearly impossible to discern any of them. One full-throated reporter, however, managed to raise the volume of his voice above the rest. If you slow down the video footage of the preacher's son at the precise moment the question is asked, you can see him look to the left, in the direction of that reporter. In response to the question asked, the preacher's son darted his eyes, smiled, and walked through the pack, past the reporters, the cameras, and the microphones, following a bodyguard to a shiny black luxury sedan with tinted windows parked curbside. Just before he disappeared into the backseats, the preacher's son turned his head; the same reporter who had grabbed his attention asked him the same question again.

"Do you plan to run for office?"

The preacher's son hesitated, seeming ready to answer this time. Then the bodyguard slammed the door shut, and within seconds the car drove off.

A few more weeks went by.

M's belly got larger.

By now, she looked unmistakably pregnant. She looked like she had a slightly deflated soccer ball tucked under her shirt. Or a small pillow.

One night, at the start of what we then presumed to be either her fifth or sixth month of pregnancy, give or take a week or two, or even three, I took it upon myself to read up on the baby's development and told M about it, reversing the roles we had grown accustomed to playing.

"The baby is anywhere between six and nine inches long now. Its fingerprints are forming. If she's a girl, her ovaries are just starting to develop."

Something else I had also discovered on my own: At this point in a pregnancy, an ultrasound scan could be used to determine the sex of the unborn child. I wanted to tell M, thinking the uncertainty of whether to call the baby a boy or girl would spur her into finally making a doctor's appointment. I decided against it because M, who had obviously done much more reading than me, told me that while a baby's sex might be apparent, gender wasn't—that did not occur until the child was three or four years old. I didn't argue with her. I had been wrong about so much already, why not this? Besides which, I doubted that M really wanted to know the baby's sex, not until the moment of birth. She always referred to the baby as "the baby," as both he and she, and sometimes they. She never talked about naming the baby nor did she ever express a desire for either a boy or girl. More than all this, M had already made it clear that she was not revealing her pregnancy to anyone until she had no choice otherwise. If she was anything, M was stubborn. She might have used another word—resilient, persistent, tenacious. Go ahead, feel free to choose any. I will stick to stubborn.

I said to M, "Your uterus is now as big as a cantaloupe or a honeydew."

She replied with what I could only describe as pure glee. "Oh, my God, I love the taste of honeydew."

She promptly sent me to supermarket to find one.

At beginning of the sixth month, the end of the second trimester or thereabouts, the child in M's womb would have weighed about sixteen ounces, which is nearly equivalent in weight to a can of black beans or a jar of peanut butter. It would have been nearly ten inches long, just shy of the length of most egg cartons. M's uterus would have grown to about the size of an official NBA basketball, and the baby would have started stretching its arms and legs, and hiccupping, too. During this time, M also started gaining weight more quickly, approximately one pound per week. All these things, I told her about, except for the statistic concerning her weight gain, which she clearly must have known without having me point it out.

While enjoyable, the role reversal was short lived. Several nights later, again in bed, while I was reading yet another article about the preacher's son, M nudged me with her elbow and said, "Right around now, our baby will be opening and closing its eyes." She wondered out loud what the child would see inside her womb. Whatever it could see, if anything at all, it didn't ultimately matter because it wouldn't remember a single experience or sensation from its time in the womb. Such an existence is as close to not existing as a living being could come, second to being a coma, third perhaps to the sleeping states of those unfortunate people who do not dream. For months, we had talked about the future human being inside of M, imagining—however much possible—the life it was coming into. Yet because M refused to see a doctor, we had not actually seen evidence of its existence. M was also among the women who did not feel their babies moving in the womb early in their pregnancies. The Internet advised these women to see their doctor or midwife by week 24, which we had reached or were about to reach. Any other woman would have been able to get a glimpse of her unborn child in the swirling grainy black and white of an ultrasound. Had M been capable of losing just an ounce of stubbornness and allowed a doctor to do that for her, we might have been witness to the actuality within her womb. M was headstrong and obstinate, and our unborn child existed much the same way life did in the unobservable reaches of the universe—invisible to us, its presence grounded in faith and conjecture, not concrete evidence.

If a pregnant woman were to have visited a clinic around this time, which M hadn't done and which I had altogether stopped bringing up as a topic of conversation or a matter of instigation, a doctor would have monitored her blood pressure for signs of hypertension. She would have also been tested for gestational diabetes. Around this time, too, many pregnant women would have complained about itchiness, a consequence of the skin stretching around a bigger, impossible-not-to-notice womb. Fortunately, M did not have this complaint. Instead, she told me about the baby's vocal cords, which would have been functioning by now. Did this mean that babies in the womb could produce sounds? Had anyone ever recorded such an instance? The answers I found online were inconclusive. A video, with more than nineteen thousand views, purportedly of a baby in the womb making a yawning sound, was unconvincing. An article I read suggesting that babies *may* begin crying while still in the womb was based not on auditory but visual evidence—babies responding to stimuli by opening their mouths, depressing their tongues, and taking what appear to be irregular breaths, which could indicate crying, but not necessarily. M also told me that around this time the baby would have eyebrows.

At this stage in a pregnancy, some women would have started complaining about bleeding gums, constipation, heartburn, leg cramps, varicose veins, hemorrhoids, swollen ankles, headaches, and nosebleeds. M had not complained about any of these signs, which came as a relief, both to her and me.

Also, at the start of the sixth month of M's pregnancy, plus or minus a few weeks, one of the original members of The Good Neighbors, the dentist, who we last saw wearing a sundress and a straw hat while picketing the funeral of the teen who killed seven children, announced she would be running for the congressional seat about to be vacated by the congresswoman who on occasion wore wear green suits. Everyone had suspected the preacher's son would pursue the seat. He played an important role in the dentist-turned-political-hopeful's announcement. At the press conference, the preacher's son gave the dentist an enthusiastic introduction culminating in a heartfelt embrace. After the hug, the dentist smiled for the cameras. Her teeth were perfectly straight and white. She rattled off, by way of thanks, a list of endorsements already in place, which included the names of people I could not place and the editorial board of a newspaper I didn't recognize. Later, I discovered that the newspaper's founder and publisher had been a controversial cable TV host who believed that the initial set of suicides—the first girl, her mother and father—was a carefully orchestrated hoax, performed by actors. As for the teen who drove his car into the first-grade classroom, the TV host/newspaper founder was a believer.

For a few minutes, the dentist spoke on a rehearsed set of talking points, and though she smiled throughout and seemed genuinely pleased to be the center of attention, she also seemed anxious to have the preacher's son speak again. That was how the press conference ended, with the preacher's son pledging his full support for her candidacy, calling her one of the strongest women he knew, adding that he could think of no other man or woman who would better serve to protect our children's freedom and safety. He brought his endorsement to a close and the press conference full circle by embracing the dentist one last time.

About the dentist announcing she would run for the House of Representatives, the retiring congresswoman never made a comment. Because so many people, professional and amateur, had wrongly predicted that the preacher's son had sights on the congressional seat, many of the same people now speculated that he had higher office in mind. Most believed he had his eyes on becoming the state's next governor. Reporters asked, but the preacher's son did not give them an answer.

M was standing a few feet from me, gazing at me, her head titled sideways. Her face was lively and flushed.

"I've got such an intense urge," she said.

We were finally going to have sex. I could hardly contain my excitement. I pulled myself together, asking calmly and matter-of-factly, "What for?"

She licked her lips and said, "Watermelon."

There was a silence during which I tried to hide my disappointment. I might have been successful, given M's reaction. Either that or she simply hadn't caught on to the presumption I had made.

"It's the middle of fall," I said. "There are no watermelons left. Not here, at least. Maybe in Mexico or California. I could probably get you a pumpkin, though, or squash, or a gourd."

I headed to the supermarket. Though the temperature outside was now chilly, requiring either the heat to be turned on or a few layers of clothing to stay warm, I drove with the windows down. The air smelled like autumn. It was a week or so before the peak of leaf fall. Above us, red and orange and yellow against a crisp blue sky. Before the end of the month, the curbs would be lined with overstuffed leaf bags. Given the time of year and the region of the country we lived in, the fruit section was stocked with bananas, blackberries, blueberries, cranberries, grapes, pears, oranges, and apples, but not watermelons. I picked out a bag of apples. Then, walking around the apple bins, I saw the sign for quince, one of the likely fruits of the tree that God forbade Adam and Eve from eating. The quince looked more like a pear than an apple. Their color, a yellowish green. Because I had never seen a quince before, I didn't know if the color indicated ripeness or not. I wanted to know the taste, and I did not want to wait to find out. I picked one out, wiped it clean against my jeans, and without checking to see if anyone was looking, I took a bite.

Had an employee caught me and a rule-abiding store manager insisted on having me punished for shoplifting, it would not have been worth it. The flesh was hard, bitter, and tart. It left my mouth dry. I wanted so badly to tell the girl from the pink bungalow that if Adam and Eve had given up paradise for a quince, the taste would have disappointed them.

A while later, I found out that around the time I had tasted the fruit, the girl underwent several psychiatric examinations to determine her mental well-being. She also went through several court proceedings, and contrary to the advice of her counsel, she pled guilty to the charges made against her. She was now awaiting sentencing. I wondered if she thought of me. If so, I also wondered whether the prevailing feelings during those moments were of fondness or regret, delight or disgust. I had been checking the news about her every so often. Early on, every few days. Then, every few weeks. Soon enough, just as I had wished for her, she faded from view. Bit by bit the stories about her dwindled and then altogether disappeared. She was no longer of interest or newsworthy. She was finally left alone.

I still looked her up but not nearly as frequently. The last time I searched her name, I read that her parents had disowned her. A local newspaper in Utah, where the parents lived, published the story, along with a photo of the girl and her mother and father. They looked nothing like her. Not the shape of their faces or noses, not the size of their foreheads or the color of their eyes or hair, not even their complexion. Had she been adopted? The article didn't say. In the comments section—there was only one posted, and it had been left anonymously—someone expressed the hope that the disowned daughter would get her just deserts while serving her prison sentence.

"No punishment is too harsh for this monster," Anonymous said.

Given when and where the girl's story was taking place, it could end in only one of two ways: life in prison or the death penalty. Because of her age, it would likely be the former. Regardless, I would not see her again.

M would, but not me.

In addition to apples, I also picked out a pomegranate, one of the other fruits God may have tempted humanity with, purportedly bringing about our downfall.

SEVEN

ON A DAY either in the seventh or eighth month of the pregnancy, I was in the kitchen, typing away on the laptop. The child inside M presumably would have been able to see, hear, and taste around this time. Also, stretch marks began to appear on M's body. Mostly around her belly, thighs, and hips, though it might have been possible that lines and streaks had formed elsewhere, like her breasts or below her thighs. I hadn't seen M without clothes in a long while and wouldn't have known. Up since 6 a.m., I had already knocked back an entire pot of coffee and was waiting for the coffee maker to beep for a second batch. Around ten o'clock, M came down. She greeted me good morning, filled a glass with tap water, and drank it while standing next to the sink. She then toasted a slice of bread. She didn't butter the toast or spread jam on the slice. She just ate it plain right out of the toaster. After she finished eating, she interrupted me.

"Let me finish this sentence," I said.

She said, "I want to get a crib. I also want to get a mobile of the moon and stars, and a nightlight, too."

She walked back to the sink, refilled her glass with water, and looked out the window over the sink into the yard. She seemed lost in thought, but her back was turned to me, so I didn't really know if this was true.

"Is a baby supposed to sleep in a crib or in the bed with us?"

She didn't answer me.

"I heard that sudden infant death syndrome occurs more with babies in cribs. Or is it the other way around?"

She stretched her arms wide but otherwise carried on with whatever she was doing. Thinking, probably. Day-dreaming, also a possibility. Or just plain staring out into the backyard. There wasn't much to see there other than grass, a couple plastic lounge chairs, the garage, and the fence behind it, both of which badly needed a paint job, and three trees. When we first moved into the blue bungalow, we had talked about putting in a garden (tomatoes, cucumbers, a variety of peppers), adding a raised flower bed along the fence line (M had pictured rose bushes), and building a wood deck off the back of the bungalow (I had pictured a barbecue grill). Our plans never materialized, largely because they had been crowded out by the other plan that for years had eluded us—having a baby. The two red lines on the pregnancy test had altered our circumstances, but I didn't anticipate any new projects on the horizon. Around this time, I was convinced that M would never again leave the house. She was anywhere from one to two months from going into labor. The timing would have been just right for revisiting our landscaping aspirations. To the picture already imagined, we could have added a play area, a sandbox, and a swing set. If every predictable platitude about the passage of time bore the slightest hint of truth, the child would be walking, running, climbing in the blink of an eye.

"And a sound machine," M said.

"But we already have a radio."

"No, a noise machine. To play nature sounds while the baby is sleeping. Rain drops on a tin roof, birds chirping at night, ocean waves crashing. I found one online that makes whale sounds and another that plays appliance sounds, like a dishwasher, a washing machine, and a clothes dryer. Most of the noise machines also play classical music on a loop. Beethoven, Mozart, Chopin, Mendelssohn. Classical music is supposed to be good for the baby's brain."

We also have a dishwasher, I thought, and a washing machine and a clothes dryer, but I kept my thoughts to myself.

For a few weeks, in anticipation of her due date, which loomed around an imprecise corner, M had been ordering supplies for the baby off the Internet: a case of diapers, a diaper changing pad, a set of covers for the changing pad (one with blue polka dots, one with red), a tub of butt paste, a baby bathtub, a set of baby towels (one green with a hood stitched to resemble a frog, one blue with a hood made to resemble either a dragon or a dinosaur). She avoided making purchases from websites dedicated solely to baby products, even though they usually sold the same wares at lower prices. She bought only from the big-box stores so there was no chance the delivery person or a neighbor or a passerby could know from the packaging that M was pregnant. Everything related to the baby, we placed in the guest bedroom, a room that had never actually been used as such because in almost a decade of marriage, we never had overnight guests. The room had been M's bedroom when she was a girl, and although I still referred to it as the guest bedroom, she had converted it into a nursery. With all the stacked cardboard boxes now lining its walls, it resembled an enormous storage closet. M aimed to change that, to make the room look like we were going to have a baby.

The coffee maker started to sputter.

"Sure," I said. "A crib, a mobile, a nightlight, and a machine that plays whale sounds, symphonies, and Laundromat noises."

I saved the document I'd been working on since the morning and then opened a browser window.

"Which website do you want to go to?"

"I don't want to order online," she said. "I'd like to get them from the mall."

I let out a sigh, which I immediately regretted. M must have noticed, and she must have judged, correctly, that the sigh was body language for the mild to moderate irritation her request caused me. She'd been sending me on errands almost daily. To the grocery store, to the pharmacy, to this or that restaurant when this or that craving struck.

"Sorry," I said. "I'm just a little crabby. I've been up for a while, and I've been writing. My brain is killing me. I'll get changed and head out. Just make a list, print out pictures, the usual."

"Actually, I was thinking that we could go together."

The coffee machine began beeping.

"You want to go out?"

She nodded.

The coffee maker let out several spurts of steam. It sounded like someone having a hard time breathing.

"You mean out, as in you want to leave the house?"

"Yes."

The coffee maker stopped making noise.

"To the mall?"

"Yes. The nice one, the Galleria."

I searched M's face for a clue as to why, why now, without warning, she was willing to go out, wanting to head out, why she was no longer afraid. In retrospect, I know that I could have been asking not why, but why not. Everything could have turned out differently had M arrived at this turnabout sooner. Maybe better. Maybe. Everything is clearer after the fact. Or seems so. In the moment, I vacillated between out-and-out embrace and downright rejection. Was her self-imposed quarantine over? Was this the beginning of a return to normalcy? I looked past M, out the window that faced the backyard and the garage and the fence and the houses on the other side of the fence, behind which were rows and rows of more houses, more yards, and more fences that went on for block after block until they reached the freeway. On a map, and in the minds of most everyone who lived here, the freeway was a line dividing east from west, the East Side from the West Side. There, in the west, was the mall, the nice one, the Galleria, which was a short distance from the grade school where the teen had killed seven children.

"Are you sure?"

"Absolutely."

What's out there? What's waiting for us? What's waiting for M?

I stood up, stood before her, and touched her hand. She touched mine back, squeezing my fingers. I leaned slightly to the left, titling my head to see over her shoulder. Before my eyes was the large tree near the fence, a bigleaf maple, according to M's father. Its leaves were already almost entirely yellow, with hints of orange near the top. On either side of the maple were trees the names of which the old man never mentioned, and I didn't know, but which I had always figured as a species of oak, the foliage still green but faded, washed out.

"You haven't left the house in weeks," I said.

She corrected me.

"Months, actually."

She let go of my hand and went to the coffee maker and said she would fix me a cup of coffee before we left. I kept looking out the window. The branches and leaves of the trees, the bigleaf maple and maybe the oak, were casting shadows on the grass and on the garage and on the fence.

"Here you go."

M handed me a cup.

"Are you sure?" I asked.

"Things seem better," she said.

She must have expected me to respond with an equal if not greater amount of resolve. I didn't, which is probably why she followed up with, "Don't they? Don't they seem better to you?"

"You're so pregnant," I said.

"I know."

"You're huge."

She laughed a little.

"Maybe people will think you're just fat."

She smiled and said, "That's not nice."

"Or that you have a beer belly."

She laughed a little louder and said, "Are you trying to be funny?"

"I'm trying not to act nervous."

"You're not very good at it."

"All right, then. Let's go to the mall."

I changed into a dark pair of blue jeans, a black sweater, and a pair of suede Oxfords. M put on a long-sleeve gray T-shirt, black overalls she had recently purchased online after seeing a pregnant celebrity wearing them on late-night TV, a black cardigan sweater that fell to her knees, and bright red canvas sneakers. She intended for the outfit to hide her body, to conceal what was beneath. She looked pretty, but she still looked pregnant. She also seemed happy. I persisted in being nervous about leaving the house.

The car was parked at the curb. I pulled it into the driveway as far as I could go, up to the backyard fence, nearly out of view from the street, so M could leave the blue bungalow through the back door, reducing as much as possible the odds that a neighbor or passer-by might see her. Before backing out of the driveway, I turned the radio on. The cabin filled with a newscaster's voice telling us that several teenagers trapped in a flooded cave had finally been rescued. The teens had spent nearly two weeks in the cave without food. Other than hungry and several pounds lighter, the boys and the adult had who led them into the cave appeared relatively healthy, the newscaster said. Upon their rescue, they asked for cheeseburgers, but the medical personnel attending them immediately rejected the request.

I switched over to another station. I didn't recognize the song being played. It was either very old or very new. I couldn't tell. Nothing about the lyrics or the music sounded familiar. It could have been made by an alien, I thought to myself. I changed stations again.

"Could we drive without the radio?" M said.

So we did.

On Lawndale Avenue, we drove past the elementary school. Its few windows were barred, which must have been a safety hazard. A chain-link fence encircled the playground. A dozen or so children chased each other, and a handful more swung on monkey bars, and even more were sitting on picnic tables looking at phones.

We passed the bus stop where no one was waiting. Just beyond the bus stop, the health clinic, which used to be the mom-and-pop grocery store where I bought my cigarettes because M never went there. Four or five blocks farther down, the trees began to thin out, and the small grassy patches along the sidewalks dwindled with them.

Then the self-service car wash, which a few years ago I stopped using after I timed its four-minute wash cycle and it ran for only three.

For several blocks, we drove past lot after empty lot overgrown with weeds and uncut grass, flanked by aging clapboard houses with sagging rooflines—the oldest East Side houses and the most neglected.

We passed two stray dogs before reaching the next bus stop. At the bus stop after that, a man was waiting, and beside him, an abandoned grocery cart.

Then a liquor store, a funeral home, an intersection with two gas stations and two tire repair shops. Then a massive parking lot, empty. Then the department store delivery warehouse, boarded up. At the far end of the warehouse lot, near the frontage road of the freeway, a rusted semi-trailer with GOD BLESS US spray-painted on its side. Then the frontage road and the freeway. I signaled a right turn, intending to take the entrance ramp, but M said, "Could we take the side streets?"

Ordinarily I avoided the side street route to the mall because it cut through the college. Should I go that way, I imagined the unlikely, purely fabricated scenario of stopping at a pedestrian crossing in the middle of campus and through the windshield spotting a former colleague who knew my story. Or maybe I would run into one of the professors I considered a friend but who'd been compelled to speak out against me (there were at least two of those) or one who had been willing to do so (there were a couple of those, too). I imagined them being overtaken by a sixth sense and coming to a halt, looking sideways in my direction, into the car, and in that moment of unwelcome and ignominious recognition, we would be gripped by a chorus of feelings. For them, disgust, contempt, and loathing. For me, the three cousins of disgrace—embarrassment, shame, and humiliation. While such an encounter would have lasted only seconds before we each went our separate ways, likely never to see each other again, I never risked driving through campus, knowing full well that no matter how fleeting the actual experience might be, its half-life was immeasurable.

I wanted M to keep feeling good though. I cut the turn signal and drove straight ahead, toward the college.

Campus was crowded. Twice I came to a full stop. Once at a red light near a student parking garage where no one spotted me and nothing eventful happened. The second time near the football stadium where, again, no one who knew me or M had caught sight of us. The street outside the football stadium was thronged with people, mostly students, even though there was no game scheduled. The students were carrying signs and chanting slogans about one of the wars overseas. There were so many of them marching, protesting, chanting that the traffic light changed from red to green to yellow and back to red three times before we were able to drive away.

"They look so young," M said as we left them behind us.

"They *are* young."

In the rear-view mirror, I watched with relief as the campus shrank and then disappeared. A mile or so past campus, we entered the Historic District, the East Side's sister neighborhood, its houses much like ours, nearly identical, same number of bedrooms, bathrooms, square footage, and lot size, built around the same time, too, at the turn of the previous century. The main difference was their value. Theirs was three or four times greater than any home in our neighborhood.

We went through Midtown, where several luxury high-rise apartment buildings were under construction, and then through the Hill, a neighborhood named after its main thoroughfare, Hill Street, on which there were as many tattoo parlors and gay bars as cafes and boutiques. Most of the storefronts in the Hill looked at once shabby and divey but trendy and chic. Just past this stretch of the city's most popular restaurants and shops, right before the Galleria, for a mile or two the speed limit dropped to 20 mph. Driving slowly, we took in with a mixture of awe and envy the city's grandest homes in its most affluent neighborhood, where the East Side teen had ended it all, the West Side.

"Look," I said. "The grass is actually greener."

A few minutes later, we arrived at the mall.

I circled the lot, passing up several empty parking spaces, waiting until I found a spot without shoppers nearby, either getting out of or into their cars. It didn't make sense to do so. I know that now, and I probably knew that then. There was no good reason for being that careful and cautious, especially because we were going into the mall regardless of where we parked, and once inside a whole host of people would see M pregnant. My choices weren't informed by logic or rational thinking but by fear and emotion. Such an ancient dilemma.

Five minutes or more later, I pulled into a spot without cars on either side. With the engine idling and the key still in the ignition, I turned to M.

"Are you positive? We could go back."

She answered by opening the door and stepping out.

Hand in hand, we entered the mall through a department store. Music greeted us, the song in surround sound, a remake of a famous hit from decades earlier recorded by a man with a gravelly voice, now sung by a woman, her voice soft and melodic, the tempo slowed down. To be honest, the cover was a better version, even though the original was far more popular. And while the song was new and the artist unknown to me, its familiarity felt welcoming. It must have also eased M's entry back into the outside world.

At every turn, we met our reflections. There were so many mirrors catching us looking at ourselves. Everything seemed to gleam. The floors, the shiny polished chrome displays, the glass display cases, the necklaces, earrings, and bracelets behind them. Even the plastic mannequins with impossibly perfect bodies were glossy and lustrous.

We cut through the cosmetics section. A woman with flawless skin complemented M's eyes and hair. She held out a bottle, called it ageless cream, and offered M a sample. M thanked her but said no thanks. Jokingly, I told the woman, "I could use some of that," and she laughed, said the lotion was formulated for women, but squeezed a drop onto my palm anyhow.

Walking away, I said, "I like her lab coat."

M took my hand, squeezed affectionately, and said, "It's called a smock."

The woman in cosmetics didn't say anything about M's pregnant body. Had she not noticed? Maybe she had but was only being polite. Or else she had noticed but willingly overlooked the fact just to make a sale.

Or, for better or worse, maybe things were not as bad as we had been telling ourselves. Maybe we'd spent too much time alone, isolated, focusing too much on the very people and ideas that worried us.

We exited the department store and made our way into the mall, stopping beside a fountain. M asked if I had any coins in my pocket to toss into the pool at the base of the fountain. I didn't, so I stole a penny from the bottom of the fountain and handed it to M, and she tossed it back in, presumably wishing for something before doing so. What she wished for, I didn't ask, and she didn't reveal. I also made a wish, but without a coin.

We stopped at several window displays to look at giant TVs, custom-made hats, high-heeled shoes a pregnant woman could never wear, and an electric car we could never afford. Then we rested underneath a hanging sculpture made of crystal glass pieces, birds or objects made to resemble birds, thousands of them suspended in successive lines across the length of the atrium's ceiling. I thought they were more beautiful than real birds.

At an upscale shop, which required us to be screened by a security guard to enter, I tried on a watch worth almost as much as the blue bungalow. The woman who showed it to me asked me to keep my elbows on the display case. The watch was attached to a thin silver chain, which was attached to a case, which was handcuffed to the saleswoman's wrist. She must have known—by the astonishment on my face when I asked how much the watch cost—that I could not even dream to buy it. Yet she still asked me if I wanted to try on another watch. I said no, but M wanted to try one on, just to feel what it was like to have something she could never really have.

Afterwards we ate frozen yogurt. I also bought a pair of casual shoes on clearance. I didn't need new shoes, but they looked good on me. M also bought something on sale, a pair of pajama pants, forty percent off the regular price, and made with a stretch fabric and an elastic waist. She wouldn't try them on in the store, though, partly because she did not want to expose her pregnant body, even though she would be in a fitting room behind a locked door, but mainly because, given the changes her body had undergone, getting into and out of clothes had become an arduous task.

Finally, we made our way to another department store, on the other end of the mall, one that sold baby furniture. There were a lot of cribs and mobiles to choose from but none that matched what M had imagined for the nursery. Still, we spent nearly a half-hour in the baby section, standing in front of this and that crib, imagining what it would be like to do so with a child of our own. My idea of what it would be like was a lot more sentimental, not to mention tremendously easier, than how it would eventually turn out, and I assumed the same applied to M's imagination. It was all we knew at the time, to imagine our future sentimentally. I'm convinced that it's a good thing that most people about to have children for the first time don't have a clue what the actuality is like. Otherwise, by choice and sheer will, humanity might abruptly end.

We headed back. In the department store through which we had entered the mall, another woman in cosmetics approached us. She, too, was beautiful and was wearing a smock that looked like a lab coat. She also complimented M, on her smile, and tried but failed to get her to sample a product, a skin cream that hides the effects of daily stress. Making our way to the exit doors, I saw myself again in the mirrors. After the fact, the thought occurred to me that no one else in the mall had paid as much attention to me or to M—to who or what we were—as much as I had. Exiting the mall, M and I agreed to go shopping again and soon.

"Tomorrow?"

"Why not?"

Back in the car, I felt something like sadness. Surrounded by what and how we could be, we had been able to forget for a short while who we were. There was nothing in the mall to panic over, fear, or get depressed about. There was no past in the mall. No dead children, no Good Neighbors, no protests, speeches, funerals, or warnings. At the mall, we suffered absolutely no confusion about what we were supposed to do. The more I thought about it, the more I realized that along with the past, the present moment had no place in the mall, either. Within its walls, the future governed. Even if only temporarily, while in the mall we lived in the future, as willing subjects, and the only law we had to abide by was to imagine ourselves becoming better, healthier, prettier, sexier, more comfortable, more content. In a word, happier.

❧

In the car, M tuned the radio to a station that featured popular songs from the decade we met. She immediately recognized the song being played and sang along without the least bit of concern over the sound of her voice or how loudly she belted out the lyrics or that she was mangling the lyrics and singing off pitch. She simply sang, badly but gleefully. Each time I looked over and she caught me looking, she returned the glance with a smile. This went on with the next song and the one after that. I was so taken by M's cheerfulness, so thoroughly lost in it, that not until we reached the East Side and I turned off Lawndale Avenue and onto our street did I realize I had gone the entire drive back from the mall hardly noticing—really, not noticing at all—all the things that had weighed me down on the drive out. I could not even recall driving through the college campus.

Catching sight of the blue bungalow, however, delivered me right back to our other reality. I pulled into the driveway, again as far as possible. I don't remember if I sighed or said something that would have articulated my discontent. I don't remember because what happened next overtook any memories of that scene. I removed the key from the ignition, and just as M opened the passenger-side door and stepped out, I saw a stranger appear in the rearview mirror.

The stranger, a woman, was walking up the driveway, and in a hurry.

"Wait," I said.

Already outside the car, M didn't hear or me or else ignored me.

Over the sound of me calling to her ("Get back inside"), I heard the woman calling to M ("Hey"), and through the rear window, I saw that she was only a few yards from M, who was standing motionless beside the passenger door. As for me, I was still sitting in the driver's seat, my seatbelt still strapped across my chest. I was stuck, as if in a bad dream, watching the woman come closer and closer. By the time I finally unbuckled and got out, the woman was already at the bumper, and once more she shouted "Hey."

"Hi," M said back.

I said, "Who are you?"

And the woman replied, "Where y'all been hiding?"

I clenched my fists and was about to threaten her. "Leave or else!" is what I was going to tell her. But before I could speak up, she laughed out loud for seemingly no reason. The laugh was not menacing but boisterous, easy-going, even affectionate. For a split second, her laughter made me wonder if we'd known each other our entire lives but, somehow, I had managed to forget who she was.

"I've been next door six months, and I ain't caught sight of you one time," she said. "You folks scaredy-cats of the sun or what?"

She was tall, taller than me, the tallest woman I ever met. She also looked strong, strong enough to knock me over with her bare hands, one of which she held out for me to shake.

"I'm Tammy," she said. "We're neighbors."

"Neighbors?"

"Not a hoot away—just next door."

"I didn't know the old man moved."

"No, he ain't moved. How I heard it, he got so sick he had to get better to die. So he upped and ate a better pill. Been so since the bluebonnets bloomed."

I had no idea what she was talking about, and she could tell.

"April, honey. He done traded in his guitar for a harp just this April."

I must have still looked puzzled.

"It don't matter none," she said. "We've howdied, but we ain't shook."

Without waiting on me, she grabbed my right hand and shook so vigorously I thought she must have been an arm wrestler. She then turned to M and placed her large hands around M's belly and said, "Oh, look at you, wide as two axes. You got one in the chute. Boy or girl? You set on a name yet? I got three of my own. All grown up. Ain't kids no more. This is your first, isn't it? I can tell. You look happy as a clam at high tide."

M blushed.

"And look at you," Tammy said turning back to me. "You make Samson look sensitive."

"You live next door?" I asked.

"Honey, I've been unpacked since this pretty little thing of yours was flat as Lubbock."

M laughed, and Tammy laughed with her.

"Ain't we joined at the hip," she told M.

"I guess we are," M said, and to my astonishment, she invited Tammy in, and without hesitation, Tammy accepted.

M offered tea. Tammy said she wasn't thirsty. Then M offered coffee. Tammy said she didn't touch the stuff. She only drank water, no ice, but on special occasions she would fix a batch of homemade lemonade.

"Don't go having the fidgets over me," she said. "Let's put our sitting britches on and chaw the rag."

Pretty quickly, we worked out that Tammy really liked to talk—a lot—and at breakneck speed. She told us that she was married to a driller who worked on an oil rig in the Gulf of Mexico, fourteen days on, twenty-one off. She hadn't seen him in over a month and wouldn't lay eyes on him for at least two more because he was on a special assignment training new drillers somewhere in the Black Sea, a financial opportunity they couldn't pass up. "Tall cotton," she called the overseas job. She called her husband "Hubbs." So not to embarrass ourselves, she told us that Hubbs wasn't a shortened version of "Hubby" but her husband's actual name. M said it was a good name, and Tammy laughed so hard I thought she might be choking. She told us that her husband was the real talker in the family. "He can talk a coon down a tree." Months later when I finally met Hubbs, he looked very much like a man whose real name would be Hubbs. Big, burly, graying moustache and goatee, shaved head, liked to wear a baseball cap. He smiled a lot and seemed kind, but he barely said a word. Tammy and Hubbs had three children. In the order of their births: Johnnie, Jennifer, and Eudora. The firstborn, Johnnie, had recently earned a bachelor's degree in communications, and the younger two were still in college. All three lived in different parts of the country: Johnnie in the Northwest, working as a copywriter for a prestigious advertising agency. Two commercials he wrote the copy for had aired during the last two Super Bowls. When Tammy asked if I had seen the commercials, I said yes, but that was a lie. The middle child, Jennifer, studied theater in New York City, and the youngest, Eudora, was a double-major in biology and chemistry at the University of Michigan. "All native Texans," she said about her kids. As for her roots, Tammy was born in Vernon Parish, Louisiana, but her father, a military man, left Fort Polk for Fort Hood, in Killeen, Texas, when Tammy was only a few months old. She said, "I might not have been born in Texas, but Daddy got me here faster than small-town gossip." After her parents divorced when Tammy was a grade-schooler, she moved back and forth between Louisiana and Texas, mostly small towns (Innis, Lufkin, and the like), until her mother finally settled outside of Houston, where a relative (Aunt Libby or Liddy, I couldn't figure out just how Tammy pronounced the name) took them in. After that, Tammy's mother earned a GED, then an associate's degree from a community college, and then she went on to become a nurse, which Tammy called the family business. She'd met her future husband, Hubbs, while they were both seniors in high school, married him while she was still taking classes at the community college, and like her mother, she went on to become a nurse, a job she held until she gave birth to Johnnie, then Jennifer, and then Eudora, whom she birthed in succession, each born about a year apart, about which Tammy said, "I was tired as a boomtown whore, but the kids come up close as stink on shit." With her children out of the house and her husband gone a lot, these days she spent most of her spare time knitting made-to-order sweaters for cats and dogs, which she sold online at $100 a pop, plus shipping and handling. All this, and more, she got out in under five minutes.

Like me, M mostly listened. It surprised me that the entire time Tammy visited with us, M didn't bring up the child suicides or The Good Neighbors or the old preacher or his son or the pink bungalow burning to the ground or anything or anyone having to do with what had worried her so much over the last several months. I hadn't either, but I had my own reasons. I was waiting to see if Tammy would. Why M stayed quiet about all that had preoccupied her for the entirety of her pregnancy, I didn't know, guess, or ask, and she didn't let on or tell.

Tammy began describing in detail the changes that her body had gone through during her three pregnancies. With Johnnie, her feet grew an inch, from a size 10 to an 11. With both Jennifer and Eudora, each time the baby had taken to crying, Tammy would involuntarily lactate. It was at this point in the conversation that I left her and M alone in the kitchen and went out back to the garage.

I rearranged and dusted off tools I hadn't used in years. A hand plane, a dovetail saw, a set of C-clamps. I also perused through some of my old lecture notes. Nothing in them inspired me. Though I had told myself I wouldn't, soon enough I brought out my secret pack of cigarettes from its hiding spot in my toolbox. I took a cigarette out, opened a matchbook, removed a matchstick, put the cigarette in my mouth, and stood there, ready to strike and light up. Hesitant, I went back and forth between acceptance of my weaknesses and resistance to them. I told myself that the original impetus for quitting no longer existed (M was finally pregnant), so I should go ahead and strike the match. I also told myself that I had to consider a new, fresh impetus (a future child), so I should throw the pack out, once and for all, and swear never again to succumb to habits I have kept longer than I should have. Both arguments were persuasive. I chose to wait on making a final decision. I put the cigarettes back in the toolbox and headed back inside.

Walking into the kitchen, I heard Tammy say, "Unbearable, honey. I ain't trying to frighten you none, but I'd liken it to the worst menstrual cramps ever known to womankind. Just about tumped me over. Felt like someone stabbing me to death, like my hips was drawn-and-quartered by bucking bulls, and when her slick towhead crowned, my vagina honest to goodness burned."

I continued walking, straight out of the kitchen, up the stairs, and into the bedroom, where I remained until Tammy left.

That night, before switching out the light on her side of the bed, M told me that she liked Tammy.

"We could be friends."

The next morning, M woke up before me. She hadn't done that in years. By the time I went downstairs for a cup of coffee, she had already showered, dressed, and eaten breakfast. She had also brewed a pot of coffee for me, and she greeted me "Good morning" and told me she wanted to go shopping. Before I could answer or check the wall clock to see what time it was or even take a sip of my coffee, she added, "You don't have to go. I can go by myself."

"You haven't been out by yourself in forever."

"I know."

"Are you sure?

"I'll be okay."

"But by yourself?"

"I can handle it."

I responded how I thought I should, which happened to be against my better judgment and worst inclinations: I showed my wife support. I wish I would have said "No, don't" or "Not alone" or "Not today."

Would have, could have, should have.

Within minutes, she was out the door. I stood on the front porch and watched her drive away. Briefly, the trees on the block looked fake. No movement in the leaves, in what leaves remained. No birds wobbling branches. For the first time in a long time, I was alone.

❦

I turned on the TV.

Soap opera, soap opera, game show, soap opera, game show.

I turned off the TV.

Upstairs in the bedroom, I read the news on the laptop. More accurately, I read the headlines and ignored the stories. The pope rebuked an unnamed but easily identifiable political leader for a comment the leader had made in a televised speech. The president threatened the press for comments they published about a speech he had made on TV. Many of the same news organizations chastised by the president also reported on the rising numbers of stock market indexes and global temperatures and the falling numbers of median income and bee populations. Someone who had vanished a half-century earlier turned up alive but not well. After reading the news, I went downstairs and watched a game show on TV. I cheered for a family from the Midwest. They all had bad haircuts and matching outfits: red tops, black bottoms. They won, beating out another Midwest family with better hair and slightly less-matching outfits. The triumphant family won $10,000. They jumped for joy when they heard and saw the buzzers and lights signifying their victory, except for the matriarch—she cried.

To my astonishment, I welled up with emotion.

I turned the TV off, and because M was not home, I drew the blinds open, flooding the room with sunlight. I went out to the front porch to get sunlight on my face and to breathe fresh air. Though it was still sunny and bright out, the air felt chilly, more so than the day before. I checked the weather on my phone. A cold front was descending on the area. The front was coming from the north, and it stretched a few hundred miles to the east and almost as many to the west. I wondered if M had taken a sweater with her for the change in temperature. Her departure, alone, threw me off, and I hadn't paid attention to what she was wearing. She got cold so easily. Lately, she'd been waking up in the middle of the night and running a hot bath to warm her feet. I wondered if this was a symptom of pregnancy, but I didn't look it up. Instead, I stood on the porch trying but failing to recall what M was wearing when she left the house. In addition to the clothes she might be wearing, I thought about when she would be back and what she would bring home. At a loss, I shrugged.

For ten or fifteen minutes more, I sat on the porch steps, looking out and about. The entire time I saw no one—no one going or coming, no one passing by. Not Tammy next door, not the other next-door neighbor, not the young couple with a Chihuahua across the street, or the retired couple to the left of the Chihuahua house, or the old guy to the right of the couple with the Chihuahua, or the short-haired woman next to him who must have owned a dozen cats, or the owner of a rusted pickup with flat tires that hadn't been moved from its parking spot in at least five years. It occurred to me that maybe M was right. Maybe things did seem different now, better than they had been. Maybe everything that had been worrying us had finally passed from our lives. As usual, I entertained a contradictory supposition. Maybe it had always been this way. Maybe our street—the East Side itself—had always been this quiet, this calm, this absent of people outside the confines of their homes, and the only change had been in our perceptions.

I faced the dilemma by compounding it with another: the desire to smoke a cigarette. The urge coming into being must have been rooted in M's absence. With her home every single minute of every hour of every day for several months straight, sneaking cigarettes came to be close to impossible. I had learned to fight the cigarette cravings by substituting the Internet and coffee, both of which blunted the desire to light up but not entirely, not until, that is, I took to sitting down every morning to type up our story. That's when I began to feel genuine relief. Now, because she was not home, and because I was too racked with questions to think or write, I surrendered. Willingly, I should add, and happily. I headed back into the house through the TV room and into the kitchen and out the back door and across the lawn and straight for the garage. I did not light up behind closed doors, either. I smoked a cigarette right out in the open in the middle of the yard. Under the sun, a relatively cloudless sky, the air cool, with cigarette pack and matches in hand, I said to myself out loud, "Yes, our perceptions have changed." M was out in public, shopping. I was out in the yard, smoking. The threats, of course, were real. We hadn't imagined The Good Neighbors or the warnings they left on our doors or the rally. Maybe, though, we had exaggerated the extent and reach of their threats. Yes, they had left us dire warnings, too, but as far as I knew, The Good Neighbors hadn't victimized a single person who looked like M or me. As for the pink bungalow burning to the ground, wasn't that an act of retribution, not against us or people like us, but against the girl, who looked like them and even sat among them unnoticed in their small church? Our conscience both demands and opposes vengeance, and as such, I could even sympathize with the arson committed. The girl had killed the old preacher, after all, and had The Good Neighbors practiced eye-for-eye, bone-for-bone justice, the girl would be dead. But she wasn't dead. Maybe M and I had allowed ourselves to be overtaken by our overactive imaginations. Maybe, all along, we had been living our life by making errors of judgment.

Right or wrong, for better or worse, I decided to bring all this up with M when she returned from the mall. I struck a match and lit another cigarette. I hadn't smoked in so long the cigarette made me lightheaded, so much so I had to steady myself against the side of the garage. By the third cigarette, I was feeling nothing but good.

In the early afternoon I ate the leftovers I had saved for M, who was still gone. Midway through a corn muffin, I wondered if she was having a good time all by herself. Probably yes. Whether she was didn't matter ultimately. Having speculated that she was, I believed it to be true, and I would continue to do so until proven otherwise.

In the middle of the afternoon, I debated giving her a call to find out if she knew when she would be heading back. Worried that my phone call would make her feel rushed, or worse, spied upon, I chose not to. I would have argued with myself much longer about the merits of calling versus leaving her alone, but the inclination to smoke another cigarette came on fast and strong, and I decided to call her to get an estimated time of arrival so I could gauge just how much time I had left to sneak in another smoke.

The call immediately went to voicemail.

"Hey, babe," I said. "It's me. Just wondering when you'll be home. Call me back."

Cellphone reception was notoriously spotty in the mall. M must still be shopping. If she were to leave the mall right then and there, after I ended the call, it would take her at least twenty minutes to head back to the car and commute back to the East Side. That was without accounting for traffic or stoplights or for M walking and driving like a pregnant woman. I gave myself a half-hour, plenty of time. My problem is I think too much. For me to have concluded that M did not answer her phone due to poor reception and no other scenario was reckless, not to mention bad logic. Another chain of events, just as likely, was that my call did in fact go through, and M intentionally ignored it because she was driving the car, and given that she would be extra cautious while driving, she might have also been so close to the East Side (a block or two away, even) that she didn't pick up because she could talk to me face to face within a few minutes or less, and not because she was far away.

Simply put, I had no idea where M was or what she was doing or when she would be back.

I smoked a cigarette anyhow, but only one. I did so in the garage, not as I had hoped, which was sitting in the lawn chair under the shade of the bigleaf maple. The upshot was that I enjoyed the experience less than some guy who kept close tabs on his wife would have. Nevertheless, I still got pleasure out of it, but not nearly as much as I had expected.

I went back inside and searched online how many cigarettes the average person could smoke before reaching the point of no return. According to the top search result, I could become a nicotine addict after smoking a single cigarette. The second, third, and fourth results reaffirmed the first. I resolved this problem by clearing the browsing history, which was when I discovered that M hadn't cleared hers. The exhilaration I felt at the possibility of discovering something my wife might have been keeping from me was palpable. I felt giddy. My heart rate doubled, my breathing quickened.

I began at the end.

Late the night before, M had read two news stories, the first about a growing wildfire out West, the second about a woman still missing after going on a hike by herself in the woods near her home. Before these stories, M had added several items to an online wish list, which included several pairs of tiny baby socks and three pairs of tiny baby shoes, which a baby would outgrow long before it would even be able to stand or crawl, much less walk. She had also added to the wish list a set of tiny feeding bottles—I imagined their smallness filling M with joy—and a product called a pee-pee teepee. I clicked on the link and read the product description:

Why is it that the act of diaper changing always seems to inspire an extra "contribution" from the little one? Parents of baby boys have been particularly vulnerable—until now. Just place a pee-pee teepee on his wee-wee during diaper changes, and the hazard is averted. An ideal baby shower gift, the powder blue 100% cotton pee-pee teepees are decorated with airplanes and hemmed with soft fringe. Made in China. Not intended for sleepwear.

Was M going to have a boy?

Before her suspicions about the baby's gender, M had visited the month-by-month pregnancy website she quoted from all the time, though either because I had already fallen asleep by then or for some other reason, she didn't pass on what she'd read.

I went further back into the past.

For several days, her history looked much the same: a combination of news, shopping, and information on pregnancy. Except for Sunday, around the time she'd sent me grocery shopping. On that day, at that time, M visited a page titled "Mom Speaks Out." I clicked on the link. A video uploaded. In the still frame, a woman I did not recognize sat facing the camera. She was in a kitchen. She resembled M. She could easily have passed as M's sister. Or mine. The video's statistics: 13.03 minutes in length, 453 views, 105 thumbs up, 6 thumbs down. I read the first comment beneath the video: "shes defending her kid even tho he killed other kids. discusting!" Below this comment, there was a reply to it: "Obviously you weren't paying attention, and you must have skipped school the day they taught spelling."

I hit play.

The woman began with a greeting and her name, and then she said, "My son killed seven children." She summarized her son's actions with a concise sentence: "He stole my SUV and crashed it into a classroom full of school kids." After this, her tone shifted. She began to speak more openly, the words she chose less guarded. Listening to her and watching her, I could see that she was sad and mournful, but it was obvious that she wasn't wretched or despondent.

That surprised me, given whose mother she was. "I'm upset," she admitted. "Of course I am. I'm upset at what my son did." Then she offered what I took to be a reasonable explanation for why she hadn't succumbed to wretchedness or despondency. Her son, she told us, was ill. She had known about his illness for a long time. In fact, she had taken measures against it, steps designed to help him cope and live with mental illness. Once a month, she said, she took him to a psychiatrist, once a week to a therapist, and every morning she made sure he swallowed the prescribed pills meant to stabilize, alter, and adjust his mind, mood, and temperament. About these conditions, she kept his teachers, neighbors, close friends, and family members up to date on the ups and downs, improvements, and deteriorations of each. She reminded them regularly of the consequences of inaction and neglect, and the catastrophic failure that could result should they disregard or not take her son's fluctuations seriously. She said, "My son talked about killing himself." He had looked up ways to commit suicide, including the most effective, the least painful, the quickest, and the least complicated approaches. Numerous times he even admitted to his mother that he felt trapped in the world, by his body and mind, and he had also admitted these impressions to a few teachers and at least two classmates. In the weeks leading up to the day he stole her SUV and crashed it into a classroom full of first-graders, he wrote in a notebook, "If I could just get even with God." She said she showed the notebook to his high school principal, the school counselor, his therapist, and his psychiatrist. She also talked about the notebook with her brother, who was also her best friend. "Do you feel cursed?" she said. She swallowed her breath. "That's the question a lot of people have asked me. Do I feel cursed?" She answered without hesitation. "No, I don't. Not anymore. I used to blame God and nature and myself, but I stopped doing that when I realized that my son wasn't cursed. He was just sick. No one should have to imagine the ways their children may kill themselves. Or worse than that, that they'll kill someone else." She turned her head slightly away from us, as though she could feel the weight of our stares and judgments. She took a long breath and let out an even longer exhale and turned back to face us. "I failed. Much as I tried, I failed. And I just want to say I'm sorry." Her eyes were now watery. "So sorry. To the parents whose lives my son wrecked forever, for the little ones he stole from you, I'm so, so sorry." Her speech was now being interrupted by sobs, but she kept apologizing. To the brothers and sisters of the children killed by her son, to their friends and classmates, and to all their relatives and neighbors. In between apologies, she wiped her tears. Just when I thought she had exhausted the list of people hurt by her son, she dropped an apology to the principal, the teachers, and the counselors at her son's school, those people who earlier she claimed had let her down. About them, she said, "What could any of you really do?"

She was slowing her speech, catching her breath, and regaining her composure. All these indicated to me that the video would come to an end soon, except the red line showing the video's progress hadn't yet reached the halfway mark. The mother wiped her face with a tissue she pulled from outside the frame, and with the following statement, she brought her catalog of regretful acknowledgments to a stop: "I failed. I did. But you did, too. You failed us all. You, those of you who went on and on about child suicides—on the news, online, on TV—you failed big time."

I turned the volume up.

"You did just about everything wrong," she said. "You talked about suicide in the most reductive terms. Glorifying, romanticizing, and sensationalizing it. Maybe you think that's okay, but when kids commit suicide, it's...it's..." She choked up, but not with grief—anger and indignation were holding her back. "It's messy, it's painful, and unlike in the movies or in the stories you told, the pain doesn't stop in real life. Pain doesn't take a commercial break or make you money or famous. Worst of all..." She took a long, deep breath, inhaling back into her lungs all the rage she had let out. "You turned the death of children into a storyline, into entertainment, fodder for a bunch of hate-filled degenerates. And for what? Self-interest. Profit. Attention. Shame on you."

The video wasn't over yet, but I stopped it. I sat for a while without moving or thinking or doing anything except sitting still. In retrospect, I could have asked a dozen questions about what I'd witnessed. Given that her son had killed kids, was she speaking from a position of unique moral authority, or was she out of her goddamn mind to tell us how to think? Was she a victim or a victimizer? Why had so few people watched her video? Why wasn't she being interviewed on prime-time television? But I didn't ask any of these questions. Instead, I kept looking at her face, at her life, frozen on the screen.

Eventually, probably within a minute, I snapped out of it and closed the browser window and cleared the history, mine and M's. I looked around the bedroom, where M and I spent so much time together, most of it sleeping, yes, but still side by side, waking up next to one another, she with the blanket pulled over her head, me with the blanket pulled off my body, she with two pillows under her head, me with one, she on one side, me on the other, which is how it's been from the first day. I got up and walked to the bedroom window. Peering down to the street below, I asked myself, where is she? I checked my watch. I said out loud, "It's getting late," and in my head I added, "Something must be wrong."

I phoned M again, and again the call went directly to voicemail. As I listened to M's voice on the outgoing message, I walked around to her side of the bed and pulled open the top drawer to her nightstand. Her gun was in there, the positive pregnancy test, too, and an old, faded photograph of when she was a little girl being held by her father when he was a young man. Both were smiling. She seemed happy. Her father did, too, which I had presumed to be an emotion utterly absent from the entirety of his life. That was when I heard a knocking on the front door. M was finally home.

I carefully returned the photograph to its place in the drawer. Later, I would realize that I had left a silent message on M's voicemail, one lasting seventeen seconds, which was apparently the length of time I spent starting at my wife and her father, thinking to myself, despite visual evidence to the contrary, that it was impossible she could have ever been so young or that her father could have ever experienced a moment of joy.

I walked back to the bedroom window facing the street to see if M had parked at the curb or in the driveway. Probably the driveway, I told myself, believing she must have purchased all sorts of items for the baby, maybe even a crib, which was also the reason why she rang the doorbell rather than letting herself in. Her hands were full, she needed help.

Instead of M or even our car, I saw parked in front of our house a vehicle I did not recognize.

I headed downstairs, and because earlier I had opened the blinds to let light in, I could see two people standing on the porch. I was one hundred percent certain that they also saw me, but I hoped otherwise.

One of the two strangers knocked on the door again, and either the same person or the other one yelled loud enough for me to hear, "Hello? We see you in there. Hello?"

I stepped to the door and raised the peephole cover. Inside its convex circle, I saw two young women, a fact that on its own should not have granted any relief whatsoever, but I let it do just that, immediately feeling less anxious about their presence.

"Just a minute."

I eyed them one last time through the peephole and wondered what they wanted. My first guess, they were Jehovah's Witnesses. I quickly rejected this possibility because the Witnesses who went door to door in the East Side only showed up on Saturdays, usually early in the morning. It was neither morning nor Saturday, and neither of the two young women was holding a Bible or any of the literature the Witnesses always carried with them when they went preaching.

One of the young women was tall, the other short. The shorter of the two was wearing a denim jacket, the taller a royal blue puffy jacket. I could tell that the shorter one was growing impatient. The two times she tried looking into the house through her side of the peephole, she sighed, and the breath of her impatience fogged the glass and blurred my vision. Because all this transpired within a few seconds, her eagerness for the door to be opened irked me, especially because I had told them to give me a minute.

I undid the deadbolt, and through an opening about a foot wide, I asked how I could help them.

"Professor?" the shorter of the two said.

Only two people had recently called me that: M, during a fight, as a wisecrack, and the girl in the pink bungalow. Otherwise, it had been years since anyone called me by my former title. Maybe these two had been students. I doubted that. To begin with, they appeared too young to have been college students when I was still teaching. However, having been so scandalously wrong about the age of the girl in the pink bungalow, I couldn't help but second-guess my estimation about their age. Ultimately, it mattered very little. Had they been former students, I probably wouldn't have recognized them anyhow. Without exception, within a year of having them in a class, I forgot most of my students, even those who dazzled me with their brilliance or their good looks. I couldn't remember what they looked like, their names and majors, or the grades I assigned them. Running into former students and not recognizing them got to be such a problem, I went so far as to concoct a script for such occasions, especially when they wanted to strike up a conversation. I always began with a smile and a nod, which was usually met with a mirroring of the gestures. I followed with a simple greeting. "Hello," "Good morning," and the like. If they wanted more, I was ready with two questions and a remark, delivered in that order. Question 1: "How are you?" Question 2: "How are your classes?" Usually—always, in fact—every student who unwittingly participated in this brief drama responded to my questions with the same one-to-two-word reply: "Good," "Pretty good," "Okay," or "Fine." Whatever their answer, I would bring the chat to an end. I would look down at my watch and say, "Well, it's good to see you," and true or not, I would tell them I had a meeting to make and was running late. Without fail, this left them looking content, perhaps even feeling acknowledged, and I walked away clueless as to who they were. M was the exception to all these forgotten students. Otherwise, a total stranger could knock on the door and claim to have been in one of my classes, and I would have to take their word for it.

I responded to the shorter of the two addressing me as professor by asking, "Who are you?"

The question seemed to throw the two women into a state of bewilderment. They glanced at each other, then at me, and then back at each other again, then at me once more. The back and forth was disorienting, so to spare all of us, I asked, "Do I know you?"

"You know our friend," the shorter one in the denim jacket answered.

Then the second one, the tall girl in the royal blue puffy jacket, added timidly, "I'm sure you know about The Good Neighbors."

I had made a terrible mistake opening the door.

"I don't know any Good Neighbors," I said.

Inwardly, I prayed that M would not show up anytime soon. If I'm being totally honest, which I've been throughout, I was gripped not only by apprehension but mostly fear, even though they were women, young women at that. Still, I managed to remain calm, or I believed that I appeared so, standing before them.

To my insistence that I did not know any Good Neighbors, the shorter one said, "Our friend, she…she founded us. She's the founder of The Bad Neighbors."

I repeated in my head what she had just said: The Bad Neighbors.

"Is this some kind of joke?" I asked.

"No," the short one said. "It's no joke."

"Listen, I don't know who you are or who your friend is or what—"

"Yes," she interrupted. "Yes, you do. You know her. You were her teacher."

"Probably not," I said.

"She said you two studied the Bible together."

"I don't teach the Bible. In fact, I don't teach."

The taller girl in the puffy jacket interjected. "She said that once a month, you two read the Bible together."

Then I knew.

Also, in that instant, the blue bungalow I was inside of, and the front porch on which they were standing, and the East Side itself, all of it felt oppressively confining. I tried even harder to present myself as calm and collected, though I hardly felt that way.

"The Bad Neighbors, huh?"

"Yes," the short one said. "That's the name of the group she formed, in opposition to The Good Neighbors, as a form of resistance—" She interrupted herself. "We," she went on, gesturing toward the taller one at her side. "The three of us met in a study group over the summer. We'd taken a course together at the college, and she founded the group after that, and she told us that you two used to meet and go over the Bible with each other, and you were a professor, and—"

Now it was my turn to interrupt.

"She was never my student," I said antagonistically.

The taller of the two reacted by stuffing her hands into her puffy jacket and tightening her shoulders. The shorter one, however, was not fazed. She echoed my antagonism back at me.

"Whether she was or wasn't your student isn't the point. The point is that you two used to meet, and I know you know who I'm talking about."

"I was never her professor. I was her landlord."

"Landlord, then. You were her landlord."

I nodded.

She smiled sarcastically, but then, with a hint of disappointment in her voice, she said, "She didn't tell you about The Bad Neighbors?"

"No, I don't know anything about...your group. And like I said, she wasn't my student. I don't have students. I haven't had a student since you two were scraping your knees and elbows learning how to ride a bike. And your friend, your *founder*—you realize that she committed murder, right? If you were in a group with her, The Bad Neighbors—super original, FYI—then you and your group got a man murdered, and that makes you an accessory to a crime."

"No," the taller one blurted out. "We didn't kill anyone."

"Be quiet," the short one told the tall one. Then to me she said, "Listen, mister, you're wrong. We went to protest. That was the plan. That was the only plan. The night before the rally, we made signs, and we memorized a few chants. That's all we brought to the rally—words, words on paper and words in our head. *She* was the one who brought a gun. She didn't tell us she was bringing a gun, and she didn't tell us what she was going to do when she got there. We didn't even know she had a gun until she pulled it out and shot at the stage."

"It's true," said the taller one. "She didn't say nothing about killing anyone. Swear to God."

"Let me guess. Your sign said, NO HATE, ONLY LOVE."

The shorter one snickered at me and without hesitating said, "Actually, my sign was GOD HATES ASSHOLES, and right now I'm pretty sure God hates you for being such a huge one. Look, Professor Landlord, we came here because she asked us to, not because we wanted to. We're bringing you a message from her, and she said you'd be nicer than you're being. We're doing you a favor, but if you don't want to hear what she wanted you to hear, that's fine by me. We're off."

"But..." the tall one said.

"Be quiet," the short one said, and then she grabbed the taller one by her puffy jacket and dragged her down the porch steps.

I opened the door wider and yelled after them.

"Wait, wait a minute."

They stopped. They turned around but didn't come closer or speak. The tall girl was looking to the short one, to follow her lead, I supposed. The short one was eyeing me sideways, disdainfully.

"What did she say to you? What did she tell you?"

"Stay here," the short one said to the tall one, and then she walked back up the steps and onto the porch and stopped about arm's length from the door, from me. On her face, a flicker of delight. "The night before the rally, she told us that if anything happened to her, we should come to you and give you a message. She said to wait a while, though—'lay low' was how she put it—until whatever would happen to her was all but forgotten. That's when we should come to you, and here we are. The thing she told us to tell you, I told her *she* needed to say to you face to face. Not me, not us, not anyone else. But she said she might not be able to, she might not make it. I didn't know what she meant by that. I figured she was just scared to tell you. Then she went and killed someone."

I couldn't tell if she was angrier at me or the college girl.

"I didn't want this burden," she said.

"Just tell me what she told you."

She couldn't have known it, but I liked her. To show such defiance, she might have been the kind of student I would have remembered.

"It's cold," I pleaded. "I'd like to get back to what I was doing before you interrupted me, and my wife will be home soon."

"Your wife?" she asked.

I nodded.

"She's pregnant," she said.

"How do you know my wife's pregnant?"

"Jesus, you're stupid," she said "*She's* pregnant, not your wife. We didn't come here to tell you about your wife."

"We didn't know you had a wife," the taller one said from the bottom of the steps.

The short one added, "In case you're as thick-headed as I think you are, it's your baby. You're the father. You got her pregnant."

She waited for me to say something. The only response that came to mind, after several moments of uncomfortable silence, was to thank her for telling me.

"You're welcome."

They stood there looking at me, expecting me to say something else, to ask for details, to do something other than step back into the blue bungalow and slowly close the door on them. I would like to tell you about the profound thoughts I had then and there. I would also like to say something about how I experienced the revelation the way the prophets of old did, as a window or a portal into a greater awareness of who I was and what I should have been doing with my life. Finally, I would like to tell you just how that singular moment changed everything that came after. But none of these things happened. Although I had been stunned by their message, I quickly regained my senses, and before the two girls had made it to the parked car at the curb, I threw the front door wide open and walked to the edge of the porch, and not the least bit concerned about who might see or hear me, I called after them.

"Wait," I yelled.

They turned around, and again they stopped, and again they stood there without saying a word. With as much dignity as I could muster, I said, "I was going to tell you to go fuck yourself. But, you know, the truth is that even if I had done that, it wouldn't have made much of a difference. All that matters to you is that you're right. You can't possibly imagine that you might be wrong. I've taught hundreds of kids like you. Worse than thinking you're always right, you all think that your ideas are original, that you and your generation are going to save the world, and that all the others who came before you weren't as smart as you, weren't as motivated, didn't know their elbows from their asses. But not you. You're different. You're special. Let me tell you, you're not. There are a million others already in line ahead of you, just like you."

"You don't know what you're talking about," the short one said.

"You're naïve," I said.

"You're out of touch," she said. "Stuck in your old ways. You know what you are? Irrelevant. Your time's up. It's a new world, and you're just an old guy with old ideas."

"I'm not old."

"You had your chance, old man, and you failed. You didn't change the world, you didn't make it better, and it's too late for you to do anything about it. But you wouldn't even try if you could."

"You can leave now."

"You know what you are?"

"Get off my property."

"A creep."

"Get off."

"A creepy professor who doesn't respect women—who violates their bodies."

"Get the fuck off."

EIGHT

PROBABLY WITHIN A year of our coming together, M and I began falling apart. Ever since, we'd been gradually pulling away from each other until, one day, the distance between us had become spectacular. How far apart? I was the Middle Ages, she the Industrial Revolution. Or she was a Romantic, and I a postmodernist. Or better yet, one of us was an arrow, and the other the atomic bomb. Call the rift between us what you will, I saw it coming long before it finally arrived, and I had counted on our marriage collapsing the way most did: little by little, then suddenly. Only a miracle could save us, and I did not believe in them.

Then M got pregnant.

Because I didn't expect her to conceive, or even believe it remained a possibility, it was nothing short of extraordinary when M showed me the positive pregnancy test. That was M's miracle. The miracle of the two red lines, which irrevocably altered our life together. Like M, and maybe even because of her, I took for granted that our marriage would be better because of the two red lines. This was a conclusion premised on an assumption I hardly thought to question. Hardly anyone questions it. I don't mean the existence of miracles. I mean that miracles are always good. That they improve the futures and fortunes of those who receive them. Who cares if what we call a miracle is in fact a bona fide supernatural act? It doesn't have to be. It doesn't need to be highly improbable or extraordinary, either, though that certainly does help. What a miracle does indeed have to be is good. That's what we take for granted. A miracle must bring about a welcome consequence. Whether it is a pregnancy or jugs of water turned into wine, the miracle is in what follows: the birth of a baby or the best wine being served after all the guests are already drunk. Had the disciples at the wedding in Cana gotten shit-faced drunk on the water Jesus turned into wine, and then fought each other, insulted the groom, and groped the bride, would we still call the act a miracle? The miracle was good because the wedding ended well. It was good. But I'm telling you now, what brings a miracle about does not have to be. Infinitely more important than any miraculous act or where it comes from or who is responsible for its presence in the world is the result it produces.

For M, the act was two red lines appearing on the pregnancy test, and what made this good was the promise of a baby, which had not come yet.

For me, the promise wasn't a baby. It was M and I remaining together. Which we did, even though by any reasonable measure, we should have been divorced.

I had taken for granted that the pregnancy had saved us—M's pregnancy, not that of the girl from the pink bungalow. Now, though, with the gift of hindsight, I know better. The phenomenon rescuing us from ourselves could just as easily have been the sudden rash of suicides or the threats posed by The Good Neighbors or the temptation of a pretty girl or an act of vengeance. Whatever the cause (the death of a child, an impossible pregnancy, a dire warning, a premeditated murder, a carefully planned arson) and whomever the agent (a depressed teen, a hopeful wife, an old preacher, a sharp girl, a skilled speaker), M and I began to come back to each other. Little by little, the distance between us contracted. Once a great chasm, it appeared to me more and more like a fissure or a crack. Something manageable, traversable. We began again to feel genuine affection for one another. We may have even felt love, or a sentiment that is much the same as love.

That was a miracle.

If you knew our story the way I did, you would have noticed the thorough and dramatic changes our marriage endured. Though these changes came to pass gradually, they were hardly subtle. To begin with, there were all the years of M trying and failing to get pregnant, and again trying and failing. What could come of such inadequacy, of such a miscarriage of conjugal duty other than heartache, bitterness, and distance? If you doubt me, let me make the case with an image. Our bedroom. We slept on a simple bed made of wood, but wood that was laminated to mimic the grain of maple. The headboard had also been manufactured with simplicity in mind—straight lines, laminate grain finish, and according to its product description, "perfect for cozy bedtime reading." The sheets on which we slept were white, no pattern, no embroidery, just like the pillowcases. The blanket, a solid gray comforter. Now imagine M on the left side, sitting upright, a pillow behind her back, the laptop on her knees, and a bluish glow on her face. On the right side, add me, pillows under my head and holding a book probably closer to my face than an optometrist would advise, and from the lamp beside me a warm incandescence. If you must, especially if it aids in making the image more real, adjust it as you see fit. If you're in your own house, take a good look around. Notice the lines, the colors, the shapes, textures, and imperfections. If you're not at home, work from memory, or create your own ideal space. Whichever you choose, imagine your own bed and your own bedroom and your own light sources. As much as I would like for the image in your mind's eye to match as much as possible what is right now before my eyes in the blue bungalow, the fact is that the objects in the room do not ultimately matter. The people in the room—what they are doing, feeling, and thinking—they matter. Whichever room you choose (yours, ours, or a composite of the two), place M and I on the bed (any bed will do), and picture M on one side, me on the other (who is on the left or right no longer makes a difference), and finally, draw a thick, dark, prominent line between us (any color will work). Let the line run not only down the middle of the bed, but let it split the entire room in two. On either side of this boundary, for years M and I inhabited our own private worlds. We were nations unto ourselves. We had our own time zones, our own weather, our own seasons. While we weren't officially enemies, we were no longer partners. We weren't friends, either, or even allies. We had signed a treaty, yes. We called it a marriage. We had come to certain agreements, yes. We called them vows. But we had become isolationists. Tensions on the border mounted, trust eroded, and even before I violated the terms and conditions of the treaty, we were each seething with resentments and regrets. Trouble was coming, and we both knew it. We both saw it on our shared horizon, but neither one of us was strong enough to stop it. There were days, in fact, when I wished for all-out war. Maybe M did, too.

For just a few sentences, let me take you back to the beginning, to when I had fallen for M and she was still a student at the college, my student. In those days, it was inconceivable that I would feel such discontent for her, or such acrimony. If anyone other than me had felt that way and expressed it openly, I would have murdered the sonofabitch. But by the time the first East Side kid killed herself, our marriage was on life support, and when I cheated on M with the girl who lived in the pink bungalow, I pulled the plug.

For all that, even after so much wreckage piled upon wreckage, you must have sensed an inkling of hope when you saw M and I together all those nights, side by side in bed, reading about the progressive stages of pregnancy. Is there any gesture more emblematic of unity in a marriage than a husband and wife reading, together, about a child of their own making? You must have also found our descriptions of the baby as the size of this and that, apples and baseballs and whatnot, heartening and heartwarming. We were finally on the same page, some nights literally reading the same page. We were going to be all right. We were going to make it.

Then two strangers told me I got a girl pregnant.

Even then, I remained one hundred percent positive that M and I would still survive. How? Why? You and I, we live in an age of eternal hope. We always have. Our ancestors, too, and the millions and billions before them. The signs we want are always right before our eyes. They wait for us, ready for any interpretation under the sun. We only need to look for them and to make use of them. After I told the two girls to get the fuck off my property, I stood on the porch until they drove away. The short one was driving. She laid on the car horn and then extended her arm out the open window and gave me the middle finger. Would you believe me if I told you her "fuck you" made me smile? I walked back into the blue bungalow and sat on the couch facing the TV. For a while, I stared at my reflection in the television, that box of fabrication, half-truths, and deception. I saw my face twisted and distorted, darker and unfocused. I could have agreed with the TV's assessment, which was not so different than the opinion of me expressed by short girl in the denim jacket. I could have said to myself, "She's right—your life *is* a perversion." But I didn't. I could have also examined my surroundings, taken a closer look at the furnishings in the room, the fake leather couch I was sitting on, the faux marble coffee table in front of it, the synthetic wool rug beneath it, and construed each as a metaphor of the sham my life had become. I didn't do that either. I just sat for a while, looking at my face in the TV and telling myself that the person staring back at me was not a creep or an irrelevant human being. "You're wrong," I said, as though they were there with me, the two girls. Only the TV was, though. I was speaking to myself.

Eternal hope.

I stood up and turned away from the self I saw in the TV, and to symbolize the moment, as well as my conviction, I shook my head at the judgment laid against me.

"Bitches," I said.

Was I wrong? Maybe. But I felt much better.

A renewed, reinvigorated faith was now guiding me. Maybe it was something else, some other kind of delusion. Right then and there, though, I believed wholeheartedly, so I decided to come clean and confess the truth to M.

"Everything's going to be all right."

I thought about that for a few seconds.

"Everything will be okay."

I let out a sigh of relief, and rather than spend the rest of my time worrying, panicking, smoking, or drinking, I tidied up the house so M would return to a clean, orderly place. I made up the bed, that sanctum of our life together. I scrubbed the bathtub in case she wanted to take a bath. I cleaned the toilet and bathroom sink. I swept the floors, upstairs and downstairs, every room, and vacuumed the rugs and wiped the countertops. I watered the potted plants, folded the clothes in the dryer, added a load of whites to the washing machine, and lit a scented candle, which I placed on the coffee table in the room with the TV. Satisfied with the job I had done, I settled back onto the couch. What I was doing and what I planned on doing felt good and right. I told myself that. I was gaining control over my life again. I told myself that, too. I knew M could end up hating me, but I had no misgivings. Maybe for the first time in my life, I looked forward to the consequences of my actions. I was unafraid of the future. A good thing, too, because what happened next would have made an average man go to pieces.

I reacted like a Stoic.

My phone rang. My phone hardly ever rang. Only M called me. My phone had been silent for half a year or more, ever since The Good Neighbors posted yellow warnings on our houses and M stopped leaving the house. It had become useless, so much so I'd given serious thought to cancelling our phone plan, which cost more than a seriously committed cigarette addiction. Hearing the ringing now, after desperately waiting all day for M's call, I couldn't imagine life without a phone. In fact, prior to this day, in what I now think of as my previous life, I might not have even heard the call. The phone wouldn't have been in my back pocket but somewhere in the house. The bedroom, usually, on my bedside table. And had I heard it ring, I wouldn't have rushed upstairs to answer. And if I happened to be near the phone when someone called, I would have identified the caller before picking up, and maybe not answer; if it wasn't M calling me, it was almost always a telemarketer or a wrong number. Even when the person trying to reach me was M, I sometimes still let the phone ring, ring, ring, and go to voicemail.

Not this time.

I reached for the phone instantly. I didn't bother checking the caller ID before answering. Simply uttering the word

"Hello" immediately relieved me of the enormous sense of urgency I was feeling.

I expected M to apologize, to say she'd lost track of time. "I'm heading home," she would say, reassuring me, and I would nonchalantly reply, "Would you mind grabbing take-out on your way back?" not because I was hungry but because I had figured that M should not hear me come clean about the girl in the pink bungalow on an empty stomach. I would suggest Chinese, M's favorite.

That was not how the call went.

I did begin with "Hello," but someone other than M replied. A woman, a woman whose voice I did not recognize. She asked me if I was M's husband.

"Yes, I'm her husband."

"There's been an emergency."

I grabbed my wallet and keys and checked myself in the mirror before stepping out. I looked fine. I walked across my lawn to Tammy's. Across her grass, I walked slowly, careful not to step on the dog shit she only picked up every three or four days. The dog I had heard barking these past few months belonged to Tammy. Composed and unperturbed, I climbed the porch steps casually, one step at a time, and I took a second or two to decide whether to knock or ring the doorbell. I chose the bell. In the time it took Tammy to stop whatever she was doing, walk over, and unlock the door, I realized for the first time since moving into the East Side that the house next to us, Tammy's, was identical to ours, except that it was white. Even the layout, which I saw through the windows, mirrored that of our bungalow.

For so long I had not paid attention to so much.

Tammy opened the door and said, "Look what the cat dragged in."

She smiled so wide I could see her all teeth. My sudden and unexpected appearance at her door must have made her happy. Or else she was just that happy all the time. That was possible. I used to think that no such people existed, but Tammy might have been the exception to invalidate the rule.

"I'm really sorry to bother you," I said, with maybe too much sincerity.

"Don't get your bowels in an uproar."

I laughed, but I sensed that under the circumstances, laughter was inappropriate. Tammy must have picked up on this, or else she finally noticed something about my demeanor (a tick I wasn't aware of, maybe) or in my physical appearance (some look of distress that I obviously did not see in the mirror).

She said, "Neighbor, you look like you fell off a turnip truck."

"I'm okay."

"I doubt it," she said.

"I need to ask you for a favor."

"Go head—I'll sit still."

"Would you drive me to the hospital?"

She gave me a once-over, head to toe.

"I thought you looked sickly and nervous."

"I'm okay," I reassured her.

Her eyes went up to mine. She looked confused, but only for a moment.

"I am okay," I repeated.

"Oh," she said, her eyes widening. "Oh, my. Oh, dear. Is she having the baby?"

"I don't know. I don't think so."

"How come you don't know?"

"I just don't."

"And the baby—the baby all right?"

"I don't know."

"How come you don't know?"

"I don't."

"Honey, is you dumb as a watermelon?"

"I don't know what that means. But if you would stop asking me questions and agree to drive me to the hospital, then we can both find out what's going on."

Tammy drove like a teenager, jerky and reckless. She made hard turns around corners. She braked abruptly at stop signs and traffic lights, tailgated the vehicles in front of us, changed lanes without signaling or checking the side-view mirror, and she nearly sideswiped a sedan and a school bus. I started feeling nauseous. I closed my eyes to keep from getting so dizzy I would vomit. About halfway to the hospital, we got stuck behind a line of cars waiting to make a left turn. It was a momentary reprieve from all the lurching and jolting, so I took the lull as an opportunity to beg Tammy to ease up on the abrupt stops and starts.

"I'm not saying you're a bad driver, but I'm going to puke all over your dashboard if you don't take it easy."

She nodded yes, and to this day, while I believe she did make a concerted effort to minimize her bad driving habits, the rest of the drive felt just as rough. In fact, it got worse when she took to asking me a slew of questions I could not answer.

How did M get to the hospital?

I didn't know.

Did she drive herself?

I didn't know.

Was she transported by paramedics in an ambulance?

I didn't know.

Who called 911?

I didn't know.

I thought she would get the hint and stop, but she persisted. How close was M to her due date, she asked me, and did I think her water broke and is that why she was in the hospital and could she have gone into labor?

"Tammy, I simply don't know. Please, stop asking me."

"How come you don't know nothing from nothing about that prettier-than-pie wife of yours?"

I sighed and said, "It's a long story."

"Sheesh. Ain't it always with men."

Up until that moment, I had been taking long breaths and keeping my eyes closed with the goal of reducing the effects the car sickness was having on me. Now I was fighting the urge to snap back at Tammy, and I remembered how good I felt telling the two girls to get the fuck off my porch. I opened my eyes, focused on my reflection in the side-view mirror, inhaled deeply, and said, "Let me ask *you* something. You've talked to my wife. I heard you two go on and on about pregnancy. Did she ever tell *you* when her due date was? Did she ever tell you about her doctor visits or what she learned during her check-ups or what she saw on an ultrasound? Did she ever tell you anything about her being pregnant other than the facts she read about on the fucking Internet?"

For a second or two, I took my eyes off my reflection in the side-view mirror to see Tammy's reaction. She did not have one. She did not say anything, either. She just drove, eyes on the road, and for once she was driving smoothly.

"That's makes two of us," I said. "I don't know the answer to any of these questions because my wife doesn't know either—because she was too goddamn afraid of those motherfucking Good Neighbors to see a doctor."

So much for being stoic.

Tammy cleared her throat but said nothing. A minute or two later, she signaled a right turn, and carefully, slowly, she made a right turn. Even though I was feeling less sick, I closed my eyes again and carried on with the deep breathing. Except for the intermittent bump and thud of tires rolling over potholes and the steady hum of recirculated air blowing out of the car vents and the unrelenting clamor of every worst-case scenario trying to make itself heard in my head, the rest of the drive was relatively quiet. Tammy and I did not speak again until we reached the medical center and she turned into the hospital's parking complex.

"We're almost there," she said.

"I didn't mean to yell," I told her.

She cleared her throat again and then added, "I'm sure she's fine."

"Yeah, me, too."

But if that were true, M would not be in a hospital.

I opened my eyes.

&

At the reception desk in the emergency room wing of the hospital, a nurse, or someone I presumed to be a nurse on account of her green scrubs and white sneakers, told us that M had been admitted to the ER but soon after was transferred to the main building. She gave us the room number and pointed in the direction of a long, brightly lit hallway and said, "Follow the signs."

Taking strides that were neither leisurely nor hurried, we walked the length of the hallway until it dead-ended at another one perpendicular to it, and here we followed a red arrow with the word MAIN beneath it down a corridor until we reached a sign with another red arrow pointing left. We went left, and that took us out of the ER and ushered us into an enclosed passageway with a skylight running its entire length. Above our heads, a cloudless sky, still blue but fading into black. Except for footsteps, the passageway was noiseless. Given the nature of the situation, I want to say that our pace quickened in the passageway, that we moved with a greater sense of urgency, but I don't remember if this was the case. There were others passing through with us, heading in the same direction, but I don't recall passing them or feeling anxious that they were holding us back. Before we reached the end of the passageway, I looked up at the sky one last time and said to Tammy, "I don't like these places," expecting her to respond with a quirky saying, a phrase or sentence that I'd never heard anyone else say before. She only looked at me and smiled, apprehensively, with a degree of pity. I tried to tell myself that Tammy meant well. Pity stems from compassion, a natural impulse indicative of our collective humanity. But for all its good intentions, pity is also a turning away from suffering, an escape from the sufferer. We think to ourselves, "That guy's life sucks so badly, just looking at him physically pains me." If the recipient of pity recognizes this, he will invariably feel much worse, not better. For better or worse, Tammy looked away. Then we reached the end of the hallway. Together, through revolving doors, we entered the main building.

The entrance hall bustled with people, dozens upon dozens, some dressed casually like Tammy and me, but most wearing clothes more suited to a corporate environment—men and women in business suits not sweats, slacks not jeans, buttoned and collared shirts not graphic tees, loafers and high-heels not sneakers. With the hall's arched glass ceiling, its gleaming granite floors, and the impossibly tall potted palm trees lining the walls, the entrance hall looked and felt like the lobby of a financial center or a five-star hotel or the shopping terminal at a busy airport that accommodates international flights.

While waiting on an elevator to come down to the ground floor, I heard music coming from an overhead speaker, a requiem mass, maybe, Chopin or Mendelsohn. From one of the shops off the atrium, a cafe that also sold flowers, I heard a Muzak version of a Beatles song. I also made out a phone ringing, a text message alert, a set of keys striking the granite floor, someone laughing, someone else coughing, another phone ringing, someone saying "Hello," someone else saying, "There's no way it's true," which was immediately followed by, "Not this, that," then the swoosh of the nearby revolving doors, then a ding, and then the doors to the elevator in front of us sliding open.

We rode up to the seventh floor. If the lobby downstairs could be thought of as a projection of the energy and chaos of everyday life, by contrast the floor to which M had been assigned spoke to the need to subdue that energy and to exact a measure of control over the chaos. No more gleaming floors (they were carpeted) or sunlight (there were no windows) or music or chatter (the only sound was the intermittent beeping of medical equipment). We did not need signs, either. The nurse's station was right off the elevators. I checked in with the nurse, who was a nurse, not someone dressed like one. I know because she told us. "I'm Nancy," she said, "one of the nurses attending to your wife." She led us down the hall to a small room with a single couch and three chairs, all the same muted green, like a faded leaf. In the middle of the room, a side table with five magazines on it: women's fashion, celebrity gossip, hunting, travel, and automobiles. Mounted on the wall a TV, turned on but the volume off.

"I'll let the doctor know you're here," the nurse said.

Tammy thanked Nancy by name and took a seat in one of the chairs, leaving me the couch. She asked if I wanted a magazine. I shook my head no. She grabbed the hunting magazine and flipped through it. I stepped back into the hallway, anticipating the doctor. The hallway was empty, so I sat down on the couch. Tammy had already set the hunting magazine down and was looking up at the TV. Enveloped in a bluish hue, a woman was sleeping comfortably, the pillow under her head impossibly fluffy, her nightie without a single crease, and for some reason the bed she was on had no sheet or blanket. I wondered what kind of commercial this was. One of two guesses came to mind: luxury mattresses or a prescription drug treating insomnia, snoring, or back pain. I reached for the volume control to find out which, and just then a policewoman stood at the waiting room entrance.

"Are you the husband?" she asked.

"I am," I said, and I looked over at Tammy. "She's with me—she's my..." I corrected myself. "She's *our* neighbor."

The policewoman was holding a thick notebook in one hand and a ballpoint pen in the other. She took another step forward, out of the hallway and into the waiting room.

"Your wife was assaulted," she said.

I took a moment before saying or doing anything. In that moment, that sentence, "Your wife was assaulted," lived in the world without interference or intrusion.

Tammy broke the silence.

"Oh, Lord," she said.

The policewoman flipped her notebook open, but immediately she decided against using it. Almost imperceptibly— but I saw her do so—she shook her head no. As I think back now on what unfolded in the waiting room, every action, every word, every feeling transpires without hurry, at a pace much slower than real life ever could, which made seeing and understanding what was happening, then and now, practically effortless. The policewoman closed the cover, and then she swallowed her breath. Taken together, these gestures spoke to her awareness, to the gravity of the situation, to the damage written in her notebook, and to the harm inflicted on M, which she had committed to memory and was about to inflict on us.

"Your wife was at the mall," she said. "It happened when she was leaving. She was in the parking lot beside her vehicle. She was digging through her purse for her car keys. She also had two shopping bags with her. She set those bags at her feet, beside the driver's side door, so she could get to her car keys more easily."

The policewoman cleared her throat. She knew what was coming next, which I didn't, which Tammy didn't, and, I suppose, when it had happened to her, neither did M.

"That's when two men came at her."

The policewoman paused.

Tammy stood up.

"Your wife didn't know the men who attacked her. Unfortunately, she didn't get a good look at them. They blindsided her, and they had their faces concealed with face masks and hooded sweatshirts."

After coming at her, the two men either shoved or knocked M to the ground, the policewoman said. Once she was on the ground, they began kicking.

"Where'd they kick?" Tammy asked.

There was no shock or horror in Tammy's voice. Her question, and her manner of asking it, was rational, straightforward, and sober. The policewoman replied in kind.

The two men kicked M in the head, the ribs, the arms, the legs, the back, and the stomach.

"Her stomach?" Tammy asked.

The policewoman nodded.

"For two shopping bags? They ain't needed to do all that. They coulda just took the bags."

The policewoman glanced at her notebook, began to open the cover, but again stopped herself. She did not need notes.

"They didn't take the bags, ma'am. Or the purse. Or the keys. Or the car. They didn't take anything. They just assaulted her."

"She wouldn't bite a biscuit. Why'd they do that?"

"She's in stable condition," the policewoman said. "The doctor will talk to you, and he can update you, give you more details."

"Hold on," Tammy said. "Church ain't out yet. What about the baby?"

The policewoman looked at her notebook again and sighed. This time the gesture was not at all subtle.

"The doctor will talk to you about that."

The whole time, I didn't say a word, probably because I didn't know what to say. I didn't know what to do, either. I just sat there, wanting to believe everything was going to be okay. Not just okay, but good. Not just good, but that everything would somehow be better.

A few minutes after the policewoman left, the doctor showed up. He was handsome, tall, fit, and looked to be about my age. He could have been younger. He wore a beard, and he seemed extraordinarily healthy, so it was hard to guess his age. He was probably much younger than I had guessed. He could have been ten, twelve years my junior. If that were the case, he was young enough to have been a student of mine. Either way, he was about to teach me something I did not want to learn.

M was doing better, he said. "But..."

"But what?"

"She suffered a few fractures. Two of her ribs were broken, and her left cheekbone, too, which is more serious. She's also badly bruised, especially about the face. There's a lot of tissue swelling. It's gone down significantly since she was admitted, and she looks much better. But when you see her, it won't look that way to you."

"What about the baby?" Tammy asked.

The doctor's arms had been at his side the entire time, but after hearing Tammy's question about the baby, he brought them up and folded them over his chest, which is the most obvious sign of discomfort. Arms folded over a chest also signifies disagreement or resistance. Whatever the message, the sign is universally negative. Clearly, the doctor did not like the answer he was compelled to give. It was remarkable to me how, in real life, we enacted every cliché imaginable, and not once do we think to say to ourselves, "React differently—don't cross your arms—be more original." He looked at me, a hard stare, and said, "I need to ask you a few questions about your wife's pregnancy."

I said, "Is the baby all right?"

Without hesitating or offering an excuse or an apology, he ignored my question, and he seemed to have no qualms in doing so. He was so good at not acknowledging or expressing regret, I couldn't help but think that while in medical school, he must have received specialized training at being unapologetic.

"What's the name of your wife's ob-gyn?"

"I don't know," I said.

"What do you mean, you don't know?"

Here we go again, I thought to myself.

"You don't know?"

"I don't know."

"Has she been to a gynecologist or an obstetrician?"

I didn't answer right away.

"When was the last time your wife had a medical exam?"

I looked at Tammy, who remained silent, but she must have been silently screaming, "Why don't you know?"

"When was the last time she saw a doctor about her pregnancy? Or any doctor for any reason?"

At this point, it was clear to me that the doctor's questions had become rhetorical. He already knew the answer I would give to each. Exasperated, he let out a sigh and asked, "Does your wife even have a doctor?"

"Please," I said, my voice the voice of a supplicant. "Please just tell me if the baby is okay."

Not only did he have his arms crossed over his chest, but his brows were furrowed and his eyes narrowed down to slits. In between interrogating me and waiting for a confession, he clenched his jaw. But the instant I begged him to tell me about the baby, his temperament changed. I don't know what I must have looked like for him to have altered so dramatically and suddenly. Whatever it was, he saw or heard something that disarmed him. Instead of looking angry with me, he now looked sorry for me. He pitied me.

"We should talk with your wife," he said. "Together. That would be best." Before walking away to check on M, to see if she was awake and capable of a conversation, he asked, "How far along in her pregnancy do you think she is?"

"I don't know for sure. Maybe eight months, give or take."

"Give or take what—a week, a month?"

I shrugged my shoulders.

To this day, I thank all the gods I don't believe in that after the doctor left, Tammy did not ask me anything or express an opinion or utter a single word. She only kept me company while I waited on the doctor to come back. While waiting, I kept my head down and tried hard to avoid eye contact so as not to give Tammy the opportunity, either out of curiosity or desire or even sympathy, to talk to me or offer consolation or even comfort. I didn't want any of it. I only wanted to see M and to know that the baby was unharmed, safe, and sound. The one time I did look up while waiting, I caught one last glimpse of the TV. Another commercial. A middle-aged man, maybe my age, maybe older, and a woman probably about the same age as M, maybe older, both seated on a sofa, watching TV. The volume was still off, so I couldn't hear what the commercial was trying to sell. Life insurance, maybe, or the latest pill for men who couldn't get it up.

The doctor reappeared.

"She's awake."

❧

I flinched when I saw her.

The left side of M's face, where the two men had broken the cheekbone, was bandaged. Streaked with blood, some dried, some fresh, the gauze was pinkish in color. The skin surrounding the cheekbone was a mix of colors that approximated blue, purple, and red. The tissue around the nose was inflamed. The lower lip was swollen, split open in more than one spot, and bruised. Until that moment I had never seen a bruised lip. I never imagined that M could look so terrible. She looked nothing like herself. She hardly looked human. She looked more like a zombie in a movie. The men who had beaten her made her monstrous.

The doctor had tried to prepare us, telling us she was in better condition now than when she arrived. But no amount of preparation could have stopped me from being wonder-struck at the thought of M, in the state she was in, having the capacity to speak. Not only to us now, but earlier to the doctor, the nurses, and the police about what had happened to her in the mall parking lot. She didn't seem capable of blinking or breathing, much less speech. A whimper, an undecipherable groan, yes, but I could scarcely comprehend how she had managed much more than that. She must have struggled relaying the details. Without the full force of her vocabulary at her disposal, she must have related her trauma in bits and pieces, having to rely on whichever words she could produce with the least amount of pain, not necessarily the ones she wanted or the best or most accurate. Despite the odds against her, M had managed to string together enough sounds and gestures to create a clear, coherent, and compelling narrative. To my mind, the achievement was no less a miracle than her pregnancy. Yet despite the accomplishment, which was godlike, seeing the aftermath of the assault in full view had a greater impact. I felt more horrified than amazed. Standing at the foot of the hospital bed, I saw in M the embodiment of pain and suffering. Later, I would revise my thinking, having determined I was wrong, and my reassessment would be worse. It was not agony that I witnessed, but innocence taken.

Terrible though it was, I would get used to the image, the memory of it. That was one of humanity's pinnacle feats, learning to live with any hardship, catastrophe, or loss life threw at us, no matter how painful or objectionable. There was no limit to the heights we could reach or the depths we could plunge.

M did not speak. She only stared, blankly. I had convinced myself that she stayed quiet, despite my presence, because she was still in too much pain. Or the experience of having to give a statement to the policewoman had exhausted her and she needed to recuperate. Or one of the nurses, perhaps even the doctor, had advised her not to talk unless necessary, to reserve her energies for the healing process. Or maybe there was no need for her to say anything. What else could she tell me? What more did I really need to know? Or, it finally occurred to me, maybe she needed *me* to be the one doing the talking. Maybe the words to comfort and ease should have come from me, not her. I could not imagine a sentence capable of realizing that goal or even coming close. I was also afraid of the words that could come out of my mouth. I had no practice for what I needed to do, and for the first time in my life, everything I had read in books or watched on TV or seen in the movies failed to provide me with a ready-made response. Rather than say anything at all, I walked from the foot of the bed to M's side, touched her hand, leaned in, and carefully kissed her forehead. And because women had done so in all those movies and TV shows that had let me down when I needed them most, I expected M to cry. She only squeezed my hand, and I promptly let go.

A nurse walked into the room. Not Nancy, the nurse who took us to the waiting room, but someone else. She didn't say hello. She didn't acknowledge the doctor. She walked past him and up to me and asked me curtly if I would move out of her way, which I did, stepping aside so she could hook up a second smaller bag to the IV line next to M's bed. Before the nurse finished, the doctor started talking again.

"Your wife," he said, as if M weren't in the room with us, listening. "She suffered what's called pseudocyesis."

The nurse interrupted the doctor.

"Excuse me," she said.

I saw her roll her eyes, and I think the doctor did, too, which would explain why he waited for her to leave the room and for the door to close before continuing.

"After the initial ultrasound," he went on, "I performed a pelvic exam and a second ultrasound."

"What's pseudo—...whatever it is you said. I don't know what that is."

"Pseudocyesis," he said. Finally, almost unwillingly, he looked at M. "False pregnancy. It's what used to be called a hysterical pregnancy."

Except for the sound of the IV drawing fluid and the monitor next to the bed beeping, the room was quiet. The doctor was looking at me, I was looking at M, and her eyes were locked on the doctor, waiting for him to say something else, which, after a pause that seemed both then and in retrospect to be too long and too dramatic, he did.

"You're not pregnant. You never were. There is no baby."

When Tammy came in to see M, I returned to the waiting room, which was empty, the TV turned off. I thought about flipping through a magazine, but I just sat there, which was much easier to pull off. Fifteen minutes later, maybe a half-hour, I don't know, Tammy walked back into the waiting room. I didn't ask her what she and M had talked about, or if they had talked at all, and she kept whatever did or didn't happen to herself, telling me only that M was sleeping, and for that, I was grateful. I thanked Tammy for bringing me to the hospital, and I apologized once more for yelling at her.

"Don't get all het up about that," she said, and then she offered to drive me home if I wanted to get some rest.

"I'll be fine. I'm going to stay the night. But you should go."

I reached my hand out to shake hers, but she threw both arms around me instead and hugged hard.

"What happened to her," she said, "that shouldn'ta happened to a dog, much less a woman."

M had missed dinner, and when another nurse showed up around 8 p.m. to take her vitals, I asked if he would bring some food back. He did, but M didn't wake up, and the food got cold; when the nurse showed up a couple hours later to check M's vital signs again, he took the tray with him on the way out. I saved the orange juice and the applesauce, and around ten o'clock M finally woke up. I asked if she was hungry. She shook her head no. I peeled the foil lid off the orange juice bottle and offered it to her.

She touched her throat and grimaced, indicating it hurt to swallow.

I stopped asking questions. Soon after, she fell back asleep. Not much later, sitting in the chair across from the hospital bed, I also drifted into sleep and didn't wake up until a few hours later, in the middle of the night, when another nurse, older, in her fifties, maybe sixties, came in to check on M. The nurse smiled and told me to go back to sleep, but I watched her do her job. She moved effortlessly. I closed my eyes for a second. When I reopened them, the nurse was gone.

M was snoring, and I couldn't get back to sleep. I went online with my phone. I searched for news stories about women like M getting assaulted by men like The Good Neighbors. I didn't find any. Not exactly. There were hundreds of articles about men beating up women, but not under the same circumstances.

I started another search. I typed p-s-e-u-d-o, and the words *pseudonym* and *pseudoephedrine* came up. I added the letter "c," and *pseudocyesis* appeared.

The first link I clicked sent me to an article about a woman in North Carolina. She showed up with her husband at a regional hospital and claimed that for two days they had tried to induce labor naturally, at home, in their bathtub, but their attempts had ended in vain. Because of their failure, or the failure of nature to do as it should, they decided as a last resort to go to the hospital. The woman told the triage nurse attending her exactly what she needed, a C-section. She was admitted and sent directly to surgery. During the surgical procedure, the doctor on call, who was not an ob-gyn, discovered an empty uterus. After the discovery, according to the article, the surgeon simply closed the woman back up. About the mishap, a dean at a college of medicine was quoted as saying, "You open someone's abdomen, you make darn sure you know what you're doing."

On another website dedicated to medical news and information for lay people, pseudocyesis, "aka false pregnancy," was defined as a disorder, a psychiatric condition during which women may exhibit all the physiological symptoms of an actual pregnancy, among them the cessation of menstruation, a distended abdomen, swollen breasts, morning sickness, food cravings, and labor pains. M had suffered all these symptoms, except for labor pains, which she might have gone through had the pregnancy not been cut short by the incident in the mall parking lot.

I clicked on another link, an article featuring historical accounts of pseudocyesis. Two thousand three hundred years ago, Hippocrates treated twelve women who believed they were pregnant but eventually realized, or were told, that they were not. Mary I of England, also known as Mary Tudor and "Bloody Mary," who reigned from 1553 until her death five years later, had endured a false pregnancy. The article's author, a self-described medical practitioner, as well as a self-described historian, surmised a reason for the queen's pseudocyesis: Her father, King Henry VIII, had a reputation for beheading women who could not produce offspring, and under such pressure, the queen produced one that was never there.

I read for a while longer, until I came across an article that claimed even dogs could be afflicted by false pregnancy. I knew then that I had read enough.

Around 5 a.m., M woke up again. I was still in the chair across from the bed, exhausted but wide awake. She asked me the time. When I told her, she asked why I wasn't at home. I shrugged my shoulders. She asked if I was tired.

I told a lie, said I was feeling fine, and added, "You should go back to sleep."

"What are you thinking about?" she asked.

I thought about it and told her the truth.

"Nothing."

A brief silence followed, and I listened to it intently. Was it this quiet when we were alone at home?

Yes, it was. Sometimes quieter.

Then, for the first time since finding out she was not pregnant, M began to cry.

Without thinking about what to do next, I went over to her and sat on the edge of the bed and took hold of her hand and gently squeezed. I wasn't worried about how the gesture came off, whether as an act of affection or pity. M didn't seem to care, either. She whispered something. Despite our proximity, the words were inaudible. I could have asked her to repeat herself, but I didn't need her to say the words to know what they must have been. Wrong or not, I assumed that what she needed and wanted mirrored exactly what I had needed and wanted all along. I crawled into the hospital bed with her, pulled the thin blue blanket over us, put my arm over her shoulder, and held her close.

"I'm sorry," I said. "I'm sorry for everything."

I could feel her muffled sobs against my body. I have no doubt she also felt mine.

❦

For the next few months, I faced the fact that there must have existed a good, rational, commonsensical explanation for why, right away or soon after she found out, the college student chose not to tell me herself that she was pregnant. Whatever it was, the explanation evaded me. She had numerous ways to deliver the message. She could have just told me. She wasn't shy or timid, after all. Even had she found herself too this, that, or the other to deliver the news in person, face to face, she had plenty of other approaches other than the one she took. She could have left me a note with the rent check. She could have left a voicemail on my phone. She could have sent me an email. Had she done any of these, I would have gone over her message a hundred times.

After her arrest, she still had options that were better than the one she chose. Had she requested that I visit her, I would have driven to whichever prison she was being held in, sat across from her, and heard her out. If that would have been too much for her to handle, she could have written me a letter, or she could have instructed her court-appointed lawyer to notify me. Instead of any or all these choices, she placed the responsibility of letting me know in the hands of two people she had met in a Bible study group, two people I judged to be acquaintances at best and at worst accomplices to first-degree murder. She chose two people who were ultimately under zero obligation to seek me out or tell me anything. They could have decided to disregard the girl's request, to not so accidentally lose the address to the blue bungalow, to never knock on my front door. Or they could have had every intention of doing her the favor she had asked but chickened out at the last minute. Or for any reason under the sun, moon, and stars, those two could have decided on their own that I didn't deserve to know the truth. They could have concluded that the burden placed on them was too heavy and not theirs to lift. Or fearing that they could get caught, or further caught up in troubles with which they clearly wanted nothing to do, they could have convinced themselves that there was no baby or that they didn't know the college girl, much less that she was pregnant, and I would have lived out the rest of my life, or at least a good portion of it, unaware of the fact that I actually, finally, got someone pregnant.

After a while, I did accept that she did indeed have a good reason to go about it the way she had as opposed to the way I would've. In the end, however, whatever reason she had for choosing to rely on and confide in two strangers, I figured it was best for me not to know. I arrived at the same conclusion about her other actions, too. I didn't need to know why she shot an old man to death or why she had sex with me. As a professor and a person, I had spent my life trying to figure out human behavior, and the best, most definitive opinions I formulated over the course of a lifetime inevitably did not matter. Except for one: People did what they thought was best, even if it wasn't—even if they knew, for a fact, that it was the worst thing they could do.

As for not telling me directly that she was pregnant, I figured it was no different than not telling the two girls who went with her to the rally that she'd brought a gun and planned to use it. Both were facts requiring no explanation, and their message was simple: The world is not all will and logic, and neither are all our decisions. In the absence of an explanation, or because the explanations available had failed to provide answers that I wanted to believe in, I did what people have been doing since the beginning of time: I made up my own. I told myself that the college student's choices to have sex with me, to pass on the fact of her pregnancy with indifference, and to kill the preacher betrayed a logical, practical, even enviable rejection of the norms the rest of us lived by. Trite as it may be to say it, I'll say it: She lived by her own rules.

For a while, I told myself that, and I believed it wholeheartedly.

It's her life, I told myself. It's her body. Her choice. Her future.

Each time I told myself these things, I accepted as true that what had happened between us was not right, wrong, good, or bad. It was just what had happened.

For a while, I told myself all sorts of things about the choices I had made. For telling the two girls to get the fuck off my property, I considered myself principled and right-eous. For keeping the pregnancy from M for as long I did, which was in fact longer than the girl had kept it from me, I deemed myself to be honest and trustworthy. Never mind the fact that I had made a promise to myself, only minutes after finding out that the girl was pregnant, that I would im-mediately confess to M but did no such thing. That I eventually did tell her, months later, was all the proof I needed of my having integrity. And for not letting the girl's pregnancy bother me or disrupt my life with M, or for not allowing its actuality to keep me up at night or intrude on my daily habits and appetites, I told myself I was not indif-ferent or unsympathetic but defiant, that I was standing up to rigid and repressive moral codes. I told myself I was liv-ing in the present, not the past. I would not bow down to conformity for society's sake. Be proud, I told myself, for what I had done amounted to selflessness.

During this time, what I would not tell myself, but which I knew to be true, is that every one of these pats on the back amounted to a large, heaping pile of horseshit. Justifying my actions to myself proved to be endlessly exhausting work. Of all the verdicts I had arrived at, about who I was and what I had done, the one that turned out to be the most incorruptible was "I'm full of it."

What thoughts colonized M's head around this time, I can't say. We barely spoke. When we did, we said little more than necessary. "Are you hungry?" "Yes." "Do you need a pain killer?" "Yes." "Do you want to talk?" "No." The first week back home from the hospital, she slept for hours at a time during the day, and I spent those hours reading about what women went through after a violent attack. And because I found nothing on women coping with pseudocyesis, I read up on its next of kin, miscarriage. Beyond recovering from the physical trauma (in M's case, bruises, cuts, and bone fractures), she might have trouble sleeping (she didn't) and nightmares (if she did, I slept through them, and she didn't tell me). I read that M might also become depressed and anxious, and she might begin to doubt her ability to take care of herself, so much so the feeling of helplessness could turn into paralysis. None of these happened. Within two weeks, M stopped asking for help. She got herself out of bed, washed and dressed herself, made her own coffee, and took to visiting Tammy almost daily. Once, I overheard them laughing on the front porch, and every time M returned from a visit, she looked, if not happy, then at least at ease. When the bruises healed, she went to the grocery store on her own.

The possible long-term effects of the attack and false pregnancy included chronic pain, stomach ulcers and other digestive complications, migraines, stress, a compromised immune system, and sexual problems. All these M had complained about long before the attack, but she did not bring them up after. Did she wake up with back pain? Did she suffer headaches? Did her ulcers flare up? Maybe. As for problems with sex, she did not once lodge a complaint. The explanation was simple. We stopped having sex. Then, M started leaving the house, twice a week, Mondays, Fridays, always at the same time, and she did not tell me where or why she was heading out. I suspected she was seeing a therapist or attending a women's support group or both.

I knew this: She looked okay, and she behaved typically, but she had changed. She could never be the same, and she wasn't. I probably did not notice immediately because, after all, I also had become different. When I finally realized so, I could not tell if the change had been for better or worse, only that M was moving on with or without me.

❧

There was no coverage of the attack on M. Not on TV or online. The local newspapers didn't mention it, either, not even the *East Side Gazette*, a free weekly that regularly published summaries of the most inconsequential neighborhood transgressions. In the days and weeks following the assault on M, the *Gazette* mentioned stolen lawn ornaments, a new wood bench outside the civic center defaced with "Ali + Salma" carved into a slat, and dog owners not picking up after their dogs at the dog park. Every week for several weeks after the attack against her in the Galleria parking lot, I checked to see if what had happened to M also happened to someone else. Every time, nothing. M's case was isolated, or else women like M were being attacked, but like M's attack, they weren't being written about. At the grocery store, the post office, the bank, the gas station, the mall, I kept an eye out for women with black eyes, bruised arms, broken bones. I didn't see any. But I don't get out much these days, so it's hard to know for sure. It may yet be happening. It probably is.

The most realistic, levelheaded explanation for why I haven't read or heard about any more assaults against women like M is that the attacks went the way of the child suicides: They grabbed our attention one day, and they lost it the next.

A handful of nights, the college student appeared in my dreams. In one of the dreams, we had sex for the first time.

The moment after climax, she told me she was pregnant. A moment later, from somewhere in the pink bungalow, which was still intact, no hint of smoke or fire or ash, I heard a crying baby. The moment after that, from somewhere else in the house, I heard M's voice. She was speaking softly, cajoling a newborn into serenity. "Now, now," she said, and "There, there." I wanted to go to them, to spring from the bed to witness M with a baby, but the college girl stopped me, climbed onto my chest, held me down, and said, "Look at me, look me in the eyes," and with that, M and the baby faded further and further into an impossible distance.

Then I woke up.

Later, I described the dream to M. Every part, every detail. As you might expect, it went badly. But it also led to an unexpected admission on M's part. She wished to visit the girl in prison. She wasn't asking me, either. She was simply telling me, being up front and honest—something I hadn't been with her.

"I'm going alone," she told me.

Outside of the confines of the blue bungalow, a fog was lifting. A bunch of people who got to voice their opinions on big stages agreed that the spirit of the times was changing, and for the better. The rules of the game were being rewritten to make winning easier. People wanted to move on. They wanted to get past it, whatever *it* was. They wanted to enter a new age, to wake up to a new day and be guided by something other than fear or hate. In short, people had grown tired of hearing about bad things happening. Despite the ills of the world, they wanted to feel good again. They wished for the things making them feel good to define their lives. They yearned for joy and happiness, not sadness and grief. To be proud, not ashamed. They wished for news, TV shows, songs, and stories filled with hope, of which they could not get enough. They wanted to be Adam and Eve again, before eating the fruit.

None of these desires was new. This had happened before. Countless times. The world was reborn every single day, even if from one day to the next nothing new happened and nothing got better or worse. Also, it was an election year. There was so much hope in the air and on TV. That was the prevailing sentiment that overtook the dentist who became the East Side's elected representative in Congress, and she embraced the new and improved mood. In her first act as congresswoman, she announced an East Side revitalization project slated, ironically, for the site of the old church where the old preacher conceived of The Good Neighbors. The preacher's son had sold the building and lot to a developer who also happened to be the congresswoman's brother. The demolished church, the leveled ground, and the construction fence set up around the perimeter all made sure that no trace of the past remained. At the groundbreaking, a sign spanning the length of the construction fence facing the main street pictured the new businesses to come: a yoga studio, a high-end boutique, an espresso cafe, a wine bar. These weren't necessarily the actual businesses coming to the neighborhood but artist renditions of what could be. Visions of the future. Hope for the future.

Also at the groundbreaking, the newly elected congresswoman took an unexpected and extraordinary step. She publicly expressed regret over her words and actions as a former member of the church, using words like "forgiveness," "atonement," "healing," and "rebirth." To ensure the success of her new image, she began to surround herself with likeable local figures. She didn't stop with pure optics, either. She made overtures of reconciliation to the East Siders she had once deemed a threat. One such conciliatory move: She vowed support for a nonprofit organization dedicated to raising awareness about child and teen suicide. Another: She spoke at a fundraising event held by the local community center offering social services to immigrants and refugees residing in the East Side. Yet another deed made with the goal of fostering friendly relations with the people she had once portrayed as menacing: She secured funding for a new gymnasium to be built at the East Side middle school. As a sign no doubt meant to repair old wounds and to rebuild community, the funding also included construction plans for the West Side school where seven first-graders perished.

The preacher's son was conspicuously absent from the congresswoman's new life. The impression I got from reading about him and watching him on TV was the opposite made by the dentist's conversion: Nothing we say or do will change how others feel, think, and act. The preacher's son all but abandoned the East Side after selling his father's church. He began spending a lot more time in other parts of the state, particularly those cities and counties where he could count on votes. His candidacy for the U.S. Senate was met with enthusiasm by his backers and political party but obviously was rebuked by his opponent and his opponent's party. Unlike the dentist, the preacher's son opted not to reinvent himself but to strengthen his commitment to the cause that had made him famous. He campaigned on a promise to protect voters from the ever-present and growing threat posed by people like us to communities across the state, even the country. That not a single East Side child, teen, or adult had killed themselves or anyone else in over a year seemed to make no difference to his supporters. Other politicians in other cities and states talked about similar threats by similar people. Almost always, the threats did not exist. Also almost always, those who wanted to believe men like the preacher's son did so, regardless.

"We're a nation of fools," I would say. "Our country is an insane asylum run by madmen."

When I made comments like this, M usually ignored me. Nonetheless, I suspected that she agreed with me.

On an unseasonably warm day in November, nearly two years after the first girl's suicide, around the time when the trees give themselves almost entirely to the changing season, the preacher's son, in an upset victory almost everyone had once thought unimaginable, won election to the Senate.

"Can you believe this shit?" I asked M.

She was on the couch beside me but not watching the TV.

"Don't say *shit*," she scolded me.

"This is the dumbest, stupidest, worst thing that has ever happened, ever."

"Don't say *stupid*," she said.

I knew it wasn't the dumbest or stupidest thing. Or it wouldn't be for long. Something dumber, stupider, and much worse always lay ahead.

I turned the TV off.

The baby started crying.

"She's hungry," M said, and then she told me to grab a bottle from the refrigerator, warm it up, and bring it back.

I was more tired than I thought possible. I had considered the idea of hiring a nanny. We could easily have afforded one. The money we received from the insurance claim payout on the pink bungalow had far exceeded any amount I anticipated. The adjuster had been on the mark about East Side property values skyrocketing, and to my surprise, when I broached the idea of selling the lot, M went along without me having to do much persuading. However, I knew that the prospect of a nanny, really of any other woman, spending an inordinate amount of time in the house with us, or alone with me, would have unnerved M. So I kept the nanny idea to myself. Without childcare, we were soloing it, and we passed the days sleep-deprived and bleary-eyed.

From the room with the TV, M called out to me in the kitchen.

"We're almost out of diapers."

I was standing over the sink, running hot water over a baby bottle to warm it up. My view out the window was the garage. It still needed a paint job, just like the fence. Still in the garage, at the bottom of my toolbox, was the pack of cigarettes I kept hidden from M. There was a single cigarette left. I had gone a long time without a smoke. After the adoption, I told myself, as I had many times before, that I was finished with cigarettes, with all vices. Just the same, the one cigarette remained, always waiting. The guns were there, too, in the garage, in a safe we purchased on the same day we bought the crib. The safe was the size of a small refrigerator and held our guns and ammunition.

"And butt paste," M shouted. "Diapers and butt paste."

The baby's cries grew louder and louder. I squeezed the rubber nipple on the baby bottle and let a few drops of formula fall onto my wrist to test the temperature. Just as the drops hit my arm, M walked into the kitchen.

"If there's a knock at the door, it's Tammy." She handed me the baby and, walking away, said, "I have to pee."

The baby formula was still cold. I put the bottle back under the faucet and ran more hot water over it. The baby was still bawling, so I held her close and made soft shushing sounds. She had my forehead and hair color and the eyes of her mother, who I hadn't seen in a year. According to M, who had seen her recently, the girl seemed to be doing well, all things considered. Last time they talked, the girl said she was looking into completing her bachelor's degree online and that the warden had granted her permission to start a Bible study group. The baby was still crying. I rocked her gently side to side and cradled her small body even closer to mine and whispered into her ear, "There, there, now, now, it's all right. Everything is going to be okay."

Acknowledgments

I WOULD LIKE to thank the following people (they know why): Rachel de Cordova, Ito Romo, Randa Jarrar, Ismita Hussain, and William E. Burleson. And eternal gratitude to the novelist Samuel Astrachan (1934-2012), who so many years ago gave me the blessing I needed.

About the Author

Born in Detroit, Hayan Charara lives and works in Houston, Texas. He is the author of four poetry collections and a children's book. Hush Little Children is his first novel.